**Also available from
Lee Tobin McClain
and HQN**

Safe Haven

Low Country Hero
Low Country Dreams
Low Country Christmas

For additional books by Lee Tobin McClain,
visit her website, www.leetobinmcclain.com.

cottage
at the beach

LEE TOBIN McCLAIN

HQN

ISBN-13: 978-1-335-08055-4

Cottage at the Beach

Copyright © 2020 by Lee Tobin McClain

This edition published by arrangement with Harlequin Books S.A.

For questions and comments about the quality of this book, please contact us at CustomerService@Harlequin.com.

HQN
22 Adelaide St. West, 40th Floor
Toronto, Ontario M5H 4E3, Canada
www.Harlequin.com

Printed in U.S.A.

Recycling programs for this product may not exist in your area.

Cottage at the Beach is dedicated to my late mother, Janet L. Tobin, and to the many young women who face their genetic predisposition to cancer with courage and grace.

cottage
at the beach

CHAPTER ONE

TREY HARRISON SLID farther down in the seat of his 2009 Chevy pickup and frowned at the blue-and-white cottage at the end of the street, deliberately relaxing his tense hands on the steering wheel. "That can't be it," he said to his dog, King.

From the back seat, King's tail beat rhythmically against his crate. He gave one short bark.

Guilt pounded Trey's already-aching head, because he knew what that bark meant. King wanted to get to work.

But because of Trey, that wouldn't be happening for either of them. No more police work. Not for a while, and maybe not ever.

His own stupidity and recklessness had stolen not only his career, but King's. He moved his seat back and opened the door of King's crate, and the big German shepherd jumped into the passenger seat and leaned against his arm. Offering trust and forgiveness Trey didn't deserve.

He looked again at the neat little cottage set off by itself, the front facing the lane, the back oriented toward the Chesapeake Bay. He'd been expecting something institutional, impersonal. Rehabilitation wasn't supposed to be vacation-like. He clicked to confirm the address on his phone, then carefully turned his head to scan the row of small, quaint houses scattered along this side of the lane. White picket fences, flowers in every yard. Audible from beyond the houses was the cry of gulls and the steady lapping of waves against the rocky shoreline.

Several of the cottages, including the blue-and-white one, had little signs hanging from gateposts or vine-covered arbors. From his parking place he could read some of them: Hawthorne Cottage, Escape on the Water, Bailey's Hideaway.

Trey squinted at the sign that hung from the vine-covered arbor in front of his destination, and read Healing Heroes.

His hands clenched on the steering wheel. He sure didn't feel like a hero.

He wanted to just drive away.

Except he couldn't. Financially, he didn't have any other options, and for whatever reason, his chief really wanted him to participate in this new program for disabled police officers. Insisted, basically. "You need it mentally as well as physically," he'd said, and had implied that it was the only way Trey had a chance of getting his old job back.

It was Trey's own fault. Even if he hadn't gotten injured, his impulsive behavior at work had been about to land him in a desk job.

He got out of the truck, let King out and walked up to the door. Bending down, he attempted to fit the old-fashioned key they'd sent him into the lock, wincing as pain radiated out from his lower back.

The key didn't want to work; it was rusty, a little bent. Didn't fit, just like he didn't. Just like King didn't.

They were supposed to be hunting down missing persons, sniffing out drugs, chasing bad guys. Or, at a minimum, doing their monthly training exercises to keep skills sharp.

Instead, they were in forced rehabilitation in a tiny, tidewater town.

He wiped sweat from his face. April in Maryland shouldn't be this hot. Weren't there supposed to be waterfront breezes?

"Just three months, buddy," he said to King. "Maybe less."

King panted up at him, his face a doggy smile, and Trey stood up straighter. He needed to stop feeling sorry for himself. He had to do his wretched physical therapy, which so far seemed to hurt more than it helped. Hide his bad attitude. That was the only way to get back to the thing that never let him down: work.

The whine of a vacuum cleaner from inside the cottage startled Trey. He knocked, then pounded on the door. When there was no answer, he pounded again, too hard, making King woof.

Get control of yourself. He had to get—and keep—control.

The vacuum cleaner stopped and then the door opened. The woman who answered looked to be in her fifties with curves worthy of an old-time movie star. He liked curvy women, or had, back when he'd been interested in romance.

"Can I help you?" the woman asked.

"Um, yeah. Trey Harrison. I'm supposed to be staying here."

"Right." The woman forked her fingers through reddish hair streaked with gray and gave him a rueful smile. "I'm Julie White. I manage the place. But we're not quite ready for you."

"We will be, by check-in time." The voice, practical and friendly, came from behind the older woman. "That's 3:00 p.m. Just take a walk along the shore, or get lunch at Goody's just a block over. You can leave your stuff."

"Sure." He caught a glimpse of a younger version of the woman who'd answered the door. A knockout, he noted with an alarming lack of interest.

As he turned away, wincing at the twisting movement, he heard the younger woman speaking. "You can't break down now, Mom. We're almost done."

"Why do you always think I'm breaking down? I'm fine!"

The conversation got harder to hear as he reached the sidewalk and looked up the street, wondering whether to go for a beach walk, get lunch or retreat to where he'd come from.

Not an option, remember? The house he and his ex-wife had bought five years ago, when Trey had dreamed of a Norman Rockwell family, had just sold. He had to go back there at some point, probably tomorrow, to clean it out for the new owners. Not to stay.

He should do as the woman had suggested, hit the beach. Light walking was recommended for his injury, and it might clear some of the gray cloud that kept sinking over him. And King could use the exercise. He turned toward the access path he'd seen earlier and nearly ran into a short, barrel-chested cop, another fiftysomething. "Excuse me," Trey said, and started to pass.

The man held out a hand. "You must be our visitor for the new program. Welcome. I'm Earl Greene."

Was his identity as a so-called *healing hero* that obvious, or was this just a really small town? Trey forced his lips into a polite smile. "Pleased to meet you," he lied. This guy would write the report that might convince his chief to give him his old job back. Depressing to be at the mercy of an over-the-hill, small-town cop. He glared at the guy's badge.

Officer Greene looked past him toward the blue-and-white cottage and lifted a hand in a wave. "Hey, there, Julie. Hey, Ria."

The guy's expression was exactly what kids looked like when they saw a toy they really, really wanted, and that made Trey look back toward the cottage, too. There was nothing to see, just the door to his new home-away-from-home closing.

Officer Greene lifted his chin and looked at Trey. "Got your volunteer gig all lined up," he said. "Once you're settled, come on down to the station and we'll talk it over."

"Volunteer gig? Oh, right." Trey remembered reading something about that in the material explaining the Healing Heroes program, but he hadn't paid much attention. He'd been most interested in the rent-free opportunity to get out of town and heal. He flicked imaginary dirt from King's head to conceal his ignorance. "I'll look forward to hearing about it, sir."

Officer Greene's eyes narrowed, just a little, and Trey realized he hadn't sounded convincing. "Hope you enjoy working with at-risk teenagers, because that's a big part of the program's mission," the man said. "You'll be helping out at an academy for them, starting Monday." He gave Trey a nod and headed off down the street.

Trey looked after him, not knowing which was more startling: the quaint sight of an officer actually walking a beat, or the idea of Trey having something to offer troubled teenagers. Yeah, he'd been one, but that didn't mean he was great at relating to them as anything but a cop.

"COME ON, ZIGGY! Let's go!" Erica Rowe clapped her hands as she ran down the steps that led from their little rental house to the waterfront, her goldendoodle leaping in hysterical circles around her. It was just after noon on a Tuesday, and a rare early dismissal from her teaching job.

The narrow little beach was empty. Good. At eleven months old, Ziggy was still a puppy, but due to his large size—already seventy-five pounds—

people understandably expected good behavior from him. That was more likely to happen if he had the chance to run off some energy.

She jogged along beside the dog, watching him leap at the waves, jump back and then zigzag off to chase a seagull.

She needed to run off her own stress, too, or so her sister said; apparently, she had lines in between her eyebrows and had gotten too thin.

That was the pot calling the kettle black: Amber had no eyebrows at all and was emaciated and pretty much racked with anxiety. Erica's heart twisted. Their move to the shore town was supposed to help Amber recover from her latest round of chemo. Or, at any rate, help her fulfill a dream.

Three months in, the dream part was looking more likely than the recovery.

To continue helping her sister fulfill that dream, Erica *had* to make a success of the academy's behavior support program. It was the only job that paid enough to keep Amber, Amber's daughter and herself living here, in the tiny town where they'd spent childhood summers.

Erica had to stay on the good side of the misogynistic principal who'd hired her, had to convince him that the academy's program for at-risk teens should be continued, not terminated at the end of the school year per the wishes of some of Pleasant Shores' newer residents.

No wonder she was stressed.

Ziggy started running faster, more purposefully,

and in the distance Erica made out two figures: a man and a dog.

Great. She sprinted after her out-of-control pet. "Ziggy! Get back here!"

By the time she reached the guy and his fierce-looking German shepherd, Ziggy was in full attack mode, which meant nose-punching the shepherd and then dancing backward and play-bowing. His big plume of a tail was wagging.

The shepherd sat stoically beside the guy, who was…wow.

Was he some movie star she didn't recognize? The guy was *built*, with blue eyes that crinkled at the corners and a square jaw beneath a day's worth of heavy beard.

Erica wasn't in the market for a relationship, not even for a fling, but she also wasn't dead. She sucked in air and then focused on catching her breath and grabbing Ziggy's collar. "Sorry!" she said. "He's young. Stop it, Zig," she added as her dog took another playful lunge at the shepherd.

The shepherd curled his lips back and bared his teeth.

The movie star grunted an order, which caused the shepherd to stop, midsnarl, and look up at him. Then he responded to another of Ziggy's lunges with a low growl that made Ziggy leap away and cower behind Erica, whimpering.

"Your dog is terrifying!" she blurted out, kneeling to comfort Ziggy. "It's okay, buddy. Mommy won't let him hurt you."

The man snapped another order at the dog, who lay down with nose on paws, looking ashamed. "You shouldn't talk baby talk to your dog," the man said to Erica. "He'll just behave worse."

She lifted an eyebrow. "Excuse me?"

He gestured at Ziggy, a slight frown marring his gorgeous face. "You'll just make him more timid if you act like there's a basis for his fear. You shouldn't let him loose on the beach, either, if he can't be controlled."

She got enough mansplaining all day, every day, from the principal of her school, and she didn't need more of it in her free time. "It's private property along this stretch of shore," she said. "Is there a reason you're here with your, uh, highly trained dog?"

"I'm staying up there." He gestured toward the row of cottages behind him.

She seriously doubted that. "Where?"

He gave her a look that suggested she'd asked something rude.

"Look," she said, "I don't want to be all exclusionary, but your dog looks ready to kill someone, and you don't seem much friendlier. We have a lot of small dogs and little kids in Pleasant Shores, and it's important they be safe. That's why…" She pulled out her phone. "Everyone has agreed to call the police if they see anybody suspicious."

"Wait." He held up a hand, eyebrows coming together. "Don't do that. My name's Trey Harrison, and the address of the place I'm staying is…" He scrolled through his phone and then looked up. "Fifteen Shoreline Way, the cottage at the end of the lane. Julie White manages it. She's the one who told me to come down to the beach until they finish cleaning the place."

While they'd been talking, Ziggy and the shepherd had settled down and greeted each other in respectable dog fashion. Both tails began to wag.

"You're staying at Julie's place?"

"Uh-huh."

Erica didn't know Julie well. She'd met the woman when she and Amber had first moved into the cottage next door three months ago, had thought she'd seemed nice. Then they'd heard a lot of shouting coming from Julie's house, and then it had gone silent and empty. Rumor had it the place had sold, although Erica had never seen a for-sale sign.

Come to think of it, though, there had been some activity there this week. So maybe the movie star was telling the truth and would be a new neighbor.

And maybe she'd been a little abrupt. "I'm sorry Ziggy jumped all over your dog," she said, "and that I jumped all over you." She held out a hand. "Welcome to Pleasant Shores."

"Thanks." He gave her hand a quick shake with his own large, calloused one, and his eyebrow lifted, just a little, his gaze lingering on her face.

She sucked in a breath. Nope, not dead. *Okay, then.* "Are you planning to stay awhile, or is this just a vacation?"

"I'll be here a couple of months, looks like." He glanced down at Ziggy, who was back to nose-punching his dog. "So if you live on the same stretch of beach, it would be good if our dogs got along."

"It would." She turned to go back the way she'd come. "C'mon, Zig."

To her surprise, Mr. Handsome-But-Cranky fell into step beside her. His dog trudged along at his side.

Ziggy leaped and tugged until she let him off his leash again, freeing him to dart after shorebirds and sniff at oyster shells.

As they walked on, the silence got awkward. Erica glanced over at her new neighbor. "Does your dog ever get to play?"

"He's a working dog," Trey said.

"Oh!" She glanced at the shepherd again. "Shouldn't he be wearing a service dog vest or something?"

"Not a service dog. He's a police dog."

"Oh! Then you're a cop." And yet he was here for a couple of months?

Suddenly, realization washed over her. "Wait a minute. You're not the volunteer for the academy program, are you?" She'd known she was getting a police-related volunteer, but not who it was or where he'd be living.

He nodded glumly.

"Starting Monday?"

He nodded again. "Yeah. I just found out about it. Not exactly my thing, but it's a condition of getting the house, which I need until my disability payments come in."

"So…you don't have any training with teenagers?"

He shook his head. "Zilch."

"Great." She wondered whether it was too late for them to choose another candidate for the position.

"I mean," he went on, "I've worked with little kids some, in classroom demonstrations about police work. But teenagers I've mostly arrested. Philly cop," he clarified, probably in response to Erica's frown.

She looked over at him without speaking while her thoughts and emotions raced. It hadn't been all that long since she'd had the surgery that had destroyed her dream of having kids of her own. Since then, she'd gotten even more dedicated to her students, especially now that she'd been hired to finish out the school year in Pleasant Shores Academy's behavior support program.

Having a volunteer assistant who thought of teenagers as criminals wasn't exactly ideal.

He—Trey, he'd said his name was—glanced over at her and something must have shown on her face. "What's your interest in the program?"

"I'm the cooperating teacher," she said slowly. "I'll be working closely with you…with *whoever* Officer Greene recommends to be my assistant in the program." And she'd be having a conversation with Officer Greene just as soon as she got back to her place. Maybe there was still time to replace the movie star with someone who actually wanted to work with kids.

She'd helped Officer Greene organize the program that would get some much-needed help for her classroom full of unruly teens. It was a big part of the proposed solution to the fears Pleasant Shores' latest, wealthiest residents had about their private junior-senior high school—the only school in town—housing a program for at-risk kids. They didn't like that, but they also didn't want to bus their kids to distant public schools up the shore.

She had to do everything in her power to make the academy a success. For the kids, of course. For her niece, Hannah, who needed stability and a good school. And most of all for her sister, Amber, who deserved to have one dream, at least, come true.

If that meant throwing the handsome movie star under the bus, well, that was what she'd have to do.

CHAPTER TWO

"I CAN'T BELIEVE you turned the poor guy in!" Amber hooted with laughter and shook her head at Erica, all at the same time.

"His attitude is worse than any of the kids'," Erica said as she lifted a second slice of pizza from the box and put it on her plate. "I mean," she said to her seventeen-year-old niece, Hannah, "you wouldn't want some giant, sulky cop helping in your class, would you?"

Hannah lifted an eyebrow. "Depends what he looks like."

"That's part of the problem!" Erica said. "He looks like a movie star. Like that guy who played Thor."

"Chris Hemsworth?" Hannah laughed. "He could sit in on my class anytime."

"No way. His looks just make his bad attitude more of a pain."

"Why?" Amber asked. "Nothing wrong with having some nice scenery in the classroom, even if he doesn't do much."

Erica stood to pour more mineral-infused water into Amber's glass, then Hannah's. It was a balancing act, trying to appeal to two picky appetites while making meals as nutritious as possible. "I can just imagine him sitting there in the back of the room, all handsome and sullen. It's hard enough to get the kids motivated without having a male role model slouching around acting like everything we do is stupid."

"Maybe you can convert him, change his attitude," Amber said, waggling painted-on eyebrows. "Or at least have fun trying. You need to get out more."

"And upset Principal O'Neil? Remember, he doesn't like his single teachers to date. He's afraid it would somehow hurt the school's reputation."

"That's not fair!" Hannah ripped the crust off her slice of pizza. "Isn't it, like, an invasion of privacy?"

"Yes, it is. And to top it off, he freaks out if any of his teachers gets pregnant." Erica looked out the window toward the bay, and immediately her blood pressure eased back down. Golden sunlight slanted low, making the scattered clouds go shades of pink and purple and turning the bay to a glowing mirror. Pleasant Shores' location on the tip of a Maryland peninsula meant that both sunrises and sunsets were spectacular.

"Didn't O'Neil just have a new baby?" Amber asked. "So he didn't mind his own wife getting pregnant."

"She doesn't work, from what I've heard, and that's the way he thinks families should be. He's old-school, he always says."

Amber snorted. "He's out of touch, is what he is."

She leaned back in her chair, furtively sneaking a pizza crust to Ziggy.

"He seems weird," Hannah said in the dismissive tone of a teenager.

Erica leaned back in her chair. "In retrospect, I can't believe he hired me, but he was desperate to find someone who could finish out the school year."

"And who he thought he could push around," Amber said.

"Right. But the academy's behavior support program is super important, and the kids are great. If I keep working hard, I hope I can convince O'Neil— and the board—to keep funding it."

"I think you should give the hottie another chance. Flirt with him," Amber said.

"No. No way. Officer Greene is going to try to find me someone else." Erica didn't want to listen to her sister telling her she needed to date, have fun, meet men. It wasn't on her agenda and she didn't want to discuss the reasons why with her big sister. "Hannah, how was your math test?"

They talked about school for a little while, all of them eating just a little pizza. Hannah constantly worried about gaining weight, while Amber, who actually needed to gain, found that a lot of food didn't taste quite right. Erica had always been someone whose appetite was affected by her emotions, and those were running a little high tonight.

After a few minutes, Hannah picked up her mother's plate and her own and carried them into the kitchen.

There was a slight slump to the seventeen-year-old's shoulders.

Erica looked quickly over at Amber to see if she'd noticed.

She had. She was looking after her daughter, biting her lip.

The sound of dishes clanking told them Hannah was loading the dishwasher. Erica raised an eyebrow at Amber. "She's a lot more responsible about chores than we ever were," she said.

"She hasn't had much choice." Amber sounded discouraged, and who could blame her? Her first bout with breast cancer, when Hannah was ten, had been difficult, but Erica and a bunch of friends had all rallied around, helped with food and with Hannah, and thrown a party when Amber had been declared free of disease.

Now that it had recurred and spread, now that Hannah was old enough to help her mom—and also, to understand the implications of a cancer recurrence—things were different. More challenging. The outcome less likely to be positive.

A glance at Amber suggested her thoughts were traveling down the same road. Time for another change of subject. "We should start on those curtains and valances we were talking about making."

"Eh, I don't know."

"If you're too tired—"

"I'm fine! Every time I don't want to do something it's not because…" She trailed off as Hannah came into the room. "It's not because I'm sick. And sure, I'll help with the curtains, though why we're making them for a rental I don't quite get."

Because it's a project, something to keep us busy. "A long-term rental," Erica said.

"Let's hope so." She glanced up at Hannah and added quickly, "I just mean we might not be able to afford this place through the high season."

"It's okay, Mom." Hannah's smile looked forced.

"Do you want to help?" Erica asked her niece. "You're so good at crafty stuff."

"Um, no, thanks. I have homework." Her phone buzzed and she glanced at it, then hurried out of the room.

Wanting to wipe the worried look off Amber's face, Erica got the bolt of filmy fabric, embroidered with tiny blue and green seashells, and started to unroll it across the table. "I'll measure. You cut," she said.

"Sure." Amber pushed herself out of her chair and walked slowly to the kitchen. "Where'd you put the scissors?" she called back.

Erica gripped the back of a chair to prevent herself from rushing in to help her sister, making her sit down, doing it all herself. "Drawer by the stove, I think. Do you see a tape measure in there?"

"Yep." Amber came back into the room brandishing scissors, handed them and a tape measure to Erica and then eased herself down into a chair. "So what's really going on with that cop you turned in?" she asked, sounding a little out of breath.

Erica measured the width of the dining room window and jotted it down. "I just really, really want the academy program to continue, help more kids."

"Because you can't have any," Amber said flatly.

"It's not just that, but…yeah." Erica sighed. She didn't like to talk about her own issues when Amber's were so pressing. "I guess that's part of why."

"That's a lot of weight to put on a bunch of troubled kids, making them stand in for all your old dreams," Amber said.

"They've lost so much in their lives. I really want to make a difference to them."

"*You've* lost so much. And was this guy possibly too good-looking?"

"Stop it." She didn't want to discuss her decision to avoid any kind of real relationship with her sister, who'd just argue with her. It was an old argument, predating the cancer and her recent resolution. Amber had loved boys as a teenager and had run pretty wild. She'd tried to get Erica to take advantage of the fact that their mother was usually too busy working to supervise them closely. But Erica had been the responsible one, trying to rein Amber in, rarely agreeing to even a simple date.

Now that she knew what she was facing, she kind of wished she'd taken Amber's route.

From upstairs, a blare of loud music sounded. Erica wrinkled her nose. "Ugh," she said.

"Yeah. The 'I hate women' music."

"Well, to be fair," Erica said, "it's what all the kids listen to."

"Promise me you'll make her know not to think

of herself that way, if…" Amber's voice tangled on the last word.

Erica's throat tightened. "Of course, but you'll be here to do that."

"Yeah." Amber cleared her throat. "Listen, I think I actually am a little too tired to help with this tonight. Rain check?" She was scooting back her chair as she spoke, hunched over, like a hollowed-out shell.

Erica wanted to hug her and reassure her that everything would be all right. But she didn't know that. And moreover, she thought as she watched Amber stare up the steps on the way to her first-floor bedroom, she couldn't even really imagine what her sister was feeling.

THE POUNDING RHYTHMS of Metallica and the throb of his muscles as he scrubbed floors and carried boxes distracted Trey from thinking about the depressing thing he was doing: cleaning out the house he'd shared with his wife.

He'd pay for it tomorrow. He wasn't supposed to lift anything over ten pounds, but come on. How could he clean out what remained of his married life without lifting a few boxes? And when his friend Denny from the force had volunteered to help, well, he couldn't sit around and let the guy work alone, could he?

The smell of bleachy cleaning solution got to him, so he left Denny finishing the kitchen floor and headed upstairs, taking it one step at a time, jaw clenched against the pain that radiated out from his lower back into his hip and leg. From his position by the front door, King rose and dutifully followed him.

As he ran the vacuum cleaner over the bedroom carpet, trying not to twist or make any sudden movements, he saw the lighter-colored squares on the walls where their pictures had hung. In a side nook was one they'd neglected to take down. A caricature they'd gotten of the two of them at some street fair was framed: him looking like a giant cartoon cop, Michelle like a tiny, cute perp begging for mercy.

She'd spent time begging during their marriage, all right, begging him to give up his notions of an Ozzie and Harriet family and come out partying, until the begging had turned to anger and then she'd stopped talking altogether. Meanwhile, his cop side had grown bigger and bigger until it had overshadowed the marriage. Chicken-and-egg thing: he didn't really know which had come first, Michelle's withdrawal or his own.

Truth was, they'd been poorly suited from the start. His growing desire to start a family and Michelle's flagging one had sealed their fate.

He stuffed the caricature into the trash bag he'd been hauling from room to room and walked down the hall to check the other two bedrooms. One painted pink and one painted blue, a relic of the previous residents who'd had a boy and a girl and then outgrown the little house.

He'd wanted a boy, some antiquated notion of building a family line. But a girl would've been fine, too. One of each, even better. He did a quick check of the two rooms and found one of Michelle's thongs and a bra in the back of the blue room closet. Strange, considering neither of them had spent much time in that room unless they'd had guests, which hadn't happened in a couple of years.

King stuck his nose into Trey's hand, a welcome distraction from thinking about what the lingerie meant. He stuffed it into the garbage and hauled it downstairs, leaning hard on the railing, King at his side. At the bottom of the stairs he checked his watch, considered taking a pain pill early and then forced the thought away.

In the kitchen, Denny finished rinsing out the mop and stood it near the back door. He checked his phone.

"Thanks, man," Trey said. "Take a break. There's cold beer in the fridge and I'm about to order us some pizza."

"I'll grab a beer, but then I've gotta go. Milo's starting T-ball and normally Laura would take him to practice, but she's leaning on me a little more." Denny didn't look at all upset.

"Are you in trouble with her?" Denny had been a big womanizer before falling for Laura and learning to walk the line.

"No, but…she's pregnant again," Denny blurted out, kneeling down to pet King.

Trey stopped in the middle of pulling out two beers and stared at his friend, ignoring the twist in his gut. "That's great, man. When is she due?"

"Six months, so end of October." Denny wiped

his forehead with his sleeve. "I've been taking some extra shifts to bring in a little more. When I'm off, I feel like I should be with her, take care of Milo so she can get some rest."

"You should. I appreciate your coming out today. I'd have hired a cleaning company, but money's tight."

"No problem. You'd do the same for me."

It was true. They'd been partners before Trey had become a K-9 officer, had dodged plenty of bullets together, had commiserated over beers about department politics and women and life. But their connection went back way further. Having spent time in the same foster home, they were practically brothers. "Give Laura a kiss for me, and tell her I'm sorry I stole you away today."

"Will do. She said to tell you she's already counting on you babysitting for us."

"Anytime." Although Denny had been sunnier and more beloved in the foster home, it had been Trey who'd helped with the babies, known for being the one who could make them stop crying, adept at changing diapers and heating up bottles. Denny remembered, and had entrusted Trey with Milo often enough that Milo called him Uncle Trey.

On some level, he guessed, he liked babies and wanted to be a dad so he could show the world he wasn't the same kind of slacker his own father had been.

"Got an offer on the house pretty quick, huh?"

Denny cracked open a cold beer and guzzled half of it.

"Inspection tomorrow. Should go well. Closing's next week." And that would be that.

"Young family, I'm guessing."

"Yeah." The little brick two-story was perfect for kids, with a fenced yard sporting a tire swing and a picnic table, and a basketball hoop above the garage. That was why the place had appealed to him, too.

"You'd think Michelle would've helped. She owns half, right?" Denny waved his phone at Trey. "Looks like she's partying instead, if you believe what she's posting."

Trey had blocked his ex-wife on social media, but he did still know her whereabouts. "She's doing a girls' week at the beach. Florida. Or so she said." He swallowed down a sour taste in his mouth.

"You're over her, right?"

Trey thought about it. It had been a year and a half since they'd separated, and their divorce had come through six months ago. The sense of failure still nagged at him, and he regretted losing his dream of a family. But Michelle?

Thinking of her partying down in Florida didn't make him jealous about the men she was probably meeting. It just made him feel like a sucker, agreeing to take on the cleaning. "Yeah, I'm over her." Then, restless, he took hold of two of the trash bags and started dragging them toward the door, ignoring the shooting pain in his back.

"Whoa, man, let me get that."

"I'm fine."

"You're not fine." Denny tried to grab the trash bags.

Trey held on. "I can get them."

"You're an idiot." Denny followed him outside, beer in hand, and watched while he tugged the bags down the steps. "You can't be a hotshot on the force, so now you're trying to be a hotshot at, what, taking out the garbage? You're gonna set yourself back."

What does it matter? Trey opened his mouth to say, but snapped it shut, realizing he didn't feel that way anymore, not exactly. The PT was undeniably awful, but he'd noticed a slight improvement in his last session. Maybe, just maybe, it would help. And he definitely didn't want to set himself back, because if he lost more of his mobility, if he couldn't get groceries or do his own laundry, where would he be?

A silver Camaro pulled up and parked at the curb. Both he and Denny stopped in the middle of the driveway. What was the chief doing here?

Chief Lincoln, whom they all privately called "Abe" because he was tall and thin like President Lincoln, came around and greeted them both, asked about their progress on the house, about Milo, about Trey's back. All of it was friendly enough, but Trey got an uneasy feeling.

"Gotta go," Denny said, waving his phone. "Wife's on my case."

As Denny drove away, Trey invited the chief up on the porch for a beer.

He was pretty shocked, though, when the man accepted. Lincoln had been a mentor to him and Denny from their rookie days, but he tended to hold himself aloof on the personal level.

"There's a reason I stopped by," Chief Lincoln said after cracking the bottle open. He put it down without taking a sip. "Heard some things from Earl Greene, the officer in charge of the disabled-officers program over in Pleasant Shores."

"Yeah? What?" Trey's heart stuttered a little, not just because he hated being called a disabled officer, but because of the censure he heard in his chief's voice. He lowered himself carefully onto the porch swing, wincing.

"He seemed to notice a negative attitude in you."

"I barely met—"

The chief cut him off with a raised hand. "Apparently, the cooperating teacher complained. Asked if there was anyone else who could come in and work with the kids, short notice."

Trey looked down at his knees, his fists clenching. Had he really been that obnoxious when he'd met Greene, and during that beach encounter with some long-legged beauty whose name he still didn't know?

You should've asked her name, made nice. "You're going to replace me," he said, dreary certainty pressing down on him. Not many guys could fail at rehab. He was a real standout, all right.

"I don't have anyone else to suggest to them, not now. And the other two departments they're working with are waiting for full approval, so they can't put anyone forward yet." The chief sighed. "I want it to work for you, but you'd better shape up. I look bad to have recommended you if you don't."

In a corner of his mind, he recognized the opportunity for a second chance, and seized it. "Will do, sir. I'll have a better attitude."

The chief stared Trey down. "A lot better, because attitude was a part of what got you in the fix you're in now. That incident shouldn't have happened. Your head hasn't been in the right place for months. If you hadn't gotten injured, I would've put you on a desk job."

The chief's words weighed him down again. He'd known he was off his game but hadn't realized it was noticeable to others. Reflexively, he reached for King, put a hand on his furry back.

"If you can't make it work, or prove to me you've changed, I won't recommend you for reinstatement to the force, even if your back does heal," Lincoln said, standing. "Look at it as a kind of a test." He turned and strode down to his car.

Leaving Trey to wonder how he was going to succeed at something he didn't even want to do, in an environment where the people he'd be working with already disliked him.

CHAPTER THREE

JULIE WHITE PULLED the baking sheet of chocolate chip cookies out of the oven just as her teenage granddaughters walked in the door from school, and she congratulated herself on her perfect timing. "Who wants cookies?" she singsonged.

Her younger granddaughter, Kaitlyn, looked at her with an open sneer. Great. She'd come on too strong. Figuring out how to navigate her new home here, living in a suite at her daughter's motel and helping with her granddaughters at their house adjacent to the motel would take some time.

Her older granddaughter, Sophia, was busy talking on her phone, but waved a greeting and snagged a cookie on her way through the kitchen. At sixteen, she was learning to drive, did well in school and had seemingly dozens of friends, including a boyfriend she didn't take all that seriously, thank heavens. Her sunny demeanor reminded Julie of her daughter, their mother. Little to no adolescent angst, just the self-absorption you'd expect from a teenager.

Kaitlyn, the thirteen-year-old, plopped down at the kitchen table with a loud sigh. She was going through an awkward stage, worsened by her parents' divorce and, probably, the fact that her grandparents had divorced shortly thereafter. It didn't help that she had a popular, gorgeous sister like Sophia, even though Sophia was actually very nice to Kaitlyn. But Julie understood why Sophia's niceness didn't sit well with her younger sister; it smacked of charity, or pity.

Julie slid the cookies from the cookie sheet to a plate and put them on the table. "Milk?" she asked, automatically going to the fridge and opening the door.

"Don't do dairy," Kaitlyn mumbled around a large mouthful of cookie.

That was news to Julie, but she knew better than to question it. She just got a glass of ice water and set it down on the table. "Would you and your sister like to go over to the big beach in a few minutes?" she asked. The big beach was on the wealthier side of Pleasant Shores, and unlike the narrow, rocky beaches most common on the Chesapeake, it had a wide swath of actual white sand.

"Why?" Kaitlyn swiped a napkin across her mouth and took another cookie. "It's only April."

"And it's seventy degrees. The heat wave will end soon, but you could still get a little bit of sun."

That seemed to pique Kaitlyn's interest; her mother wouldn't let either girl go tanning at the salon…though Julie suspected that Sophia had finagled a way past the parental-permission-under-eighteen rule, since she looked continually healthy and golden-bronze.

"Hey, Soph," Kaitlyn yelled. "Grandma wants to go to the beach."

That wasn't strictly accurate; Julie would rather have stayed home, in her cute little suite at the far end of the motel, with the latest mystery novel. But she was justifying living here, at least temporarily, by keeping an eye on her grandchildren during the notoriously dangerous after-school period: making an after-school snack, starting dinner and suggesting wholesome activities.

Besides, as her friend Mary said, she needed to get out of the house. To combat her gloom with sunshine and meet new people.

The meeting-new-people part had exactly zero appeal, but it wasn't likely to happen today. Having Kaitlyn plodding sullenly at her side would protect her from all but the most intrepid extroverts in town. People were afraid of teen girls.

Soon enough they were walking the three blocks through Pleasant Shores' little downtown to the beach, carrying beach towels and, in Julie's case, a folding beach chair. Both of the girls had insisted on wearing jean shorts and T-shirts over bikinis, over her protests. It was an optimistic clothing choice since, even with the unusually warm temperatures, the breeze at the beach would be cool and the bay's water frigid.

Julie caught a glimpse of herself in a shop window and winced. Capris and an old hoodie of Ria's: she'd let herself go since the divorce, the eighth deadly sin according to her ex-husband, Melvin. Not that it had done her much good to keep herself in shape for him.

He'd fallen out of love with her. He didn't want to be married. Even though it had happened seven months ago, she still had trouble believing that thirty-five years of marriage were over, just like that. That Melvin had moved up to Saint Michaels and was living in some business-suite hotel close to his job.

She glanced up and down the quiet main street of town. She hoped she wouldn't run into someone she knew, but then again, who cared? It wasn't like she was out to impress anyone.

Still, she ought to try harder with her appearance. *Look good, feel good*, her determinedly perky, stylish mother had always said. "What do you think about a top like that for me?" she asked her granddaughters, pausing to look through the window of Pleasant Shores' only "better women's clothing" shop. Read: middle-aged and expensive. But for now, while she was getting alimony, she could still afford to shop there. The top in question was a dusty pink and had the forgiving waistline she needed.

"It's cute," Sophia said, glancing up from her phone and giving Julie an encouraging smile. Of course, she'd barely looked at the top.

Julie turned to Kaitlyn and lifted an eyebrow. "What do *you* think?" Partly, she was encouraging Kaitlyn to express an opinion, showing she valued it, but she did in fact expect more honesty from Kaitlyn.

Kaitlyn shrugged, her forehead wrinkling. "It's fine. It's just like everything else you wear."

In other words, what did it matter what Julie wore? She was old, a grandma.

"You should get that one," Kaitlyn muttered, jerking her head toward a purple-and-turquoise tie-dye tunic.

"Really? It's so bright."

Kaitlyn shrugged and they walked on, but Julie gave a glance back at the top Kaitlyn had pointed out. It would definitely be a new look.

As it turned out, Julie did see people she knew: a friend from the bookstore, then someone she'd met recently at church. She'd been a year-round resident for ten years, but to the locals, that was nothing; she was only now differentiating herself from the summer visitors.

Sophia saw some girls she knew and ran screaming to hug them, then started an intense conversation. Kaitlyn and Julie slowed their pace. "Do you know who they are? Old friends?" Julie asked. "Seems like she hasn't seen them in a while."

"They go to our school. She saw them an hour ago." Kaitlyn's lip curled. "That's just how they act."

Julie remembered, then, the shrill excitement Ria had exhibited every time she saw a girl she knew. "Should we keep walking?" she asked Kaitlyn. "She can catch up. Or we can wait for her at the benches." The benches adjoined the big beach and were a gathering place where music groups performed and tourists clustered during the season.

"Whatever." They trudged along, and Julie felt marginally glad that she'd gotten the girls out and about. She worried about Kaitlyn's morale, in particular.

The sun was warm on her face, the breeze not too strong, the bay's smells rising up as they got closer to the water. Julie loved the Eastern Shore, always had; it had been her idea to use her inheritance from her grandfather to buy a summer cottage here.

They reached the benches and sat down, and moments later Sophia joined them, breathless. "Sorry! Let's go down."

They walked through the shipped-in sand, debating where to sit. As they found a place to set up the chair and towels they'd brought, Sophia put an arm around Julie. "This was a good idea, Grandma."

Her heart warmed. "It's fun to spend time with you girls. Now, be sure to put on sunscreen."

There were several groups of people on the beach, even though it was way too cool to swim. Cabin fever, she guessed.

Kaitlyn grunted and nudged her sister, and they both looked toward a group of boys, closer to Kaitlyn's age than Sophia's.

Kaitlyn finger-combed her hair and checked her appearance in her phone camera. "I look bad," she said, tossing the phone down.

"You should totally go talk to them," Sophia encouraged.

"No way!"

"Well, just…walk by them, then. Give them a chance to talk to you."

"Will you come?"

"Okay, sure." Sophia got up and grabbed her phone and slid back into her denim shorts. Kaitlyn had never taken hers off, and the two of them started in the direction of the boys, who were throwing Frisbees. Then Sophia turned back. "Is this all right, Grandma?"

"Go. Have fun." She felt successful now, like she'd had a good influence on her granddaughters, getting them to come outside. She pulled out her mystery novel and leaned back in her chair, looking out at the water, watching as the girls got farther away. A buzz let her know that Kaitlyn had forgotten her phone, and idly she picked it up.

Make sure you spend time with Grandma like we talked about, was the message on the lock screen.

Oh. So it wasn't that she was helping her granddaughters; it was that they were helping her, per their mother's instructions. Embarrassed, she leaned her head against the back of the chair and closed her eyes.

Apparently, "spending time with Grandma" was a topic of discussion between her daughter and her granddaughters. She was a project.

She looked down at her pale legs and counted two more age spots. Great.

Grabbing her novel, she tried to read, but her thoughts kept returning to that text. If she wasn't really helping her granddaughters, then she felt sort

of…pointless. And that annoyed her. She had no intention of being one of those divorced women who
dwelled on problems or pitied herself. She'd always
been someone who took action.

She needed to make a change. But what?

MONDAY MORNING, TREY got lucky.

He walked with King down the rocky coastline
toward the school. Walking on uneven terrain wasn't
the easiest thing for a guy with a spinal injury to do,
but today, the outdoor setting gave him an advantage. Or at least gave him access.

Erica and her students—ten or eleven teenagers,
mostly boys—were out on the beach. The kids stood
or knelt in a rough semicircle, and Erica was talking to them, gesticulating with her hands, bending
over to pick up something and hold it up.

Looked like a science lesson, and they'd chosen
a rotten day for it. After that unseasonable warm
spell, the temperatures had plummeted and the sky
had gone heavy. Now a cold wind whipped Erica's
dark, shaggy hair. She forked it back with an impa-
tient gesture and kept talking.

Businesslike. Serious. That was why he figured he
was lucky. He didn't think she'd have let him into her
classroom, given what his chief had told him about
her attitude, but anyone could walk on the public part
of the beach, right?

As he got closer, he could see that the kids were
sketching and taking notes, most seemingly engrossed
in what she was saying. Not all, of course; one boy

was daydreaming, and a couple of others seemed to be arguing, one giving the other a subtle punch in the arm. No serious misbehavior, though.

He seized the opportunity to study Erica more closely. Know thine enemy.

She was skinny enough that it verged on un-healthy—you could see that even through the thick sweater she wore. Khaki pants and duck boots—nothing to emphasize those mile-long legs. Practical. Not his type; he'd always liked curvy women who dressed up pretty.

And yet when you looked at her face—those huge eyes, those high cheekbones—you realized she was, in her own way, stunning.

She looked up, caught him staring and strode over, parking her hands on her hips. "Why are you here?"

He gave his friendliest, most ingratiating smile. "Reporting for duty," he said.

She didn't smile back. "Students, keep working," she said over her shoulder. Then she faced Trey. "I thought they were assigning someone else."

So she wasn't even going to pretend she hadn't requested that he be replaced. Fine. "I talked them into giving me a chance."

She glanced back at the kids, who were gawking or goofing around rather than writing. One glare from her, though, and they mostly hunched over their notebooks again. Then she looked back at Trey, equally severe with him. "This is supposed to help?" she asked. "You're distracting the students."

Beside him, King stood and whined a little. Trey gave the settle command, which King did, but with a glance up at him that spoke volumes.

King was still a police dog in his heart, just like Trey was an officer, and he'd noticed something wrong. Trey dropped the leash. "Search," he commanded without thinking it through.

Almost instantly, he realized that was inappropriate; he wasn't on duty. But it was too late. King ran into the group of kids, several of whom reeled back in fear. King was large, focused and panting, which showed his mighty teeth.

"Get your dog away from them," Erica said.

"Just a minute."

"No, now!"

Suddenly, King sat. Utterly still, focused on one boy's backpack.

Trey called him back, watching the boy. He said something to another kid beside him and shifted the backpack out of sight, blocking their view with his body.

"That kid has drugs in his backpack," Trey told Erica.

"What?"

"That kid in the red jacket," he said. "He's carrying drugs. King found them. He's a drug dog," he explained as he reached into his pocket for King's favorite tug toy and knelt for a quick play session, King's reward for a job well done. He tried to keep from wincing as King's enthusiastic yanks on the toy shot pain down his back.

Erica blew out a breath. "You're sure?"

"Uh-huh." He was still watching the kid. "You'll find it, unless he manages to ditch it somewhere."

She pulled out her phone and walked away from Trey, spoke into it for several minutes while Trey stood awkwardly near the group of students. He ought to reach out to them, try to connect. Coming in and catching one of them in an illegal act probably wasn't the best start.

Erica walked back toward him. "Officer Greene is on his way over," she said. "It'll just take him two minutes to get here." Then she walked into earshot of the kids. "Okay, gather your things. We'll head back to the building."

Trey usually felt good, triumphant, when King had made a find. But looking at the boy in the red jacket walking along, desperately searching from side to side for a place to dispose of his stash, he felt like a jerk.

In his normal life, he knew what to do in such a situation, his role well-defined, that of a K-9 police officer. Now he had no idea of how to act. He was way out of his element trying to be a teacher type rather than a cop. It made him remember his own days as a troubled teen, the problems he'd had with school due to his father's frequent moves and his own shifts in and out of foster care.

"I didn't mean to get him expelled or anything," he said to Erica.

"When you told me that he was holding drugs, I had to call the police." She bit her lip. "I hate it, though. The academy is often their last chance before juvie."

Trey felt worse. He'd grown up with some kids who had gone the juvie route, and it had been the end of anything good for them.

There had to be some other way to survive this period until his benefits came in, some way that didn't mess up kids' lives and make him look like a chump in front of a pretty but annoying woman.

Maybe he could find a way to hurry the notoriously slow disability paperwork along. He'd submitted all the required documentation, finally, but the hearing process took a ridiculous amount of time.

As they reached the schoolyard, a police car approached, and he could feel the tension coming off these kids in waves. Normally, he'd have been in the car and he wouldn't have felt it; he'd just have come in and taken charge, made arrests.

From the car emerged not only Officer Greene, but also... Abe, Trey's chief? Why? Now *he* was the one who felt like he was in big trouble.

Trey moved with King toward the two men, ignoring his own qualms.

"Which one?" Greene asked.

He almost didn't want to say. He'd never been arrested as a kid, but he'd gotten in plenty of trouble, and he found himself identifying with the teenager with the backpack, weirdly enough. Maybe it was because he was here to help kids, not to uphold the law.

He'd been trained not to identify with perps,

though, and he called on that training now. "Tall one in the red jacket."

Greene nodded, walked over and pulled the kid aside, while Erica shepherded the rest of the students into the building.

His chief patted his back. "Not the start I'd envisioned, but good job," he said. "Get the bad seed outta there and the place will run more smoothly."

Trey had the feeling they were all bad seeds to someone, but whatever. "You here to check up on me already?"

"Um, no. Not actually." The chief looked uncomfortable.

Trey waited.

"There's no easy way to say it. I have a potential new handler for King."

The words slammed into Trey's chest and, instinctively, he looked down at King, whose alert chocolate eyes stared back at him. King, so naturally talented that he'd detected drugs in a random kid's backpack. King, who was aching with boredom, who wanted to work.

The chief was going on about a K-9 officer whose dog had gotten sick, who needed a highly trained dog, who did the kind of drug detection work at which King excelled, who worked just thirty miles up the shore. Might be temporary, but probably permanent unless Trey got back on the force and another dog came available for the other guy.

Trey had known this day could come. He'd signed

off on the possibility when he'd gotten King five years ago.

He opened his mouth to say that would be great, fine, but the words stuck in his throat. He'd lost his wife, his job and his home, and he could handle all that. Maybe not well, but he could handle it.

Losing his best friend? Not so much.

CHAPTER FOUR

BACK IN THE CLASSROOM, Erica told the agitated teenagers to take their seats, and they did, eventually. Venus had tears in her eyes—she and LJ were good friends—and Rory kept getting up to pace, then sitting back down when she frowned at him.

How would they trust her now?

Erica's own eyes kept going to LJ's empty desk. His defiant smirk as he'd been led away hadn't concealed the fear in his eyes, and her heart ached. She'd thought she was reaching him, had spent extra time with him, found him books that played to his interests, encouraged his friendships with a couple of the more stable kids.

With one little bag of drugs—had it been marijuana or something worse?—he'd thrown it all away.

The ache stayed as she got the kids started writing up their findings from their outdoor session, then straightened the old, dusty shades on the classroom's single window.

The academy had been assigned the smallest room in the school and been lucky to get even that. She'd tried to warm it up with prints of great artwork and motivational posters, but the overall impression was still pretty pitiful.

The lack of ventilation meant the room full of sweaty teenagers smelled terrible, too, despite her discreet use of plug-in air fresheners.

After what had happened to LJ, all of her efforts seemed inadequate. Losing LJ, losing any kid, wasn't an option for her. She fingered her mother's crucifix, tucked inside her shirt. Mom had known how traumatic it had been for Erica to have the preventive surgery that slashed her likelihood of getting ovarian cancer, but also destroyed her chance to bear a child. On her deathbed, Mom had made Erica promise that she'd use her nurturing abilities to help kids somehow, even if it wasn't through mothering as she'd hoped.

Picturing her mother's wasted frame, her intense, faith-filled eyes, Erica swallowed the lump in her throat and straightened her spine. She'd go to the station right after school to further discuss LJ's situation with Officer Greene. Maybe she could get him a second chance.

A movement out the window caught her eye. Trey and his dog were walking toward his car. Trey's shoulders were slumped and he was limping a little, but what did he have to be upset about? He'd made an arrest, or at least helped with one. He had to be feeling great.

He'd gotten a second chance, starting over in the program for officers who'd been injured, volunteering at the school.

He was supposed to start working with the kids today. But now he was leaving his responsibility behind, and wasn't that just like a man? He'd come in, wreaked havoc and then left when the going got rough.

She pushed the window open. "Hey! Mr. Harrison! Trey!"

Behind her, the students started to murmur. She wasn't a yeller normally, so no doubt her unusual behavior made them curious.

Trey turned around.

She beckoned to him.

He shook his head.

She nodded vigorously and pointed toward the school's front door. "Check in at the office," she said in her most bossy teacher voice. "Then come to room sixteen."

She walked around checking the students' work and encouraging the slackers to get started, and a few moments later, Trey appeared outside the classroom door, his dog obediently beside him.

He looked bad. Well, he looked good—still a movie star—but his shoulders sagged and tension lines bracketed his mouth.

But she wasn't going to pity him, she decided as she walked over and stepped out into the hall. "Hi," she said, partially closing the classroom door behind her. "Are you ready to work?"

"Not really. I…thought I'd start tomorrow instead."

She pinched the skin between her thumb and

forefinger to keep from giving him a piece of her mind. "I'd rather you went ahead and started today," she said, keeping her voice level. "Your introduction to the students didn't exactly build trust, and I'd like to see you start to mend that."

"It's not a good day."

She narrowed her eyes and studied him. "It's not a good day for LJ, either. He's the one you had arrested."

He lifted his hands, palms out. "I didn't mean for it to go down that way necessarily. You called the police."

"True," she admitted. "But it still holds. Some of these kids never have a good start to their day, but they still have to come to school. I'm sure that was the case when you were working a police job, so I'd like to see you stick to the same philosophy as a volunteer."

He looked almost ill.

She frowned, studying him. Maybe he actually *was* sick. "I can't make you, of course."

"No, you're right. I can do it." He straightened his shoulders. "Why don't I do my standard 'introduction to police dogs' talk?"

"Okay, sure, if… Do you think it'll work for teenagers?" It sounded too basic.

"I don't know," he said, "but it's all I've got today."

Fair enough, it was his first day, but the problem was his attitude. He didn't seem to care. She was definitely talking to Officer Greene about his selection of volunteer, as well as about LJ.

Inside the classroom, the kids weren't even pretending to work. Paper wads flew across the room, Rory was playing a game on his forbidden cell phone, and Venus and Shane were punching each other, maybe playfully or maybe for real, or a little of both.

She walked to the front of the room, gesturing for Trey to follow, and clapped her hands to get everyone's attention. "People. We have a special guest. Two of them, actually."

The kids talked on, ignoring her. She was reaching for her whistle when King gave one sharp bark.

The room went silent.

She introduced Trey and King. Trey sat on the edge of the desk and gave a practiced spiel. It was obviously targeted toward younger kids, and her teenagers showed signs of restlessness until Trey got King to do a couple of tricks. That, they liked.

They didn't ask any questions, so she did, grilling him about King's training and his own, how he'd gotten started in K-9 work, whether he'd go back to it. He answered, but there was no spark in what he said, and the kids started whispering and, in a couple of cases, nodding off.

"If there aren't any more questions…" she began.

"I have a question," Shane said.

"Go ahead."

"What does your dog do, now that you're not a real cop anymore?"

Trey looked down at his dog and didn't answer.

"I think it's kind of like being president of the United States," Erica joked, trying to fill the awkward silence. "Once you're a police officer, you're always called one, even if you're no longer active. Is that right, Officer Harrison?"

He looked up and cleared his throat. "It's just Mr., for now," he said. He cleared his throat again. "And I actually just found out that King is going to another officer. Back to work, huh, buddy?" There was something wrong with his voice. He looked down and ran a hand roughly over King's head, scratching the big dog's upright-pointed ears.

The kids were dead silent now, looking at Trey, but he wasn't looking at them. He was staring down at King, running his hand down the dog's back.

King whined and leaned against Trey's leg. And now they didn't look like a K-9 team; they looked like any pet and owner, attached to and dependent on one another.

And Trey was about to lose King.

Unwanted sympathy twisted her heart. She knew all too well what a comfort dogs could be. Her rescue Maltese mix had gotten her through the horrible pain of her mother's death, her sister's diagnosis and her own preventive surgery. Losing him early last year had nearly broken her heart. It hadn't seemed possible she could feel for a dog again, but now Ziggy had become almost as dear to her.

If Trey could feel that much for his working dog, he couldn't be all that bad. There must be emotions, a real person, beneath that gruff cop surface.

She stuffed her sympathy away. The last thing she needed was to find out that Trey was a good human being, because that, along with his amazing looks and macho appeal, would be a lethal combination.

And she didn't dare open that door. "Thanks, Officer…er, Mr. Harrison. We appreciate your work today. Let's give him a round of applause, shall we, students?"

The kids' applause was more enthusiastic than she'd expected, probably because they, like her, felt sorry for Trey and King.

But pity wasn't respect and there was no denying Trey had done a half-baked job today, though she now understood why: he'd just learned he was losing his dog.

She told the students to clean up for lunch. "You can go now," she said to Trey.

He nodded without speaking, grunted something to King and left without meeting her eyes. But she'd seen their shininess.

A man who could cry about losing his dog might have untold depths, but there was no denying Trey was a hot mess.

She sat down at her desk and focused on her stack of paperwork, ignoring—or trying to ignore—the heavy footsteps, and her own heavy heart, as the two of them left the building.

WEDNESDAY AFTERNOON, TREY sat on the front porch of his cottage and watched King walk away with his new handler. His heart was a rock in his chest.

King trotted alongside the other officer, Cochran, and Trey reminded himself that this was good for King. He'd get to do the work he loved. Cochran said he was looking forward to working with King. He seemed like a nice enough guy, so it was wrong of Trey to want to punch him.

When they reached the car and Cochran opened the back door, King hesitated and looked back at Trey.

Cochran jerked King's leash to the side and spoke sharply, forcing King's head front again.

Trey stood up too fast and his back went into a spasm. He gripped the porch rail to keep from falling. When he looked up again, King was jumping into the back of the police vehicle.

It was just a leash correction. He has to show King he's the boss. Heart pounding, Trey sank back down onto the steps and watched the cruiser's taillights disappear.

It had just been a leash correction, but…

The image of King's confused face wouldn't leave his head. King had been his dog since he'd left his puppy raiser. He'd never known anyone else. What if he wouldn't work for Cochran? What if that one leash correction was indicative of a harsher training modality than King was used to?

Trey wanted his dog back. The chief had said it was a possibility—slim, but a possibility. *If* he returned to the force.

Which meant he had to get back into police

work...which meant he had to do well at the volunteer work as well as his physical therapy.

He'd missed both his volunteer job and a PT session today, though. Not good.

"You okay?"

He looked up, startled. The voice belonged to Julie, the older woman who owned the Healing Heroes cottage, or managed it at least. Automatically he started to stand, but his back went into another spasm that had him grasping the porch railing halfway up.

"Don't stand up." Julie sank down onto the porch steps beside him. "Listen, I just came over to check on you. Is everything okay?"

No. Nothing's okay. "Sure. Cottage is great. Why do you ask?"

"I'm friends with Earl Greene," she said. "He seems concerned."

Erica must have given him another bad report. Trey thought of King's eyes, looking back at him, and stiffened his aching spine. "It's been an adjustment," he said, "but I intend to make the most of the opportunity." He had to heal, get back on the force, for King's sake as well as his own.

Julie nodded. "Do you have family waiting for you back home? You know you can have your wife and kids stay with you here. There's plenty of room."

She was probably being nosy, probing for information, but since she was a friend of Earl Greene's, he needed to display an open attitude rather than letting it bother him. "No kids, no wife," he said. "Divorced."

"Me, too," she said, to his surprise. "You doing okay with it?"

Something about the way she asked the question made him suspect she wasn't doing okay with hers. "I don't miss my wife, to be honest," he said. "I miss the dream."

She raised an eyebrow.

"You know," he went on, "the whole two kids and a yard with flowers and a dog thing."

"Oooooh." She nodded in understanding. "If it makes you feel any better, I had the dream, for more than thirty years. It's not always perfect, and it doesn't always last."

"I guess."

They sat quietly for a few minutes then, but the silence was companionable. Trey had never known his mother, never liked his dad's girlfriends and never paid much attention to his scolding foster mom. The police hierarchy was dominated by men.

This might be one of the first times he'd had a real conversation with an older woman. He found himself liking Julie.

And the fact that she'd offered up her cottage to the Healing Heroes program, helping officers like him who needed to get away from their pasts and start over—yeah. He liked her a lot.

Next door, he heard the same loud, excited barking he heard multiple times per day, and moments later, Erica emerged from her cottage with her goofy dog on a leash.

She didn't even train her dog, and she gets to keep him.

That wasn't fair. There was no comparison between a police dog and a pet dog, between a shepherd and a designer doodle mix.

Erica waved as they passed, and then the dog spotted a seagull and lunged, nearly jerking her off her feet. "Ziggy!" she cried, bracing herself and holding on to the big dog's leash with difficulty. "Ziggy, heel!"

The dog glanced over his shoulder at her and then continued pulling toward the seagull.

Looked like she'd *tried* to train him at least. Trey stood, grimacing through the back pain, walked toward the dog and snapped his fingers. "Hey. Sit." He kept his voice low and calm. It was worth a try, considering it was the first command most dogs learned.

The dog stopped, turned and came toward him, sinking down into a perfect sit.

"Nice." He reached in his pocket automatically and realized he did, in fact, have a biscuit he'd meant to give to King. "Give paw," he said, holding out a hand to the dog, and sure enough, the doodle lifted a large, white-gold front foot for him to shake.

He handed over the biscuit. Ziggy inhaled it, nuzzled him and then jumped up, putting his paws on Trey's chest and nearly knocking him backward. His back twisted painfully as he caught himself and he couldn't restrain a grimace.

"Ziggy!" Erica jerked the dog's leash. "Sit! Down."

The dog obliged, slowly, then leaped up to snap at a butterfly.

"I'm sorry about him," she said to Trey as she planted her feet and tugged the dog back into her radius.

"Looks like Erica could use some help with training Ziggy," Julie said from the steps. "You're a dog expert, aren't you, Trey?"

Just what he needed: the responsibility of training a huge, out-of-control mutt.

But if it would get him back into Erica's good graces…help him succeed here, get back on the force and get King back… Yeah. That was a plan.

He looked directly at her. "Would that buy me another chance to work with you and the kids?" he asked. "I know I've done poorly so far, and I apologize."

She hesitated.

He knelt in front of the foolish dog so he wouldn't have to face that steady gaze. "I can teach him to mind his manners better, act calmer around people."

Erica stepped closer and rubbed Ziggy's head. "He's already calmer around you. He can tell you know what you're doing. But what I need is to get him calmer around me."

"Oh, I'd need to work with both of you," he said. And then he thought about that.

Erica was a beautiful woman. Not the kind of woman he'd go for romantically, but he felt a strange kinship between them, something he'd never felt before.

He didn't need any attachments here in this town. He just needed to stick to business, get done what he needed to get done and go back to his real life.

If that meant training Erica's dog, and teaching her to work with the dog—while keeping his emotional distance—well, that was what he'd have to do. It shouldn't be that hard. She wasn't his type.

"I always wanted him to be a therapy dog," Erica admitted. "To work with cancer patients. But I don't think he's capable. He's too wild."

"He's just untrained. He can get there." Of that, Trey was confident.

"You should give it a try," Julie encouraged.

Still kneeling in front of Ziggy, Trey looked up. Erica was chewing her lip and there was something in her eyes that suggested she was aware of the weird vibe between them.

Finally, she let out a sigh. "I guess, if it would help him be better with people… I guess it's worth it."

"You sound like it's a prison sentence." With difficulty, Trey rose to his feet. "It won't be that, I promise. I'll work hard at that and at the school, but you have to have an open mind. Toward the training and toward me."

"All right, then." Erica held out her hand. "It's a deal."

He took her hand in his, and sudden warmth shot

up his arm. Her skin was just so soft. He'd never felt anything like it.

She tugged her hand away and he realized he'd been clutching it. Should he apologize? Or pretend it never happened?

Ziggy solved the problem by going nuts over another dog walking by, and Erica waved and hurried off down the street, tugging Ziggy along.

"You just took on quite a project." Julie sounded amused.

"Yeah, I did." In more ways than one.

CHAPTER FIVE

THURSDAY AFTERNOON, ERICA headed to the teachers' lounge for her end-of-day planning period.

Trey followed her. Aaack! He'd been sticking to her so close he'd actually bumped into her a couple of times. All a part of his new effort to be the perfect volunteer, and it was wreaking havoc with her blood pressure.

Not that she was attracted. At least, no more than she would be to any handsome guy. It was just annoying when she was used to being a free, independent agent. That was it: annoying. Annoyance could make you feel flushed and feverish, right?

A few other teachers who had free periods were in the lounge, working or chatting before going to their after-school duties or lesson planning.

The gray-haired Maloney twins, who taught art and music respectively, were deep in discussion at a table in the corner. One of the math teachers was marking tests, and a couple of the social studies teachers hunched over a laptop. The smell of stale coffee blended with someone's slightly burned popcorn from the microwave.

After Trey had met everyone—and Erica didn't

miss a couple of the female teachers raising their eyebrows at each other, an obvious commentary on Trey's good looks—the two of them sat in a corner to talk about the next day's lessons and activities.

"Sorry we have to do this in here," she said to him. "We only have the one classroom for the academy, so when Paul—that's the other teacher for the behavior support program—has the kids, I usually work in the lounge. It's a little dingy."

"Conference room's empty," the math teacher said without looking up.

Aaack again. For whatever reason, she didn't want to be alone with Trey. "Oh, well, we're settled in here," she said, pulling out her folders of materials to make it so.

"No problem." Trey looked around, surely noticing the stained floors and ripped upholstery. "No worse than most police stations. I'm used to it." He settled back into the chair with a sigh. "Truth is, I'm just glad to sit down."

At least he wasn't snobby about the surroundings. "You did better today," she told him. He had taken over half the kids and helped them with lower-level math while Erica had worked with the more advanced kids. Then, because objectives called for lots of breaks for physical activity and community service, they'd walked into town and cleaned up litter in a couple of streets and alleys.

Trey had made an obvious effort to be friendly and patient with the kids, and they were starting to respond. "Here's my tentative plan for tomorrow," she said, showing him, and they were soon deep in discussions of how to give the kids real-world applications for the math they were learning.

The bell rang, signaling the last class change of the day. Minutes later, the door flew open.

"Fight," the school secretary exclaimed breathlessly, and pointed to Erica. "One of your kids, Venus, is involved. Your niece, too."

"Hannah?" Erica stood, knocking her chair back in her haste. She steadied it and hurried to the door, Trey following her. "What happened?"

"Venus said some rude things to Hannah. Kaitlyn Martin got involved and threw a couple of punches, supposedly to defend Hannah. And then Hannah jumped in and fought."

"Call the parents," Erica said, and hurried in the direction the secretary had indicated.

In the school's central court area where four halls came together, several teachers were holding back Kaitlyn and Hannah. A security officer had Venus and was tugging her toward the office.

It figured they'd be hardest on a kid from her program, although by size and angry expression, Kaitlyn looked like more of a threat.

Hannah turned toward Erica and big tears started rolling down her cheeks. "I'm sorry. I didn't know what to do."

"Don't apologize," Kaitlyn snapped at her. "That'll just make people tease you more, if you act all wimpy." She tried without success to shake off the teacher's restraining grip.

"We'll do worse than that if you don't stop resisting us," the teacher snapped, and Kaitlyn went still, looking shaken.

"Are you calm enough to walk to the office?" Erica asked both girls, and they nodded, Hannah still leaking tears.

"Thanks," Erica said to the two teachers who'd gotten involved. "We'll take it from here." She glanced back at Trey to make sure he was on board, and he nodded, his expression blank, lips flat. A cop expression, which made sense; he'd probably broken up some teen fights in his day.

No time to psychoanalyze him now. "Come on," she said to the girls. "Let's go to the office and wait for your parents."

"You called Mom?" Hannah's voice cracked on the last word. "She can't come in. I don't want to make her do that!"

Erica's heart twisted. Hannah was so careful not to add to her mother's burden, but all Amber wanted was to mother her, to do all the things she worried she wouldn't be able to do in the future. "Of course the secretary called her, and I'm sure she'll be in right away."

"My mom won't," Kaitlyn said glumly. "She's at some hospitality convention."

"Your grandma, then." They were all walking toward the office now, the girls dragging their feet.

Erica could identify. Any encounter with Principal Micah O'Neil meant a long, patronizing lecture at a minimum.

Worse, he was already dead set against the academy's support program, and he was sure to blame the fight on Venus. More ammunition to discontinue the whole thing.

They sat in the outer office, awaiting the arrival of parents and guardians. Venus, though, rode a bus quite a distance to get to school, and she looked at Erica miserably. "My mom is at work. She can't get here in time."

"I'll stand in for her," Erica said. "That means stand up for you in the meeting, and discuss it with your mom afterward."

Julie White burst into the office. "Kaitlyn, what on earth?" She gave a distracted wave to Erica and Trey and then beckoned her granddaughter over to the end of the row of chairs. They got into an intense discussion.

"Kaitlyn's grandmother?" Trey guessed, and Erica nodded.

Amber appeared next. She wore ripped jeans and a concert T-shirt, a baseball cap covering her head.

Hannah jumped up and ran to her, Erica following behind to lend support. "I'm sorry, Mom," Hannah said, her voice choked.

Amber wrapped her arms around Hannah. "I kinda want to high-five you for standing up for yourself," she growled into her daughter's ear, loud enough for Erica to hear, "but I'm going to have to act like I'm mad at you."

Behind them, a door opened, a throat cleared loudly. Principal O'Neil beckoned them all into his office, and they filed in, crowding into the chairs in front of the large desk. Trey was at the end of the line, and when he reached the door, O'Neil raised an eyebrow and took a step forward, subtly blocking his way. "What's your role here?" he asked.

"I'm a volunteer." Trey lifted his chin and met the older man's eyes, clearly no stranger to displays of male dominance. "I'd like to sit in, if it's okay with Ms. Rowe and the other girls' parents."

That made O'Neil's chest puff up, and Erica knew why: he wanted it to be *his* decision whether having Trey join the group was okay, not the parents' decision. He wanted everyone to defer to his authority at all times.

"He's shadowing me to learn about the kids," Erica said, aiming for a docile tone that was far from how she felt. "We'd really appreciate it if you'd let him stay."

Behind O'Neil's back, Amber rolled her eyes. "Of course he can stay," she said.

"Fine with me," Julie added.

"It would be an education for me, sir," Trey said.

"All right, but just listen and learn," O'Neil snapped. "And you'll have to stand. We don't have enough chairs here in the office."

Erica opened her mouth to offer to give Trey her chair—she knew his back was hurting from the way he'd winced after their cleanup activity—but he caught her eye and gave a tiny shake of his head.

The last bell rang, and the hallway filled with kids headed toward the car pickup line, the parking lot for the lucky few older kids who had cars, and the bus area.

O'Neil sat down and glared out at the three girls. "I want to hear what happened from each of you, and make it quick. Don't bother to lie, because I already spoke to the two teachers who witnessed the fight."

Venus and Kaitlyn looked away, faces identically sullen.

Amber nudged Hannah. "Tell the man what happened."

She bit her lip and nodded, then looked up at the principal. "It shouldn't have been a big deal," she said. "Someone in the hall made a comment about me. I don't even know if it was her." She nodded toward Venus. "But Kaitlyn got mad and started shoving her, and then it was a fight, and... I got involved."

Venus snorted audibly, but her face had relaxed a little. She'd clearly expected something worse to be said about her.

Kaitlyn provided it. "Venus called the new girl a name. A bad name. And we're supposed to stop bullying. That's all I was doing."

Julie put a hand on Kaitlyn's arm, but the girl snatched it away. Julie sighed and then spoke. "It's great you wanted to help, honey, but shoving or hitting isn't the answer, and you know it. You've been raised better than that."

"You can't make the excuse that you're protecting the new girl. Hannah's been here a couple of months," O'Neil contributed, and then added, "Your sister has never gotten into this kind of trouble."

Julie and Kaitlyn clenched their jaws in identical fashion. Their family resemblance would have been funny in different circumstances.

"And your story?" O'Neil looked at Venus.

"I joked along with some other kids. It wasn't anything. All of a sudden she—" she pointed at Kaitlyn "—starts shoving me into the lockers." She shrugged. "I was raised to fight back."

"And you know better, too," Erica said firmly, conscious of her surrogate parent role. "Do you have anything to say to Hannah?"

Venus pushed her lips together and looked over at Hannah. "Sorry," she said.

"Not sincere," O'Neil snapped. "Three days' after-school detention for all of you, starting tomorrow." He stood, indicating the meeting was over, and then raised a finger. "In fact, rather than relaxing in a study hall, the three of you can work on the garden in front of the school. Separately, not together. And since you're such an advocate—" He turned to Erica. "You can supervise."

Erica drew in a deep breath and let it out. No use to call him on being patronizing, treating her like one of the kids. Anyway, she'd rather be here than not, rather try to help the girls get along. The lost planning time, worrying about Ziggy stuck at home needing exercise…those were minor problems to solve later. "I won't be able to supervise them closely unless they're working together," she said, keeping her voice humble and mild.

The others had started to walk out, which was probably for the best; they wouldn't be treated to O'Neil's sneer. "I have real reservations about the way your kids mingle with the mainstream ones," he said. "Consider this a test."

Erica felt her jaw clench and consciously relaxed it. "Yes, sir," she said, and hurried to catch up with the others.

They all walked out together and then Venus veered off to meet her friends. Julie left with Kaitlyn.

Amber turned to Trey. "I hear you're going to help train Ziggy," she said. "Lord knows he needs it."

"He really does," Hannah agreed.

The side of Trey's mouth quirked up into a half smile. "I can't argue with you on that." They headed toward the parking lot, Trey, Hannah and Amber chatting amicably.

He wasn't treating Amber any differently than anyone else, despite her obvious status as a cancer patient. Erica liked him the better for that.

But liking him *too* much would be a mistake. You could be nice to a cancer patient, but that didn't mean you'd want to be in a relationship with one. And despite all her health efforts and surgery, Erica still knew her family history left her at increased risk. Not to mention that she couldn't have kids. Not exactly a good bet for a relationship.

Which was why she was devoting herself to her students. Why she needed to keep her distance from Trey.

A little hard to do when she was teaching with him every day. And having him help her train her dog. Yeah, a little hard.

Erica tuned back in to the conversation in time to hear Amber mention Italian food. Trey's face lit up. "Sure thing!"

"Terrific," Amber said. "Let's meet at seven." She smiled innocently at Erica. "Trey's going to join us for our Friday night dinner at DiGiorno's. As a thanks in advance for his help with Ziggy."

"See you later," Trey said, and headed off down the street.

"You just had to do that, didn't you?" Erica said to Amber.

"Yes, I did. You won't make a move for yourself, so sometimes your big sis has to take over."

"You two," Hannah said, but her face had lifted for the first time that afternoon. She liked to hear them bickering because it reinforced her sense that things were normal in the family, normal with her mom.

"Maybe I'll stay home," Erica said. "Leave you to Mr. Handsome."

A shadow crossed Amber's face. "Nope," she said. "This one's for you."

Hannah's face fell, too, and Erica could have kicked herself for ruining the good mood. In her darker moments, Amber talked about how she might not have another relationship, might not have time for one.

So if her sister wanted to play matchmaker, Erica wasn't going to spoil her fun. Amber had precious little of it these days. "Fine," she said. "I'll be there. But you two can't abandon me with him."

ON FRIDAY MORNING, Julie walked into the bookstore for her early shift and sighed with relief as she felt the calm descend around her. Getting a job at the bookstore had been the best thing she'd done since her divorce. She loved the books, loved the fragrance, the muted colors, the amazing ambience of a bookstore set in a squat old lighthouse that had been moved into downtown.

Mostly, she loved the friendship she'd developed with the bookstore's owner, Mary Rhoades. The sixtysomething woman was model-thin and gorgeous, and rumors abounded about her history among the rich and famous. Despite her appearance and background, she was warm and down-to-earth. When she'd moved to Pleasant Shores, she'd given up all traces of her earlier life except her Maltipoo, Baby; she carried the chubby old dog to work in a designer handbag every day.

What no one else in town knew was that Mary was the silent partner in the Healing Heroes cottage. The whole thing had been her idea, but she didn't want to be visibly involved. She'd brought up the idea to Julie when she'd seen how living in the cottage was bringing her down. She'd encouraged Julie to move into Ria's motel, even though her name would remain on the deed and she'd manage the property. Mary just paid the mortgage and, Julie assumed, took the tax write-off.

Whenever Julie tried to talk to her about why she would develop and support a venture like that without getting any credit for it, Mary gently changed the subject.

Baby woofed a greeting and then settled into the heart-shaped dog bed where she spent most of her waking hours. The light traffic sounds from outside were muted in here.

Julie's new tenant, Trey, was at the register buying a couple of paperbacks, and her heart warmed toward him. If he was a reader, that raised him up in her estimation. She greeted him with a smile, and he gave her a nod and a smile. "You look pretty, if you don't mind my saying so," he said, and waved as he limped out.

"You do look nice," Mary said as she surveyed Julie's outfit. "Special occasion?"

Julie's cheeks warmed. She *was* dressed nicer today than usual, and she couldn't pretend about why. "Meeting Melvin to work through a tax issue with the accountant," she said.

Mary's perfectly shaped eyebrows lifted. "Dressing up for your ex?"

"Not exactly, but…yeah. I don't want to look bad in front of him."

"He doesn't deserve it, but I understand. You want him to see what he's missing."

"Exactly." And maybe he'd want it back. She'd gotten an impression from him that he was nostalgic about their relationship when they'd talked on the phone.

He hadn't wanted to be married anymore, but maybe a little time being alone had reminded him that single life wasn't perfect, either.

And he'd fallen out of love with her, but didn't that happen, off and on, in most marriages? Love wasn't a steady, unchanging thing; it ebbed and flowed.

"How are the grandgirls?" Mary asked.

Julie rolled her eyes. "They're fine, except for some fighting in school." She told Mary about Kaitlyn's altercation and its fallout. "Plus, Ria told the girls they need to spend time with me. It's as if they set up some kind of a schedule."

"That's rather sweet."

"Right, but it makes me feel like an invalid who's the family burden."

"Why don't you offer to help Ria at the motel? If Ria and the girls realized that you actually have business and marketing skills, they might treat you with more respect."

"I've offered." She had, hadn't she?

"But with energy behind it? She probably doesn't want to take advantage, but I've seen the woman. She's exhausted most of the time."

It was true. Ria always acted cheerful, and was alarmingly competent, but she carried a lot on her shoulders, especially since her divorce. "I'll offer again," she promised, and meant it.

When the time came for the eleven o'clock meeting with Melvin and the accountant, Julie walked along the Pleasant Shores waterfront, eschewing her car. Good exercise, walking. The sun shone warm on her shoulders, and the breeze was brisk but not terribly cold. Most of the businesses were closed or operating on limited hours during the off-season, but the breeze brought the scent of one that wasn't: Goody's Emporium. In addition to serving lunch, Goody made fudge and other confections for the tourists. The emporium also housed a little ice cream shop, which the locals tended to gather at during the off-season.

Julie inhaled appreciatively and briefly considered stopping in for a chocolate fix, but she restrained herself. She'd started entering her calories into a fitness app a few days ago, and she knew a piece of Goody's fudge would push her over the day's limit.

As she approached the accountant's office, she saw Melvin striding toward it from the other direction. He was wearing those tighter dress pants that young men tended toward these days, along with a sport coat. Brown shoes, even though the suit was blue.

He used to make fun of clothes like that.

It was endearing, kind of. He almost had the figure for the clothes, marred only by a small potbelly, but he couldn't hide the fact that he was in his fifties. Maybe he was dressing up for her, just as she'd done for him?

As they approached each other, she tilted her head to one side, studying him. His hair was definitely less gray than it used to be.

Had he dyed it? Really?

He gave her a stiff half hug that nearly broke her heart. He'd always been a little self-conscious; she'd smoothed the way for him socially. "Would you like to get a cup of coffee after our meeting, just to catch up?" she asked impulsively.

"No, I...I can't. I don't have time, but thanks. We should go in."

He sounded nervous. Why nervous? It was no big deal to her whether they had coffee or not. She'd just been being kind.

The meeting went well, though, and they got their final tax issues figured out. Next year, they'd be able to file separately.

Afterward, they said goodbye and then, awkwardly, both ended up walking in the same direction. "Where did you park?" he asked.

"I walked down. I'm working at the Lighthouse bookstore now."

"Ahhh," he said, his voice faint. "See you later, Julie. I'm down this way."

Even if Melvin *did* make moves toward getting back together, she wasn't sure she'd do it. She wouldn't mind seeing him socially, dating even, but she definitely wanted to continue being independent. At least for a while.

The bookstore was busy, and she helped customers, feeling surprisingly good.

Melvin had been a bit of a downer, actually. Today, and when they were married, come to think of it. Life was more fun without him. She liked getting healthy, looking good, making her own decisions.

She felt a presence behind her and turned to see a tall brunette in ripped jeans and a T-shirt.

"Hi, um, could you help me find the cookbooks?" the woman asked.

"Of course. This way." She led her toward the side wall of the shop. "Was there a particular title you were looking for?"

She twisted a lock of hair around her finger. "Something easy. I'm a terrible cook."

"What made you want to learn?" Julie asked, making conversation. She knew that often closed the sale.

The woman blushed. "I want to impress my boyfriend."

Julie laughed. "He should be trying to impress you."

"Make him take you out to dinner," Mary chimed in from the cash register. "Cooking at home is overrated."

"Oh, he does take me out! He's very generous." The young woman picked up one title, then another. "But he's older, and it's like…he kind of expects the woman to cook, you know?"

The woman was picking up low-calorie and diet cookbooks. Why would a skinny woman want to buy that kind of cookbook? And what man would eat that type of meals?

Julie held up one of her own favorites, featuring home-style comfort food. "If you really want to impress your man, this will do it," she said. "Worked for me." Until it hadn't.

"Oh, really, did it?" The woman put down the other cookbooks and looked at the one Julie handed her, her forehead wrinkling as she looked at the glossy photos of pot roast and beef stew. "Do people still eat this kind of food?"

"Of course they do," Julie said.

A text zinged on the woman's phone and she immediately looked at it, dropping the conversation. Julie always found that annoying.

"He wants me to come meet him, but no way. He can come get me." She tapped a text reply. "Okay, I'll take that one." She took the comfort food cookbook out of Julie's hands.

"Here's another one that focuses on traditional dishes, but it's easier," Julie said, and Mary nodded approvingly from behind the counter. She pounded the principle of up-selling into her employees: if a customer bought one book, she'd likely buy two.

"Thanks. I'll take that, too." The younger woman headed up to the counter, paid with a credit card while scrolling through her phone and hurried out of the store.

Julie and Mary both watched as she climbed into a car.

A familiar car.

"Isn't that—" Mary asked, then snapped her mouth shut.

Heat rose from Julie's chest up her neck and into her face. Her stomach dropped as if she'd just gone over the peak of a roller coaster and was headed down, down, down. "Melvin's car. Melvin." Slowly, she turned to face her friend. "Did I really just help Melvin's new girlfriend figure out how to impress him?"

Mary stepped closer to the window, watching as the car moved off down the street. "Wonder if she knew his ex worked here?"

"She couldn't have." That was a level of setup Julie couldn't stand to think about. "Melvin didn't know when I told him earlier today. He seemed surprised."

"Doesn't mean she didn't know. She could have easily looked you up online. You're on our website, and Pleasant Shores is a small town." Mary clicked her tongue disapprovingly.

Julie plopped down into a chair in one of their customer seating areas. "Why would she do that? Why would anyone do that?" She felt like she'd been had.

"Sizing up her competition," Mary said.

"But I'm not..." Julie looked down at her new dress pants and heeled shoes, her scarf in Melvin's favorite blue.

She *was* competition, or trying to be.

And at least she knew how to cook a pot roast.

She unwrapped the scarf from around her neck,

marched over to the trash can behind the counter and dropped it in. She'd never liked that particular color of swimming-pool blue. Never liked pot roast, either, for that matter.

"If she thinks I'm her competition," she said, "that's kind of funny. Because I wouldn't have him back if he crawled to me on his knees."

A voice inside reminded her that she'd sung a different tune when she'd thought he did want to come back.

"That girl actually looked familiar," Mary said. "Didn't she work at the school for a time?"

"I don't know her."

"Pretty sure," Mary said.

Julie's stomach lurched. If the girlfriend had been living in Pleasant Shores, or at least working there, did that mean Melvin had known her for a while? How long? And how long had he been interested in a skinny woman half his age?

CHAPTER SIX

FRIDAY NIGHT DINNER at DiGiorno's didn't go as badly as Erica had feared. Even with Trey at his charming best.

They spilled out of the tiny establishment holding their stomachs, laughing and waving to Nonna, the ancient lady who worked as hostess every Friday night and knew all the gossip in town.

Word that they'd all had dinner together thus would spread, but Erica wasn't too worried. It hadn't looked the least bit like a date, and Trey had paid equal attention to Amber, Hannah and Erica. For all she knew, the others had felt the laser focus of that smile as much as she had.

"Let's go get ice cream!" Hannah, who'd walked out ahead, spun to look at them. "Please, Mom? We haven't done that since we moved here."

An uneasy feeling slithered through Erica's middle. No, the dinner hadn't gone badly, but that didn't mean it would be wise to prolong it. "Most of the ice cream shops are closed until Memorial Day," she said.

"Not Goody's." Hannah spun back around and pointed to the pink-and-white building partway down the block from them. "It's open late on Fridays, just like always. Look, you can see people going in now."

Amber pursed her lips and nodded. "Fine with me." She put her hand on her stomach reflexively, and Erica could guess why. Since her surgery and chemo, she didn't have a big appetite. She'd eaten more than usual of her pasta platter tonight, but that meant she wasn't likely to eat ice cream; it would make her sick.

"I could go for ice cream," Trey said. "Even though I'm stuffed. There's always room for ice cream."

Hannah smiled brilliantly at him. "I agree. Especially after spending the afternoon working on the flower beds at the school with Kaitlyn and Venus. Talk about stressful!"

"You girls worked well together. I was proud of you."

"So we deserve ice cream, right?"

Then everyone looked expectantly at Erica, like she was supposed to make the decision. Why was that? And how could she be the wet blanket who said they ought to go home, especially when Hannah and Amber were having so much fun? "All right," she said. "Let's get a quick ice cream, but then I'm beat."

"Way to live a little, sis." Amber wrapped an arm around her shoulders as they all headed toward Goody's. "Having fun?" she whispered into Erica's ear.

"To a degree."

Amber snorted. "Why do I even try to help you get a life?"

They strolled along the sidewalk that fronted the water. Erica wrapped her sweater tighter against the cool breeze and glanced over at Amber to see if she was getting chilled. She'd worn a leather jacket and baseball cap, though, and seemed fine. Hannah, who'd just worn shorts and a T-shirt, had Trey's jacket wrapped around her.

Soon enough they pushed through the door of Goody's, and immediately the scents of cupcakes and cookies surrounded them.

"You know we're going to have to take some baked goods home," Amber said.

Erica nodded. Reflexively, she patted her stomach and started to make a remark about gaining weight, but she closed her lips in time. Both because she didn't want to overemphasize weight in front of a young girl like Hannah, and because, for the first time in her life, she wasn't carrying an extra ounce. In fact, she was downright bony and should probably get a double-decker cone.

Except with Trey here looking so good and being so friendly, she didn't know if she could eat a bite.

Several families, all local ones Erica had seen before, were clustered around the bright tables on the ice cream side of the place. One set of adorable twins, about three, stood taking turns licking an ice cream cone while the mother and father laughed.

Jealousy tugged at Erica's heart. Once upon a time, before Mom had gotten sick and they'd learned more than they wanted to know about cancer genetics, she'd anticipated having just that type of family. One that enjoyed time together at the beach.

She'd babysat and taken child development classes in high school, not, as people assumed, because she wanted to be a teacher, but because she wanted to be a mother.

Now that option was closed to her.

Don't pity yourself. Look at Amber.

Amber was a mother, and when she'd gotten pregnant way back when, Erica had been thrilled. Even though Amber had been too young and her boyfriend had bolted, both Erica and their mother had barely been able to contain their excitement.

Now Amber was so terribly sick and their mother was gone. Being a mother hadn't made Amber's life easy, and now… Erica's throat tightened. She glanced over at Hannah and was glad to see her looking carefree. She waved to someone across the shop, and Erica recognized Pete, one of the boys from the academy, there with his dad. "Get some ice cream and go talk to them," she encouraged Hannah.

"No! I'll look like a dork!"

Amber and Erica exchanged glances. Hannah wouldn't have said that unless she liked the boy, or at least cared about what he thought of her.

Hannah ordered her ice cream, and Trey insisted that Amber put her money away; he was paying.

"Come on," Amber said to Hannah. "Let's go talk to them."

"No way!" Hannah glanced over and then back at Amber, her face pink.

"I want to meet his dad," Amber said. "You're just my excuse. Come on." She marched over and Hannah wrinkled her forehead at Erica and then followed her. Soon the father and son had scooted over, making way for Amber and Hannah in their booth.

"What are you having?" Trey asked.

Erica studied the flavors. "I think… S'more," she said. "Two scoops."

"I like a woman who likes ice cream," Trey said approvingly. He ordered his own chocolate cone and they went to one of the tables.

It was next to the family with twins, who were finishing up, and then Erica realized they had a small baby, too. Again, jealousy swept through her. The baby flung his binky on the floor, and Erica and Trey both leaned over to pick it up, nearly bumping heads.

"Here you go," Trey said, handing it to the mother. "Cute baby."

"Thanks. He's already a handful." But there was pride in the mother's voice.

Trey bent lower to be on a level with the little girls. "I bet you were handfuls, too, when you were babies." He glanced up at the parents. "I had foster brothers who were twins. It's not easy."

"You haven't lived until you've parented two colicky babies at once," the mom said.

"Ouch. Only one of my brothers had colic, but I remember the crying like it was yesterday."

Erica realized she didn't know anything about Trey's family of origin. Hadn't known he was in foster care. Moreover, she hadn't realized before that he was comfortable with little kids. A lot of men weren't.

As the family packed up and left, Erica watched them, until she felt Trey's hand on her arm. "You'd better start licking. You have a drip."

Sure enough, a trickle of ice cream overflowed onto her hand and she hurriedly tried to catch up with the melting cone.

When she looked up, Trey was watching her. Their gazes tangled, held.

Heat climbed her cheeks. "You'd better look to your own cone," she said just as his began to drip onto the table.

As she finished her ice cream, she tried to calm down with some deep breathing, but a feeling of attraction to Trey kept making her heart beat faster.

She should deny it, get rid of it, leave. But it was so sweet and pleasurable, something she hadn't felt in ages.

Why couldn't she allow herself a secret crush on Trey?

Because he likes kids and he's only here for a little while anyway.

But since he was only here for a little while, would it be so awful to enjoy his presence?

"How's your sister's health?" he asked, jolting her out of her confusion.

She looked at him and met eyes dark with compassion. "Not so good. We go scan by scan."

He nodded. "I figured it was cancer. Must be tough on all of you."

"It is." She looked over to where Amber and Hannah were smiling and laughing with Pete and his dad. "She has an amazing spirit, though. And when you're a mom, you have no choice but to fight it as hard as you can."

He shook his head. "Life sucks sometimes."

So he liked kids and he was sympathetic toward a family suffering through illness, rather than blurting out platitudes about how everything would be fine or God was in control.

She *hoped* God was in control, but nothing felt certain these days. That made it hard to listen to people who seemed to know it all. But Trey wasn't like that.

"Do you want to go for a walk after this?" he asked abruptly.

"What?"

"A walk on the beach, or through town," he said. "We could take Ziggy and work on some heeling."

"Oh, so…a training walk? At night?"

"It's not a bad idea for a reactive dog. Fewer distractions."

"Ziggy's not reactive. He's a puppy!"

"Right, well…" He tilted his head. "Your call. I just thought I'd offer."

Amber and Hannah came back then, and they all finished their ice cream and strolled back to the car.

Your call.

It was her call whether she wanted to go for an

evening walk with a guy who, she'd just discovered, was a great family man in addition to being incredibly good-looking.

Her head gave a clear message: no. No, don't get more involved. No, you've already spent way too much time with him. No, you're feeling vulnerable.

Her heart gave a different message: Why not? Just because your family has health problems, just because you can't have kids, does that mean you can never, ever have fun with a nice-looking guy?

Who's willing to train your goofy dog?

As they reached the house, Erica's tension rose. She had to decide between her head and her heart.

Amber and Hannah went on inside and, feeling cowardly, Erica started to follow them.

Trey cleared his throat. "So...you coming?"

She looked over her shoulder and caught a trace of insecurity on his face. Her heart melted, just a little. "Sure," she said. "I'll come."

TREY HELD THE door of Erica's place, waiting for her to get Ziggy calm enough to put his harness on him.

She was coming. His idiotic impulse hadn't alienated her, although her glances at him were plenty wary.

"Ziggy! Be still!" Her exasperated commands only made the big white dog jump higher.

He'd been right to ask her, because the dog needed training big-time.

Although he couldn't pretend that was the real reason; in fact, he'd only thought of it as additional motivation after she'd looked like she was going to turn him down.

Finally, she got the harness on the dog and they headed out the door, Ziggy pulling hard on the leash. As she passed, Trey caught a whiff of perfume and his entire body leaped to attention.

Had she been wearing that all evening, or had she put it on for him?

"Want me to take him for a few?" he asked, glad for the distraction.

"Um, sure. He'll settle down in a little bit."

"He should be calm from the get-go. You can't have him dragging you around." He took the leash from her hand, ignoring the hot spot where their fingers touched. He tightened the leash and pulled back.

Ziggy glanced back over his shoulder, his eyes confused.

For a moment, Trey was flooded with thoughts of King, those alert brown eyes of his signaling his bond to Trey and his readiness to work.

He'd punched King's new handler's phone number into his cell at least ten times, but he'd forced himself to turn the phone off before he hit the "call" button.

And he needed to stop thinking about King and focus on this silly, untrained creature in front of him. "Sit," he said a little more sharply than he'd intended.

Ziggy sat, then started to get up again.

Trey gave the leash a quick, sharp tug.

"Hey! You're hurting him!"

"I'm showing him what to do." When Ziggy sat again, Trey handed him a bit of dog biscuit.

Ziggy smiled up at him, tongue out, panting, and once again, Trey felt a sharp pang of missing King.

"Let's walk," he said, holding a treat directly in front of Ziggy's nose. "Heel, Ziggy," he said.

The dog trotted along beside him, nosing at the treat.

"I can't believe he's being so much better for you than for me!"

Trey shrugged. "He loves you the best, but dogs respond quicker to a deep voice. The women in K-9 training always complained about it."

"Makes sense, I guess. Glad it's not just me."

They walked slowly through Pleasant Shores' downtown, talking a little about dog training. Erica questioned some of what he was doing, but she did pay attention, leaning forward to watch how he was holding the treat and the leash, listening to his words.

And he was doing a good job of keeping this walk non-date-like; in fact, he could tell he was sort of annoying her because he was, in a way, criticizing the dog she considered as her baby.

And while he didn't approve of owners infantilizing their dogs, Erica was so cute about it that he didn't mind.

He needed to stop thinking about how appealing she was. "What brought you to Pleasant Shores?" he asked. "Did you have a background here?"

"Yeah." She looked around, smiling a little. Crickets chirped, and a light wind rustled through new leaves. "My aunt actually lived one street over, in a little place just like that." She indicated a modest cottage surrounded by flowers and trees. "We came here every summer and it was the highlight of our year."

That brought up something he'd wondered about. "How come Pleasant Shores has all these little places— older places on this side of the peninsula—and then the mansions on the other side? I'd think the smaller homeowners would have been bought out." It had happened all up and down the coast, he knew.

"Have you noticed that the beach on the little-house side isn't nearly as wide as the other, and that it's rocky? That's why. The big homeowners have the beach tended to every year. They ship sand in and have it groomed, but the way the tides run, that won't work on the other side."

"Haves and have-nots?"

"Yeah," she said, "but when we were growing up, everybody here was a have-not. Pleasant Shores used to be where the poorer folks lived when they worked at one of the tourist towns up the shore."

He looked around at the quaint streets and little yards, the neat picket fences, the colorful little cottages. "Why wasn't this a tourist area? People love visiting this kind of place."

"Harder to get to. The neck of the peninsula used to flood every tide, so you could only go over to the mainland at certain times. Tourists find that inconvenient."

"But now…"

"But now the road's a lot better. They've built up the land to keep it from flooding, so the tourists have started moving in. Plus, now that the shore is so busy, places like this are more popular. It's considered unspoiled." Her nose wrinkled.

"But it's more spoiled since the tourists came."

"Yeah, the locals think so. My aunt was a local, so I identify with them more. Hoping to become one, actually."

That was interesting. He'd guessed that she and her sister and niece were here more temporarily, but she made it sound like they'd like to make it permanent.

He got the briefest flash of what it would be like to live in a place like this, to raise a family here, in one of these little homes.

It was him being ridiculous. Just like he'd been with his wife. His sentimental dreams were never going to come true.

Erica was still talking about the town. "Plenty of people are glad that they can finally earn a living right here in Pleasant Shores, rather than driving up the coast. I mean, there's always been the fishing industry, but now there's a lot of work involving tourists, at least during the season."

"And I bet houses have increased in value," Trey said.

"They have. People could make a lot of money

if they sold their houses, in many cases, but most Pleasant Shores families wouldn't dream of selling. They'd rather keep their little homes and make a life here."

"So it's now a mix of tourist and local. Nice." He frowned. "I assume that's why the school is here?"

"Yeah," she said. "It used to be the public school for all grades. But bigger, more modern schools were built up the peninsula, and all the kids started getting bused there. So the old public school building became a private school."

They both paused while Ziggy lifted his leg by a fire hydrant.

"That makes sense, but what about the academy program? That doesn't seem to fit."

"It doesn't fit that well, not anymore." She sighed. "The program is a vestige of the old Pleasant Shores public school. Because it was the poor community, I guess, they got the honor of hosting the kids with behavioral problems. Plus, the idea was that Pleasant Shores was remote enough that at-risk teens couldn't find any trouble to get into."

He nodded, watching the moonlight play on her face, getting a little lost in how pretty she was.

And he didn't need to be staring at her. Where had the conversation been going? "So things have changed with the school?"

She nodded. "With all the new people, the rich people, there's a group that doesn't want to have behavior-support-type kids around their kids. And Principal O'Neil, well, he was hired specifically to increase enrollment. They need more paying students since there are a lot of scholarship students, kids of local crabbers or women in need. Even Hannah, she gets to go free because I teach there. So they need to balance that out by bringing in more tuition. That's why he wants to get rid of the program. He hopes that'll make the place more appealing to the high-income families."

"And you want to save it."

She nodded. And didn't say why, and he wondered at her intensity around the school and the kids.

Apparently, though, she wanted to change the subject, because she nodded down at Ziggy, now trotting along at their sides again. "He's doing pretty well," she said. "Of course, there are no other dogs around, and not very many squirrels and such. That helps." She looked at him and sighed. "Sometimes I wonder if he'll ever calm down and get trained."

"He will." He touched her arm, and then quickly pulled his hand back. *It's not a date, it's not a date.* "Listen, don't feel like Ziggy is a bad dog. I'm more used to dogs that have been raised by a certified puppy raiser and have had a lot of training all their lives. We get the canines when they're at least a year old, sometimes two years old. They're through their puppy craziness. Ziggy isn't."

"Thanks." She smiled up at him, and he was a little bit blown away. She had that chestnut hair, untamed and shaggy, and enormous eyes. She tended toward plain, practical clothes. She wasn't his type, or his old type, but he couldn't deny her appeal.

He kept getting more and more fascinated by her, the more time they spent together. She was a woman with a lot of layers.

The last thing he needed was to fall for a woman like Erica. She wasn't the type for a quick fling, and that was the most he could offer. He needed to keep this professional and make his plans to move on as soon as he'd finished his time here.

She went on talking about Ziggy. "To tell you the truth, I didn't realize what a handful he was going to be. The dog I had before was completely different, an older rescue. He got me through a lot of stuff. I was heartbroken when he died." Her eyes actually filled with tears.

He put an arm around her shoulders and gave them a quick squeeze. She was so, so thin. She felt a little fragile, and not just physically.

It was hard to remember that, because normally what she displayed was her strength, that spine of steel.

"Believe me," he said, "I understand how intense it can feel to lose a dog." The image of King, the feel of his working leash in Trey's hand, all of it washed over him, and his throat tightened.

They turned onto the street that ran beside the bay. Piers jutted out into the water at regular intervals, some with boats, some stacked with crab traps. The water lapped against the pilings, a soothing sound.

"So how are you dealing with losing King?" she asked, her voice hesitant, as if she knew it was a sore subject. "Have you heard anything about how he's doing?"

He shook his head, looking out over the water, cut with a silvery, moonlit path. "When you make a transfer of a dog, it needs to be complete. You can't go and visit or anything, because that would confuse the dog."

"Maybe, but it seems kind of harsh. I would think that being able to visit him would help both you and King."

He shrugged. "Department rules."

She reached out, put a hand through his arm and squeezed, laying her head down on his bicep for a fraction of a second. It was an innocent gesture, a shared sympathy, but her touch electrified him in all kinds of noninnocent ways.

Maybe she sensed something, because she let go quickly and took a half step away, creating a little distance between them. "Do you think you'll continue being a K-9 officer?" Her voice sounded tight, tense, and it seemed like she was trying to get the conversation onto neutral ground, to avoid the attraction that sparked between them.

"I'd like to." He reached back reflexively and rubbed his spine. It was definitely starting to hurt from walking. "It's a competitive process to become a K-9 officer, so it seems like a waste to let it go. But if my back doesn't get better, then I can't do it anymore. Can't do active police work anymore."

"What went wrong?" The question was soft, hesitant. "I mean, if you don't mind talking about it. I know it's none of my business."

Should he tell her? She seemed really sympathetic, not judgmental, but he hated looking like a fool in front of her.

It was better she knew, though. He'd let his wife glorify him in the early days and it had backfired. "A routine door-to-door turned up a meth lab," he said. "I should have stepped away and called for backup, but I...didn't. I went in."

"Why?" She glanced over at him but kept walking, which made it easier to talk.

"Heard a baby crying and I lost my head and went in alone. There were three guys inside, couple of teenagers and an older dude, all big and all high. They jumped me."

"What happened to the baby?" she asked softly.

"We saved the baby, but the perps got away. I put my fellow officers at risk coming in to pull me and the baby out, because the place was ready to blow." As he spoke, he remembered the pain from when two of the meth-crazed perps had thrown him down the stairs into the basement. More than that, though, he remembered his terror for the baby's safety that had made him crawl his way up the stairs even after he'd called for backup. He'd done even more harm to his spine that way, and had reached the wailing infant at the same time the other officers did.

"Sounds like you did the best you could," she said.

"Not good enough." That was why he couldn't trust himself or his impulses anymore.

She didn't press, didn't argue with him. Just gave his arm a quick squeeze and then tilted her head back a little and sniffed appreciatively. He did, too, then, and inhaled the sweet fragrance of some night-blooming flower.

By the time they reached the park, he couldn't hide the fact that he was limping, and she suggested they stop and sit down on a bench. He was grateful for that, and so, apparently, was Ziggy, because he flopped down on the grass in front of them and started chewing on a stick.

They sat there in companionable silence for a couple of minutes, sheltered by a few long-needled pines. Trey inhaled their resinous fragrance, thinking over the conversation. It was good to be able to talk to someone who listened. He liked that in anyone, valued it in a friend.

But with Erica, he also appreciated how beautiful she was, how good she smelled, how warm she felt beside him. He hadn't been this close to a woman who wasn't a physical therapist in a long time.

It was just too much to take. He slid his hand along the back of the bench, reaching with his other hand to touch her face.

She looked up at him, eyes wide, lips soft, full, yielding.

He leaned closer, let his thumb play along her cheek, feeling the fine sheen of sweat.

His heart started a heavy pounding in his chest. She was just too kissable. He leaned closer.

She seemed to move a little toward him.

Yeah, he was going to kiss her.

But just as his lips were about to touch hers, she jerked back and pulled away, her hand going to her mouth.

"What's wrong?" he asked her, because he really wanted to know. Almost as much as he really wanted to kiss her.

"No, Trey, this isn't a good idea," she said.

He couldn't get out of the mood that fast. "Why not?"

Her breath was coming quick. And it wasn't anger; it was desire. He knew enough about women to understand that.

"It's just not a good idea," she said. "We're working together, all that kind of thing."

"Okay, I get that." He pulled back, but left his arm along the back of the bench. The last thing he wanted was to violate her sense of what was appropriate, in the workplace or anywhere else. He didn't want to be that guy, ever.

"Thanks," she said, her voice shaky.

"Are you always so logical?" He softened the question with a smile as he took deep breaths to try to calm down his body.

"Yeah," she said. "Yeah, I am. I've had to be." Her eyes were still a little warm, dreamy, but reality was starting to come back into them. She scooted away on the bench, then stood. "I should get back to the house," she said. "I don't like to leave Amber and Hannah alone too long."

He was pretty sure that wasn't really the reason.

Amber seemed like a very competent adult, for all that she was struggling with a serious illness, and Hannah was a responsible teenager. Erica was just making an excuse.

She's being smart, he told himself. Getting involved would be a mistake, not just because of their connection at the school, but also because he was leaving in a couple of months. He wanted to go back to his job, which was notoriously hard on marriages. Especially in his case.

"Here, I'll take Ziggy," she said. "If you just want to, you know, stay here a little while."

"Do you want me to do that?" He wasn't sure what made him keep needling her. Maybe it was the passionate woman he glimpsed beneath the proper schoolteacher.

"Honestly? Yes. I'd be more comfortable." She held out her hand for Ziggy's leash.

He didn't give it to her, not right away. "Do you want me to work with him a little more and bring him back to your place later?"

"No!" She looked nervous, maybe at the thought of seeing him again later on tonight. His good mood started to disintegrate, because that look on her face was definitive. She definitely didn't want him around.

He handed over the leash, and she clicked her tongue to the big dog, who stood amicably and leaned against her.

"See you later. Thanks for the walk." She turned

and walked off toward the direction they'd come from, not glancing back even when Ziggy did.

Leaving Trey to wonder: How were they going to go forward as colleagues after that awkward moment? After realizing they were totally attracted to each other?

Or had the attraction really been just on his side?

CHAPTER SEVEN

SATURDAY MORNING, ERICA woke up with a smile on her face and realized she'd been half dreaming. Unfortunately, she was half dreaming about Trey and the fact that he'd nearly kissed her.

Which was not a good thing. She couldn't get involved with her volunteer, for heaven's sake. Her boss would use that against her and eliminate the academy program faster than she could turn around.

Besides, she'd seen how Trey acted with that family at Goody's. He liked kids, and he should have the opportunity to have them.

Even that thought was just her being ridiculous. The man had tried to kiss her in a casual moment, while walking a dog. It wasn't like he'd proposed marriage and asked her to bear his children.

The thing was, she'd been really drawn to him last night. He'd been sweet with her family, and lovely on the walk. He was good with Ziggy. And he'd intuitively understood about the situation on the island, how the place was changing, how the wealthy tourists contrasted with the locals' ordinary way of life. She didn't know a lot about his background—he didn't volunteer much—but if he'd grown up in foster care, it probably hadn't been an affluent one. Maybe that was why he had empathy for the working-class people of Pleasant Shores.

She threw off the covers and got out of bed, startling Ziggy into an excited yelp. "Shh," she scolded in a whisper. "You'll wake up Amber and Hannah."

She opened her bedroom door and held Ziggy's collar as they walked quietly downstairs. As they passed Amber's room, though, she heard her sister's low, raspy voice. "Hey, sis. Erica."

She opened her sister's door. Amber sat up in bed, wearing a hoodie, the covers pulled to her waist.

Erica looked closer and saw that her sister's face was more pale and drawn than usual, and a claw of fear gripped her stomach. She sat down on the corner of the bed. "How are you doing?"

"Not great." Amber's voice sounded weak. "Didn't sleep well last night and I can tell this is going to be a bad day. Do you think...?" She trailed off.

"Whatever you need. You know I'm here for you."

"Could you take Hannah out to do something fun today? I hate for her to see me like this. Last night did me in."

Why hadn't Erica kept a closer eye on her sister, watched for signs of fatigue? "Oh, honey, I'm sorry. It was so much fun, but I didn't think about how it might tire you out."

"Don't be sorry. You know I treasure every memory I can make with Hannah. And with you." Her mouth twisted. "It's just…there's a cost. So if you could get her out, have some fun with her, I could get some extra rest." She hesitated, then added, "Maybe you could even get her to talk to you a little. She's so careful with me."

"Absolutely." She studied her sister's face, took hold of her ice-cold hand. "Do you want me to run you to the doctor, though?"

"No. I just need rest."

Erica bit her lip. Worrying went with the territory of having a seriously ill sister, but she had to trust that Amber would ask for medical help if she needed it. "Do you want us to take Ziggy, or do you want him here with you?"

"If you can go run him around first, I want him to stay with me. C'mere, Zig."

The giant dog obligingly jumped up onto the bed and started licking Amber's face, then backed up into a play bow, tail wagging.

"I will definitely run his energy off," Erica promised. "I have some energy to run off myself today. We'll go out on the beach." Hopefully, she wouldn't see Trey there. He walked on the beach sometimes, but not on any regular schedule that she could discern.

"Take your time. Hannah will sleep in." Amber leaned back against the pillows and Ziggy flopped down beside her. The big dog seemed to know to be more gentle with Amber than he was with Erica or Hannah. "How'd your walk with the movie star go?"

"It was a nice walk, but…" She trailed off. On

the one hand, she'd like to confide in her big sister. On the other hand, she'd likely get a lecture in return, something about letting love in and enjoying the moment and life being short.

"But what?" Amber pressed her.

"Nothing. No big deal. I just...I just need to make sure I don't see too much of him. He's a little overwhelming."

Amber snorted. "And that's a bad thing? Didn't you ever just want to be overwhelmed by a guy?"

Erica thought. Had she ever wanted that? Yes, in fact she had. She'd wanted it last night. But she knew better than to go for it, because it would upset so many other parts of her life. "I think that I'll leave the overwhelmed part to you," she said. "I'm just the boring schoolteacher."

"That's not how he was looking at you last night." Amber tilted her head, smiling at Erica.

How had Trey been looking at her? Or was Amber making it up to make Erica feel good? "Come on, Ziggy," she said, standing up and snapping her fingers. "Let's go for a run."

Ziggy bounded off the bed and rushed out the door.

"We'll say bye before we go if you're awake," Erica said, and blew her sister a kiss. "Love you."

LATE THAT AFTERNOON, Erica glided after Hannah into the bike rental lot. She was breathing hard, her face was hot and she felt worlds better.

Unfortunately, she hadn't gotten her niece to open up to her like she'd hoped to do.

"Thanks for riding with me," Erica said as she parked her bike. "I know it wasn't your first choice of activities."

"Thanks for taking me shopping," Hannah said. "It was nice to get back to civilization again. I mean, I like Pleasant Shores, but there's not a whole lot going on there."

"Speaking of not much going on," Erica said, "where's the guy we rented the bikes from? This place looks deserted."

Hannah looked at the sign on the bike hut. "They'll be back in fifteen minutes," she said.

"Off-season attitude," Erica said. "Let's sit and look out at the bay and wait."

They plopped down onto a bench that faced the water. Now that they weren't moving, the sun felt too warm, and Erica slipped off her jacket and leaned back, face to the sun. "I'm so relaxed right now," she said.

"Me, too." Hannah was looking at her phone, rearranging her hair.

They'd taken turns choosing activities. First, at Hannah's suggestion, they'd spent a couple of hours at the outlet mall. Hannah had gotten two new outfits for summer. Erica had, at Hannah's urging, bought a cute shirt that fit a little tighter and looked a little younger than what she usually wore.

Then Erica had talked Hannah into bike riding, and they'd rented bikes at one of the few stands that was open throughout the year, in a town halfway between the outlet mall and Pleasant Shores. Trinity Bay was a slightly bigger town with a bike path that wove through the marshland and along the bay. A kid from the school worked at the bike hut, and Erica was pretty sure that was the reason Hannah was reapplying mascara.

It was good to see Hannah doing what teenagers did normally. She was overly responsible at home. But she still had a slightly fake smile on her face, a veiled look to her eyes. Erica's hope of getting her to open up hadn't happened. She took a risk, asked a question deeper than whether Hannah liked a particular style of dress. "How are you and Kaitlyn and Venus getting along?" she asked.

Hannah shrugged. "I mean, it's not like we're best friends, but we aren't fighting. I talk to Venus at lunch sometimes."

"That's good." She hesitated, then plunged ahead. "Look, Hannah, it has to be tough, having your mom so sick. You take on a lot, too much."

Hannah looked out over the water. "Yeah," she said. "It's hard sometimes."

"Of course it's hard. It would be hard for anyone. But how are you feeling?"

Hannah's jaw tightened. She glanced sideways at Erica as if assessing how much she'd have to reveal to escape this conversation. "I get sad sometimes, but I'm fine."

Should she confront her niece on her stonewalling, as she would one of her students? Erica leaned forward, elbows on knees. It was worth a try. "Can you just let go of being the perfect daughter and niece for once? It's pretty clear that you're able to manage a tough situation well, better than most kids could. You don't take drugs or commit crimes or even get bad grades. But you don't let it hang out, show your real self."

Hannah's head snapped around to face Erica. "You're telling *me* I'm not being real? What about you?"

"What do you mean?"

"You act like a social worker or a nurse with Mom and me."

Erica's face warmed as she thought about what Hannah had just said. Was she being fake, so fake she didn't even know it herself? Or was Hannah just doing a skillful dodge to escape the spotlight? "Today I want to talk about you," she said firmly. "If you want to be happy—not fake happy, but real happy—you need to let people in. Your mom, me, your friends."

"I let people in!" Hannah stood, shoved her hand in her pocket and pulled out a couple of bills. She walked to the soda machine against the bike rental hut and fed them in. "You want something?" she called back over her shoulder.

"No, I'm fine."

"Sure you are," Hannah called back in a snotty voice as she made her selection.

Erica felt her mouth curving up into a smile. At

least she'd gotten a rise out of Hannah, a moment of normal teen snarkiness.

Hannah came back and sat on the bench, but farther away from Erica than she'd been before.

Erica drew a breath and dived back in. "You know, you're kind of stuck with me here. You might as well tell me how you're doing with your mom's illness. Or, shoot, I'll take anything. Your friends. Missing your old home. Grades."

Hannah turned toward her, slowly, eyebrows lowered over blazing eyes. "You really want to know how I feel?"

"Yes, honey. I do."

"I'm scared, okay?" Hannah bit her lip, then spoke again. "Really scared. I can't imagine a world without Mom in it, but you and her and her doctors have as much as said she's going to die. Then what am I going to do?"

"Oh, honey." Erica moved closer, arms reaching for her niece.

But Hannah crossed her arms over her chest and turned away from Erica. Staring—glaring—out toward the water, she went on. "You know what else? I'm mad at Mom for not taking care of herself better. Why didn't she get more tests and eat more vegetables and exercise, instead of going out on dates all the time? Doesn't she love me enough to take care of herself? I don't have a dad. What'll it be like when I don't have a mom, either? When there's nobody at graduation, or my wedding, or when I have a b-b-baby?"

Her heart twisting, Erica put a hand on Hannah's back, swallowing the lump in her own throat. When Hannah didn't flinch away, she rubbed in slow circles. She had a feeling there was more.

She was right.

"And that's if I can even *have* a baby. What if I have the bad gene, too? What if I have to get my girl parts removed, just like you?"

Ouch. Was that how the teenager saw her?

But this wasn't about Erica; it was about Hannah. "I had my ovaries removed, and I can't have children anymore. There's a fifty-fifty chance you could carry the gene. But by the time you're old enough to think about your options, there might be new solutions. There's all kind of research going on now."

Hannah barely seemed to hear her. "I know I shouldn't even be complaining about this. You're in worse shape, because of how bad you always wanted to have kids. And Mom's in the worst shape of all. I'm just worried about some stuff, and that's why I don't waste everyone's time talking about it!" She jerked away from Erica's touch, scooted to the end of the bench and started scrolling through her phone, shoulders hunched.

A clear "leave me alone" stance.

Erica sank back against the bench, feeling defeated. It looked like she had just succeeded in making an unhappy girl more unhappy.

Maybe she shouldn't have probed into Hannah's feelings. After all, the teenager was doing pretty well in school and at home. Erica wasn't surprised to learn that Hannah had a lot going on beneath the surface; she'd always been a rather private child, even before her mother's illness.

She should have reassured Hannah that she, at least, would be there for her in the future. She'd already talked with Amber about taking care of Hannah if need be, if Amber got too sick or, God forbid, died. Of course she would be there for Hannah's wedding and the babies she might have. She had always been the most involved of aunts, but maybe Hannah needed continued reassurance that she would be there.

On the other hand, no matter how great an aunt was, what you really wanted was your own mother. And it looked like Hannah had had about all the deep discussion she could take today.

"Sorry, sorry." That young man who had rented them the bikes came rushing back toward the bike stand. "Had to run down and take my mama some food. Hope you weren't waiting long." He slid open the garage-type door of the little hut.

"It's fine," she and Hannah said, almost in unison. They both stood to help push their bikes inside.

"Sit. I'll do it," he said.

Erica looked over at her niece, who was watching him in a rapt kind of way. He was a cute kid, probably about Hannah's age or a year or two older, with brown skin, black hair and muscular shoulders on an otherwise slender frame. No wonder Hannah had puppy dog eyes. She hadn't been willing to put herself out for Pete at the ice cream parlor, not without an assist from her mom, but she appeared a lot more enthusiastic about this boy.

"Go talk to him," Erica suggested quietly.

Hannah's forehead wrinkled. "I can't. I don't know what to say."

"Go ask him if he knows what else is open in town," Erica urged. "We might want to come over this way again, and I don't know what else there is to do."

Hannah bit her lip.

Erica smiled and nodded sideways. "Go on. Do it. Be brave."

Hannah gave her a half smile and walked slowly over to the guy. He was backing out of the storage area, and the moment he saw Hannah he straightened and smiled, making it obvious that he was glad she'd come over to socialize. That was good; it would make it easier on Hannah.

Erica watched as the two of them talked. Hannah pushed her hair back with one hand, and the bike guy raised his eyebrows and smiled and touched her arm ever so lightly. He pointed at a flyer in a plastic holder at the side of the bike stand, and soon the two of them were studying it, standing close, laughing together.

It was sweet, and Erica was glad that Hannah was beginning to be open to those kinds of feelings, was beginning to have something good and new and normal in her life.

Watching the teens made her think of Trey and last night. He'd wanted to kiss her. He, Mr. Movie

Star, had wanted to kiss her! Her stomach churned with butterflies, excitement and worry all at the same time.

No denying she had acted like a dolt, running away. She'd probably insulted Trey.

But what choice did she have? She couldn't get involved. That was simply off the table for now. She wasn't going to be what she'd always wanted to be, the wife of a wonderful man and the mother of lots of kids. Her future was coded differently, coded in her very genes. She hoped she'd be around to help Hannah, but could she really guarantee that? No. She still had increased risk of several kinds of cancer, and no matter how many vegetables she ate, no matter how many supplements she took, the cloud of it hung over her.

She simply couldn't inflict that on a man.

But does that mean you can never kiss a man, never in your whole life?

"C'mere, Erica!" Hannah was beckoning to her. Both she and the boy looked excited.

"What's up?"

"Santiago says he saw King!"

Erica tilted her head to one side. "How do you know King?"

"From the school. I'm a senior there, and I saw him a couple of times. His coloring is unusual for a German shepherd, more black on the muzzle."

"And tell her, tell her what was happening," Hannah urged.

"This big guy, he was yelling at him," Santiago said. "Yelling kind of mean."

Erica thought of how sternly Trey had corrected Ziggy during last night's training. "Maybe that's just how they do it with police dogs," she said.

"I felt like it was more than that." Santiago waved his arm toward the northern part of the beach. "If you don't believe me, come back and see. He is there mostly every morning and also in the evenings, trying to train the dog." He frowned. "The dog does not look happy."

"We can come back, can't we, Aunt Erica?" Hannah said.

All of a sudden, Erica wondered whether this was really about King, or whether it was about two young people who wanted another excuse to get together. "We'll see," she said, keeping her voice neutral.

But as they bade Santiago goodbye and headed for the car, Erica kept thinking about what Santiago had said. Should she tell Trey about King? Or was she as bad as the young people, trying to make an excuse to get together with him again?

MONDAY AFTERNOON, TREY glanced around the semicircle of bored-looking kids and almost groaned aloud. Whose idea had it been to have these students tour the Pleasant Shores police station?

Of course, Trey knew the answer to that: it had been his idea. Just not a very good one.

Initially, he had thought that putting together an

excursion outside of school, visiting the local police station, might get him on Earl Greene's good side. And since his own chief was using his success or failure as a volunteer as part of his criteria for re-instating Trey on the force, a good word from Earl could only help.

Getting back to his own force seemed even more desirable since Erica, who was currently snapping pictures of the teenagers as they listened to Earl Greene's jovial speech, had rejected him. He'd never intended to stay here, but the way she'd shunned him Friday night made him want to get out fast.

He looked around at the cinder-block walls, the shelves overflowing with boxes and equipment, and felt at home. This was where he belonged, a police station, no matter how shabby. Not a school where all he was doing was working—badly—with under-age minors.

The school principal had insisted on coming along on the field trip, but he was making his dis-taste clear. Trey was starting to get a bead on the guy: he was a wannabe, eager to please the board of directors, who'd tasked him with recruiting more students from among the wealthy residents of town. The academy's behavior support section, a charity-based program for at-risk kids, detracted from the school's appeal to those residents, at least in the principal's eyes.

The kids were restless listening to Officer Greene go on about how records were stored. The dispatch room was a little more interesting, but it was so small that only one kid could look in the door at a time, leaving the rest of them to poke and jab at each other and generally cause commotion in the little police station.

He stepped over to Greene. "I think they'd like to see the holding cells," he said. "In fact, if you wanted, you could lock them in."

Greene laughed. "That's tempting."

"No, I mean it. We used to do that in my old department, lock people in and give them a feel for what jail is like."

The barrel-chested officer studied Trey with a half smile on his face. "You wouldn't be trying to tell me how to do my job, would you?"

Trey lifted his hands, palms out. "No, no way," he said. "Just a thought."

But Greene did take the kids down to the holding cells next. Since they were empty, he let the kids go inside if they wanted to, and closed the door on them, although he didn't lock the door and turn off the lights as had happened on one dramatic tour Trey had witnessed back at his own station.

Still, the cells had an impact on the kids, especially when the old-fashioned, barred metal gates closed. That clank was definitive.

"They can't even go to the toilet with privacy," Rory said, looking around the cell.

"Can't do nothin' with privacy," Shane added.

It was true—privacy was one of the biggest losses prisoners faced. Trey was just glad these kids were now in a program that would hopefully keep them out of a place like this.

"Stinks in here." One of the girls wrinkled her nose. "Is this where LJ was held?"

"I'm not at liberty to talk about specific cases," Greene said.

"Hey, is it true LJ's coming back?" Shane asked.

"What?" The principal had heard that, and he glared from Shane to Erica. "Surely you haven't told the students that we're bringing that criminal back into our school."

Erica met his eyes steadily. "He is exactly the kind of kid who needs to be here," she said quietly. "He'd never gotten in trouble before. I'd like to offer him another chance, once his detention is served."

"Having a criminal element in our school is just why I want this program terminated," O'Neil huffed.

Greene, Trey and Erica exchanged glances, and the kids who weren't busy taking pictures of one another in the jail cell started to whisper. Fear and resentment crossed several faces, and Trey could guess why. This program meant a lot to the kids, and they didn't want to lose it.

"We have no reason to keep him out," Erica repeated, "and it's in our charter to accept all kinds of kids and help them to the next level." Her voice softened. "LJ is a terrific kid. I've missed him, and I know he'll be a great addition when he comes back to our class. I'm almost sure he'll stay out of trouble."

"Can you guarantee that?" the principal asked.

"No, of course not," Erica said. "But I *will* vouch for him, to the board if need be. I believe in him."

How great it would've been, Trey thought, to have a teacher like her when he'd been going through his troubled times in school. Someone who would've seen past all the truant periods when his dad had come to take him away, someone to realize he actually had some smarts.

Erica was vehement but savvy in how she spoke with the principal, not letting him bully her, but not antagonizing him with a lot of attitude.

Trey wished there was something he could do to help the boy, since he'd been the one to get him in trouble. Trouble LJ had brought on himself, sure, but Trey still wished him well, remembered what it was like to be the bad kid. If LJ came back, he'd see what he could do.

As the students' visit ended, Officer Greene pulled him aside. "If you can help her keep this program alive, it would go a long way toward my making a good recommendation for you."

"Really, you're that on board with it?"

"Whatever we can do to get kids off the street and keep them out of trouble, I'm in favor." As Erica came over, Greene changed the subject. "Any word about that dog of yours?"

"Oh," Erica exclaimed, looking at Trey. "I meant to tell you. We heard a little bit about King, Hannah and I did, on Saturday while we were in Trinity Bay."

Trey had forced himself not to seek out information through the police grapevine about King, but he pounced on Erica's words like a thirsty man would grab for a pitcher of water. "What did you hear?"

"Well…" She looked a little troubled. "A source—and I don't know how reliable he is—said that the new owner is being harsh with him."

The idea of Cochran being harsh with King made the breath leave Trey's lungs. As they walked back to the school, he probed until he'd gotten some details, shrugging aside her reluctance to talk about it and her reminders that she wasn't sure the kid who'd seen Cochran was an accurate and believable witness.

"I'd like to go over there and see King." He paused, then added, "Especially if you'll come with me."

CHAPTER EIGHT

AFTER A FEW days hiding out in her room, eating chocolate and stalking Melvin's new girlfriend on social media, Julie woke up on Wednesday with a plan. By the time she got to her 10:00 a.m. shift at the bookstore, she was hot, tired and sweaty, but determined.

"Have a seat. You look like you're about to pass out." Mary waved her toward the high office chair behind the cash register. "What have you been doing?"

"Walked four miles." Julie sat down, grateful for the chance to catch her breath. "After Zumba class."

Mary laughed. "Ever heard of moderation?"

"Moderation won't get me where I want to be," Julie said.

"Which is where?"

"Right about where I was when I married Melvin," she said. "I have at least fifty pounds to lose."

"That's ridiculous," Mary said. "You look perfect just the way you are, and if men don't appreciate it, there's something wrong with them."

"Easy for you to say." Julie gestured at Mary's model-thin figure, her stylish clothes. All the men in town loved her, and several of the over-fifty crowd actively pursued her, to no avail.

"It's true," Mary scolded. "You have a lovely, curvaceous shape, and if you dressed to accentuate it, you'd be gorgeous. And in high demand, if that's of interest."

"Thanks." But Mary was a kind friend, not an age-appropriate man. "Want me to work on that diet book display we were planning?"

She knew she wasn't the only one in Pleasant Shores who was trying to drop a few pounds. With swimsuit season coming on, lots of folks would be cutting the carbs and desserts. Or at least buying books about how to do it.

"You mean the books that poor child Melvin has taken up with was looking at?"

"Yeah." Julie gave a disgusted sigh. "Though, technically, she's not a child. She's definitely young, and definitely skinny. Except…up front." She cupped her hands in front of her own average-size breasts to show what she meant.

"And lacking in other qualities, I imagine," Mary said. "Youth and skinniness are overrated. And so often, they're just fleeting."

"Even when I was young, I wasn't skinny. Not like that *poor child*, anyway." Julie headed over to the cookbook section. She pulled the books out one at a time, focusing on the most colorful and appealing low-calorie books for the display.

And, yes, they were the ones Melvin's skinny girlfriend had handled.

She studied the glossy photos of vegetables and read the cover testimonials. They had to be fake, didn't they? Did anyone ever lose half their body weight from using one cookbook?

That was about how much she'd have to lose to even be in the same ballpark as Melvin's new squeeze, she thought darkly. Even then, she'd still be old. Well, Melvin's age, and men didn't want women their own age; they wanted younger, fertile ones who could prop up their sagging manhood.

A younger woman was less likely to be patient with Melvin's older-guy issues than Julie had been. Except maybe he didn't have those issues when confronted with a body like the *poor child* had.

Still, Julie was determined to show Melvin. He'd get tired of the vapid interior of his new girlfriend, and he'd miss his wife's good conversation, her insight. Add a newly muscular, shapely figure, and he'd be crying into his hair dye.

Mary came over and helped her arrange the diet cookbooks on a table in the front of the store. "So, how are you doing?" she asked, her voice neutral. "With regard to Melvin, I mean."

"I'm doing fine. I'm gonna lose this weight and get some new clothes and see if I can get him back."

Mary's forehead wrinkled, her lips pursing to one side. "Are you sure you want him?"

"No. Not really. But I want the option. And I don't like seeing him with someone else."

"Something to think about," Mary said. "You started wanting him back more when you saw him with someone else. Wonder if the same would hold true for him?"

"Meaning what?" Julie straightened a book about intermittent fasting that claimed you could eat whatever you wanted as long as it was within a six-hour window each day. That sounded good, as long as it didn't interfere with her nightly ration of wine and pretzels.

Which it probably would.

"You could do some dating yourself," Mary suggested.

"Ugh." Julie kept rearranging books, not looking at her friend. "Even if I wanted to date some new guy, which I don't, where am I supposed to meet a single guy my age in this town?"

"Haven't you ever heard of online dating?" Mary picked up her phone and scrolled with an elegant, perfectly manicured finger. "Look, I have an app."

"You *do*?" To Julie's knowledge, Mary had never gone out on a date. Mary never talked about it, but the rumor was that she'd been widowed at a young age and had never had kids. Now she seemed to be married to her bookstore.

"I'm not in the market, no, but I always did like shopping," Mary said with a lazy smile. "Take a look."

They sank down onto the edge of the front window display together, and Mary showed her the app. "Swipe right if you like what you see, swipe left if you don't," Mary explained. She punched in some parameters that she said would fit Julie—age, body type, educational level—and they looked at the results.

Seventy-five men within fifty miles were apparently looking for someone like Julie. Who knew? They giggled over a couple of bare-chested mirror shots and rolled their eyes over usernames like "Stud4U" and "RichSexyRetired."

"Seriously," Julie said, "these are *not* the guys to make Melvin jealous. He'd laugh if he saw me with one of them."

Mary quirked an eyebrow. "He's not such a prize himself."

"I look at these guys and think I'd rather spend an evening with my granddaughters. Or you. Or a good book."

"Fair enough," Mary said. "Like I said, it's fun to shop for men. But you don't notice me making an actual purchase."

The bells on the door jingled, and Earl Greene's friendly, bespectacled face peeked around the door. "Just my daily check-in, ladies," he said. "Everything good here?"

"Better than good. We're looking at some online dating for Julie," Mary said.

Julie elbowed Mary, hard, as Earl came all the way in, turning down his police radio. "You don't have to tell the whole world! She's showing it to me," she called across the store to Earl. "I'm not actually doing online dating."

"I'm not telling the whole world. I'm just telling Earl," Mary said. And then, in a whisper, "Why don't you go out with *him*? He's always had a crush on you."

Julie elbowed Mary again, harder, as Earl crossed the bookstore to lean against the counter. "Finding any good prospects?" he asked.

"At least eight millionaires," Julie said. "And they're all six-two and good-looking, according to their bios."

Earl snorted. "Yeah, I know how that goes. I've met a couple of women who didn't quite match their profile pictures."

"You've done online dating?" Julie looked at him, fascinated. She'd never thought about the love life of her and Melvin's nerdy friend.

"Uh-huh. At least, I used to. But it's an expensive proposition, taking out women who are ten years older and twenty pounds heavier than they claimed to be online."

"They're just trying to be what men want!" Julie lifted her hands, palms up. "Young, skinny women. Even old guys with no hair and giant bellies are sure they deserve a Victoria's Secret model. They're not going to click on a realistic-size woman their own age."

"Men," Mary said with an indulgent smile. "Their overconfidence is adorable."

"It must be nice. And it even seems to work," Julie added bitterly, thinking of Melvin. Who'd have thought he could date a girl like the *poor child*? Did she have a clue about how much time he spent watching golf and football on TV, or how irritated he got if his hairbrush, wallet and keys weren't lined up just so on his dresser at night?

"Not all of us guys have that kind of confidence," Earl said, his face twisting into a rueful smile. "That's why it's hard for someone like me to get a date. When you present yourself as what you are—a short, chunky small-town cop—the winks and waves don't exactly rain down on you."

Julie looked over at Earl with fondness. They'd been couple-friends since their kids were young together, at first during summers in Pleasant Shores and then full-time. Melvin had seemed to enjoy the time they'd all spent together, but he'd often talked Earl down for his weakness for doughnuts and pastries, called him a living stereotype.

They'd drifted apart even before Earl's wife had been killed in a freak accident, partly because of Melvin's attitude. Still, Julie had always felt warm toward him. Earl wasn't likely to hit the gym anytime soon, and yet surely there must be a woman who would overlook his Pillsbury Doughboy figure and see his heart of gold.

For herself, rather than seeking a man who'd overlook her flaws, she was determined to get rid of them. She reached over and set aside the intermittent fasting book. She was going to give it a try.

The bells on the door jingled again, and this time, Ria came in. "Do you still want to go to lunch, Mom?"

"Just as soon as she's done finding her dream guy online," Mary said, and then waved a hand, laughing. "Sorry, sorry. Not the kind of thing you want to know about your mom."

"I'm *not* doing online dating," Julie said, though with less conviction than she'd had before. If Earl had done it, it couldn't be too bad.

"It's not a bad idea," Ria said. "You're beautiful, and young, and you deserve happiness."

Julie put her arm around her daughter, appreciating her kindness anew. "Thanks, honey." But inside, she wondered how much Ria knew about her father's shenanigans. If she knew he was seeing someone, would she tell Julie? Or try to protect her from potentially hurtful information?

"Let me see what kind of dudes you're looking at," Ria said, leaning closer, and Mary showed her RichSexyRetired. "Wonder if he really looks like that?"

"Wait a minute," Julie said, struck. "Have *you* ever done online dating?"

Ria shook her head. "I have friends who've tried to talk me into it, but when do I have time to date?"

Julie recognized an excuse when she heard one. She worried about her daughter. She was too young to give up on men.

"You need to make time," Earl said. "Don't wait until you're my age and all alone."

"You're not all alone. You have us." Ria put a friendly arm around Earl's shoulders. "Come over for supper anytime. The girls would love to see you."

"You know I can't resist your cooking, Miss Ria," he said. "I'll definitely stop over." Then he looked at

Julie. "If that's okay with you. I know you're living there now, too, or right next door. You must spend a lot of time together as a family."

"It's fine with me if you come for dinner," Julie said. "Why wouldn't it be?"

He looked at her for a moment longer. "Right," he said, sounding a little less enthusiastic. "I'd better get back to work." He gave a general wave and headed out the door.

As Julie gathered her things, she thought about how much better she felt with her women friends than she had either alone or with Melvin. With Earl, too—he was almost one of the girls, with his stories of dating woes.

She was still going to lose the weight, though. That was the way to snag a guy who would make Melvin crazy with jealousy.

Life wasn't complete without a man in it. She hated to even have the thought, and Mary would flay her for it, but after all those years of marriage, she felt it to be true, at least for her.

She rang up the book on fasting and both Ria and Mary looked on.

"You're really going to do that, Mom?" Ria asked.

"I might."

"Let me know how it works," Ria said. "I could always stand to lose a few." She wandered off toward the new mysteries.

Mary leaned toward Julie. "If you're making all your plans around trying to be what Melvin wanted," she said, "seems like he's still controlling you."

"I know, I know."

"Decide for yourself how you want to look and act. Don't just try to live up to Melvin's expectations."

Julie sucked in a breath. "Maybe I *am* still being controlled by him," she said, thinking again about how happy she'd been in the company of Mary, Ria and Earl. "But I don't know how to stop." She slid the book into a bag, tucked it under her arm and headed out for a last decadent lunch with her daughter. She'd start her diet tomorrow.

THURSDAY NIGHT ABOUT SUNSET, Trey pulled his truck into the parking lot of Trinity Bay's small public beach. He looked sideways at Erica. Dressed in jeans, a dark T-shirt and black high-tops, she looked all of fifteen. "You sure you want to do this with me?" he asked her.

"Yes! You need a lookout." She was bright, peppy, in a good mood. Her sister had had a good doctor appointment apparently, and Hannah was making new friends.

Erica was the type of person whose happiness came from the happiness of others. The complete opposite of his ex-wife, who'd barely noticed other people's feelings. He couldn't help admiring Erica for that.

They climbed out of the truck and walked down to the beach, taking it slow and craning to see if anyone was there. It was cool tonight, and they'd both pulled on dark sweaters before exiting the truck.

"I know sneaking around is no big deal to a cop like you," she said, "but to me, this is fun. It's like spying." She clapped a hand over her mouth. "Although I'm taking it seriously, I promise. I know it's important business. We have to make sure King is okay."

"I'm glad you're having fun. And I'm sure he's fine." He'd been trying to tell himself that since Erica had reported the conversation with the bike rental guy. Most likely, the kid had misinterpreted normal police dog training as something abusive. Training a working dog wasn't like training a pet.

And if he wasn't convinced King was being abused and needed his help, then why was he really here?

He had to admit the truth: he was looking for a reason King's placement wouldn't work. Looking for it because he wanted King back, so that when he left Pleasant Shores and returned to police work, King would be at his side. As an officer with a trained K-9 partner, he would be that much more appealing for his own department to hire back, or for another department to add to its numbers.

Without King, he was just another out-of-work cop.

He heard something in the bushes and twisted, but it was just a squirrel. Still, his back complained, and he grimaced. Unlike Erica's sister, he hadn't been getting the best of reports from his physical therapist and his doctor. "There's a possibility that this could become chronic," the doc had said yesterday at Trey's appointment.

Well, a possibility wasn't for sure, and he was trying to work a little harder at each session of PT. His therapist had given him another set of at-home exercises to supplement his sessions at the office, and he intended to surprise her by completing them religiously and showing big improvements at his next session.

He hadn't gotten where he was in life by accepting other people's predictions about his abilities.

"There he is!" Erica gripped his sleeve and pointed. "At least, there's a guy and a dog."

In the dim light, it was a little hard to tell, but then the dog barked.

Recognition of the sound made Trey smile. "That's King," he said. "Now, let's watch and see what kind of training he's getting."

"Won't the new handler see us?"

"We'll pretend to be a couple of lovers," Trey suggested, then wished he hadn't when he saw Erica's quick frown. "Sorry. Kidding."

"No," she said slowly, "it makes sense for us to do that, because if he glances over…" Suddenly, she wrapped her arms around him.

"What the…?" He trailed off, engulfed in the sweet feel and smell of her. She wasn't skin and bones after all, and she wasn't fragile. Her back felt strong beneath his hands, her soft feminine curves nestling against him in all kinds of interesting ways. Some basic male instinct made him nuzzle her neck.

"He sees us!" She hissed out the words and shifted. Was she trying to move away or trying to get closer?

He couldn't tell, but he also couldn't resist her. He pulled her tighter against him.

She turned so more of her was visible than him. "Duck down! He knows you and he doesn't know me. I'm trying to shield you!"

That made sense.

Not that much was making sense with her clenched against him.

He tried to care that Cochran might see him, recognize him, report him. That would be bad. Sure it would, but compared to the fruity smell of Erica's hair... He drew in another appreciative breath. "This is nice," he murmured into her ear.

"Is he still looking?" Her voice sounded strange, choked.

He forced himself to open his eyes and focus on the officer and King. The guy had King in a sit-stay and was walking away. "No."

She unwrapped herself and sat down on the breaker wall at the edge of the beach, her chest rising and falling rapidly. "Sorry," she said. "I shouldn't have jumped you like that. I didn't think."

"It worked." Boy, had it worked. He sat down next to her and slipped his arm around her.

She tensed and glanced uneasily at him.

"Just keeping up the facade," he said.

"Oh. Okay." She seemed to be breathing slowly, through her mouth, almost yoga breathing. In through the nose, out through the lips. Yoga breathing or having-a-baby, labor breathing like he'd happened to see on a show about childbirth.

Truth to tell, he'd kind of liked watching that show, hadn't been able to make himself click away, and now he thought about what it would be like if Erica were carrying his child. He'd definitely be the kind of husband who went along to every appointment and gladly coached her through labor and birth. Some guys were squeamish about that, but not him. He was into the miracle.

She shifted beside him. "So, anyway," she said, sounding nervous, and suddenly he realized what was going on: she'd been affected by being close to him. Maybe? He could hope.

As for him, he'd never felt anything sweeter. He'd wanted to keep holding her forever. Felt like that was how long it would take to get to know her, to unpeel all her layers, to understand the woman she was beneath the professionalism and the guardedness.

They heard a command, carried to them on the breeze, and Trey put his focus back where it belonged, on King. At that point, Trey realized the dog had been made to stay for a long time, longer than Trey would ever put him through.

King was a pro, though. He stayed still, and then, on command, he trotted to his new handler.

Trey would have knelt and praised him, but Cochran yelled something, grabbed King's leash and jerked it upward, forcing King into a sit position.

Trey's fists clenched.

King obeyed, but even from this distance, Trey could tell his ears were flattened back a little. The dog wasn't happy. That correction must have hurt.

"That was mean," Erica whispered. "Why'd he do that?"

"King should've stopped and sat in front of him." Trey forced his hands to relax. "It's more of an obedience thing than a police thing, but some guys consider it essential."

He was trying to give Cochran the benefit of the doubt, but it wasn't easy. The guy uttered another sharp command—using German, it sounded like, which was common among police handlers—and King fell into step beside him.

Cochran put King through a series of maneuvers, giving orders in a sharp voice, offering no praise or treats.

King's head drooped and his ears lay back.

Which wasn't Trey's business. Every handler did things his own way. King was a dog who needed to work, and for that to happen, he had to get used to a new handler, learn his style.

The officer put King into another sit-stay and walked away. This time, he waited an even longer time. Finally, he called King to him.

King trotted forward and sat directly in front of Cochran.

There was no praise, but at least he'd avoided a correction.

Cochran snapped his fingers and King stood and moved to his side, tail between his legs.

Trey's heart felt heavy, like a rock. "Man, I hate to see him like this. I want him back."

"Is there any way you can—"

"Nope." Trey cut her off as a way of cutting off his own hopes in that direction. "Unless he absolutely won't work for the new handler, they'll leave him there." His throat tightened on the last word.

"I'm sorry." She leaned her head against his shoulder and hugged his arm. "It's so hard to lose a dog. Especially when you see him being treated like this. I wish you could get him back."

"So do I."

All of a sudden King stopped, raised his nose to sniff the air. His tail started to wag.

"Uh-oh," Trey said, and Erica's hand tightened on his arm.

King gave a short, joyous bark and strained toward them. They were half a football field away, but King's senses were keen. He'd caught wind of Trey.

Part of him wanted to tell King to go back, stop, halt, stay. The other part wanted to run forward and pull his dog into his arms.

Cochran shouted a correction, but King ignored it, pulling toward the scent he'd caught, the scent of Trey, his longtime, well-loved handler.

Then everything seemed to happen in slow motion.

Cochran's voice rose into a scream. He yanked King's collar—probably a prong collar—hard. King ignored what had to be severe pain, continuing to pull toward Trey.

Cochran got in front of the dog and kneed him square on his side, knocking him to the ground. Then he kicked King in the chest.

King let out a yelp.

Cochran kicked him again.

And then Trey was flying over the sand, legs pumping, shouting, the pain in his back barely at the edge of his consciousness. "Leave him alone!" he yelled.

"What the—" Cochran turned in their direction and let out a curse. "Harrison! What are you doing here?" He yanked King's collar, trying to pull the whimpering dog to a stand.

Rage pounded through Trey's head like wild horses. Enough was enough. "Give. Me. The. Leash." His fists were clenched.

"Trey." Erica's hand was on his arm, "Sir," she said to Cochran, "you need to hand over the dog, now. We saw you abusing him."

"Abusing…" He cursed again. "Harrison, this is against protocol. You're not supposed to be anywhere near my dog."

"Protocol probably also dictates that you shouldn't kick your K-9 partner," Erica said hotly. "You may have hurt him, damaged his organs."

"He's not hurt. He's a tough dog."

"He's *my* dog." Trey knelt and ran his hands over King, checking for lacerations or broken bones. King licked his hand, his brown eyes fixed on Trey's.

Cochran leaned down and grabbed King's prong collar.

King snarled and went for the man's arm just as he'd go for a perp.

"Release!" Trey snapped.

Cochran yanked his arm away with a howl. "He bit me!" He clutched his arm, his face a mask of horror as he backed away.

And it all fell into place for Trey. The guy was afraid of dogs. Or, at least, afraid of King. That was why he'd trained with such harshness.

Strange for a man who feared dogs to become a K-9 officer. Strange, but not unheard of. Some men felt they had to overcome any and all fears; some feared only one particular type of dog and so normally worked with other types.

"Are you all right?" Erica went motherly, taking Cochran's arm, studying it, patting his shoulder.

Trey wondered why she was acting so nice to the jerk, and then he understood. Clever girl. She was investigating the extent of damage King had done to Cochran.

"Your jacket's ripped," she said after a quick examination, "but it doesn't look like any skin is broken."

"I'm reporting this. You'd better believe I'm reporting this," he said, glaring at them.

"Okay." Trey sighed. He shouldn't have done what he'd done, probably, but watching King get kicked without helping him wasn't in his skill set. He could already imagine the consequences that would start to rain down on him.

"That dog's not fit for police work," Cochran blustered. "And neither are you. Spying on a fellow officer, stalking me… You're out of line."

"He wasn't..." Erica started, then went quiet, knelt and scratched King's ears. "Look. For now, we'll just take the dog. We can work out the details later, during the day, when everyone's not so upset."

Cochran looked down at King and spit. Then he turned and stomped away, already punching numbers into his cell phone.

Trey stood and clicked his tongue to King, who struggled to his feet. He looked up at Trey, awaiting a command, mouth open and panting in what looked like a smile.

Trey tugged the dog against his leg, and the familiar weight and smell of him was a balm to his heart.

"Do you think he needs to go to the vet?" Erica asked. "Those were some hard kicks."

"We'll see how he does on the way back to the truck."

They strolled together, slowly, both watching King. The big dog walked, then trotted along, tail curled high over his back, ears alert. He was moving and breathing fine, and Trey's tense shoulders relaxed.

He'd make a report, of course, and Cochran wouldn't end up looking good. There was a witness, Erica.

But Trey could already hear what his chief would say: she wasn't objective, because she was Trey's friend.

If Cochran pursued his claim, emphasizing the

fact that King had turned on him, King's career as a police dog could well be over.

In a way, it was because of Trey's rash action.

But what else could he have done?

CHAPTER NINE

"CALM DOWN, ZIGGY." Erica pulled the leash tighter as she and the excited goldendoodle walked up the sidewalk to Trey's cottage.

With the hand that wasn't holding the leash, she fluffed her hair and checked the corners of her mouth for excess lipstick.

Should she have even worn lipstick? They were just going to the town's May festival, a small, weekend-long event where local residents celebrated the start of their own special season: the weather was nice, and the tourists weren't here yet. Lots of people considered May the best time of the year around here.

She cupped a hand over her mouth to check her breath, rolled her eyes at her own foolishness and then rang the doorbell. She hitched up her ankle-length jeans. They had been snug in a good way last year, but now they didn't seem to want to stay up. Maybe she should have worn her usual ancient faded ones she'd appropriated from Hannah.

King barked inside Trey's place, and then she heard heavy footsteps. Butterflies fluttered inside her chest.

She'd always felt a little fluttery around Trey, but

last night had marked a new level in their relationship. Her face heated as she thought about the way she'd flung her arms around him. That had been forward, but he hadn't seemed to mind. Not at all. He had gently tugged her closer and they had fit together like long-lost puzzle pieces.

But it was more than that. Remembering how he had run to King's defense, admiration washed over her anew. He was a protector to the core. He hadn't been able to stand by and let an animal be hurt, even when revealing his presence would potentially cause him professional problems.

Joining with him to help King made her feel like they were part of a team together, a feeling that had started when they had begun working more smoothly together with the kids at school, but had been cemented last night.

In class today, it had felt perfectly natural to go out into the hall with him to talk about how King was doing and whether he had heard anything from the other officer. When he had said, "So far, so good," she had spontaneously high-fived him and they had shared a quick little hug.

It felt so easy to be close to him. Was that normal? She didn't have enough experience to know.

He opened the door, and her heart did a double thump. His hair was damp, as if he'd just gotten out of the shower. His button-down shirt was open, revealing a very muscular chest. He wore low-slung jeans and his feet were bare, and he was so handsome she was blown away.

And he was looking at her as if she were a delicious pastry in the bakery case.

He was looking at her like he wanted her.

Heat rose up her neck to her face. She knelt down beside Ziggy, who was actually being pretty calm, and rubbed his sides until he got excited and started jumping around.

Anything for the distraction from how excessively warm Trey was making her feel.

He cleared his throat and held open the door. "Come on in," he said. "I'm just about ready. Would have been ready, but I've been giving King some extra attention. I hate to leave him." He rubbed a hand over the German shepherd's back.

"Why don't you bring him along?"

Trey shook his head and, thankfully—at least, Erica *thought* she was thankful—started buttoning his shirt. "We had agreed this would be a good time to train Ziggy. I don't want to detract from that, or take attention away from him. He needs our focus."

"It won't detract." Erica reached out toward King, and the big dog pushed his nose into her hand, seeming to recognize her as a friend. Contact with the animal steadied her, brought her mind back from Trey's good looks to where it should be. "King will be a good example," she said. "Our goal is to have Ziggy be calm around other dogs and people, and he can start slow, walking to the festival with King."

"Well…" Trey hesitated, then smiled. "I should probably argue with you about that, but the truth is, I'd love to bring him."

While she waited for him to grab his things, she looked around the cottage, curious since she'd never been inside it before. It was neat, but not obsessively so; there was an opened paperback book facedown on an ottoman, and a stack of unopened mail in the middle of the table.

Pretty much the same level of messiness as her own place. Yet another way they were compatible.

And she did *not* need to be thinking about that.

Ten minutes later, they were strolling through increasingly crowded streets toward the sound of music and the flash of colorful lights at the town park where the festival was being held. They weren't walking any closer together than usual, weren't touching each other, and yet there was a heat and a sense of promise that was hard to ignore.

You have an ax over your head. You can't have kids. You have scars, and may have more eventually. But even as she recited to herself the reasons why she needed to keep a distance from Trey, her chest tightened with yearning. She'd never felt like this before. And she hadn't realized how heady it would be to, well, start to fall in love with a guy.

Committing herself to a life of celibacy had been a lot easier before she had met Trey. Before she'd felt the strength of his arms around her.

She blew out a breath and tried to focus on something nonromantic. "Have you heard anything more about King? Any word from that awful Cochran guy?"

"Still nothing." Trey reached down and scratched

King's ears, and the big dog looked up at him, mouth open, tongue hanging out. "I'm thinking no news is good news. Cochran ought to be ashamed to show his face, let alone report what happened. Although eventually we'll have to talk to our departments about why King is with me and not with him."

"I guess there are some politics involved in it," Erica said. "All I know is, King looks happy."

"Let's hope he can stay that way. I'm hoping that jerk will decide to lie low."

They had reached the edge of the festival now, and the smell of kettle corn and saltwater taffy swept toward them on a cool bay breeze. Crowds of people walked past the booths or stood in line at concession stands. Mary and Julie were there, at a booth stacked high with books and a big cardboard sign depicting the Lighthouse bookstore. From his heart-shaped bed beside Mary, Baby yipped at King and Ziggy, making sure the larger dogs knew who was boss.

Principal O'Neil sat at a booth advertising the benefits of private schools. He was occupied talking to a couple of adults and grade-school-age kids. Good. Without discussing it, Erica and Trey went in the other direction.

Some of the teenagers had on shorts and flip-flops, but as darkness fell, the air cooled and Erica was glad she had worn something a little warmer. They strolled through the festival, dogs at their sides. When Ziggy got overexcited, Trey showed her how to give him an alternative command, making him sit or lie down or give paw until he forgot about whatever had distracted him. As the crowd thinned and Ziggy got more tired, he seemed content to just trot along beside her.

"You're doing a good job with him," Trey said finally. "He does best when he's right at your side. Most dogs do."

"I think he learned a lot from a couple of lessons you've given him about heeling," she said. She reached down to scratch Ziggy's ears.

But they were near the hot dog stand, and suddenly a little kid dropped a hot dog. Ziggy spotted the food on the ground and ran for it, taking Erica by surprise, yanking the leash out of her hands.

"Ziggy!" Erica rushed after him, but he quickly snatched the hot dog and scarfed it down. Just as she reached him, he glanced back, saw her and took off again, grabbing a little girl's cotton candy out of her hand and holding it high as he pranced and trotted through the crowd. He kept glancing back at Erica. Obviously, he thought this was the best game of chase ever.

"Ziggy! I'm sorry," she called to the mother of the girl whose cotton candy had been swiped.

"He stole my fluffy snack!" the little girl wailed.

As Ziggy dashed past another group of children, several of them started to cry, as well.

"Catch that dog," the cotton candy mother yelled, picking up her child.

"I'm sorry. I'm trying," Erica panted out, still chasing Ziggy. "He's not dangerous," she called to the crowd generally.

Now a couple of men were trying to help her, dodging in front of Ziggy, but he was an old hand at that game and danced away from them.

"Ziggy. Halt." Trey's deeper voice rang out behind Erica, and Ziggy did glance back, but obviously he was having too much fun to listen to his new trainer.

Finally, Shane from the academy held out his hot dog to Ziggy and managed to lead him into a fenced corner, and Erica grabbed his leash as he wolfed down the food. She gripped it tightly and gave Shane a quick side hug. "Thank you so much. You're a lifesaver."

"No problem." Shane ducked his head, blushing, but he couldn't hold back his big smile. He glanced at the couple of girls from the mainstream school who were standing nearby.

"You're a hero, dude," one of them said, and he blushed harder.

"Good job," Trey said as he reached them, barely breathing hard, King at his side. "I gave some money to the lady whose daughter's cotton candy got swiped," he said to Erica. "But you might want to talk to her because she's still mad her kid got upset. I'll hold Ziggy."

"Thanks." Erica jogged toward the angry-looking woman and, after multiple apologies, talked her into bringing her daughter to where she could see Ziggy. Soon, the little girl was begging to pet him, and even the mom was reluctantly converted after her daughter touched Ziggy's soft fur and smiled hugely.

After it was all over, Erica and Trey took the dogs a little apart from the crowd and sat on a bench to regroup, but it wasn't to be. Principal O'Neil came marching toward them.

"That was quite a spectacle," he said. "Not the image we want our teachers to portray."

Trey opened his mouth, obviously intending to defend her, but she nudged him with her foot. "You're right. It was a mistake to bring my dog here when he's not well trained. I won't let something like that happen again."

Trey's eyebrow quirked up, but he didn't speak, and Erica was glad. She had learned that arguing against her boss was less effective than giving in to him, letting him have his sense of power. Besides, he was right. Ziggy had been awful, and it was her fault for bringing him into the situation.

"Could you step aside with me a minute, Erica?" O'Neil asked.

Her heart sank. "Okay." She held out Ziggy's leash to Trey and he took it before she could ask him to hold the dog for her.

As soon as they were out of earshot of Trey and the other fairgoers, O'Neil turned to face her. "Are you aware that our rules regarding a relationship with a coworker also apply to volunteers?" he asked.

Her stomach went tight. "No, I guess… I hadn't thought about those kind of rules."

O'Neil's eyebrows came together, his mouth twisting to one side. "I knew allowing this program to continue was trouble."

"But it's nothing to do with the program. And I don't have a relationship with…" She trailed off. It was true, she and Trey didn't have a relationship that you could name, but their feelings for each other were becoming hard to hide.

"There are reasons for this type of regulation. It can lead to all kinds of problems in the workplace," O'Neil lectured on. "What if the relationship ends? Are you still going to be able to work with the man?" He shook his head. "I don't like this."

"We aren't dating," she said. She had to keep the academy going, had to keep this job. For the sake of all the kids who depended on it, of course. But also for Amber and Hannah, who were loving their life at the shore.

No other work around here—crab picker, waitress, retail worker—could provide anywhere close to her teacher income. If she lost her job, they would have to move away, and Erica had promised herself she would make this dream come true for her sister. "There's nothing to worry about," she said firmly. "Trey and I are not seeing each other."

"Uh-huh," O'Neil said, obviously not believing her. "There's something else. I noticed more and more mingling between the support program kids and the mainstream kids. I don't like it."

"You mean here at the fair?" Erica's voice rose to a squeak and she swallowed and took a breath. "We can't control what the kids do during their free time."

O'Neil frowned and was opening his mouth to

reply when Erica heard Ziggy bark. She looked to see that Officer Greene had come over to Trey and was talking to him intently. The discussion didn't look like it was going well.

O'Neil noticed, too. "We'll talk more about this," he said, and marched back over toward Trey and Officer Greene.

"You'll need to get in touch with your chief right away," Greene was saying to Trey.

"What's going on?" Principal O'Neil asked.

"Police business," Greene said with a smile and a wave of the hand as he turned away.

Erica could guess what that police business was from the troubled expression on Trey's face and the protective hand he put on King's back. The other officer must have reported what had happened last night with King.

After Officer Greene walked away, O'Neil frowned at both of them and then at the two dogs. "Having a cop connected with the school was supposed to help enrollment, not hurt it, but this kind of episode…" He shook his head. "And we can't have a teacher in a relationship with a volunteer."

Trey raised an eyebrow and glanced at Erica, obviously wondering what to say.

"I'm very concerned," O'Neil said. He opened his mouth as if to say more, but a woman with a baby— must be his wife and child—came to the fence beside them. The woman held up the baby and gestured to him. "This isn't over," he said, and headed toward the pair.

Erica was concerned, too. Concerned about King, about Trey and about her own job.

THE FIRST SUNDAY in May was always the church's outdoor picnic, and Julie looked forward to it every year. Melvin had come to church with her most weeks, but he'd usually begged off the picnic, so it wasn't like she missed him. She'd brought her usual fabulous deviled eggs, and she'd even managed not to sample more than a few of them.

Her intermittent fasting was just that, intermittent. Okay, she actually hadn't started yet, but she'd read through the diet book and she had cut way down on the Ben & Jerry's. She'd lost three pounds so far.

So it was okay to fill her plate now, right?

She put an arm around Sophia as they found a seat at one of the long tables. "Thanks for coming to church with me, honey. I was surprised you wanted to, but I'm glad for the company."

"It's fun, Grandma," Sophia said.

That wasn't what Julie would call a church service, but teenagers were different; they gauged everything in terms of fun. She sat down across from Sophia and took a moment to just look around and enjoy. To her right, she could see the bay, off beyond the pretty little bluff where the church sat. To her left, the church itself, small white clapboard against a clear blue sky. Beyond that was Ria's motel and her house, which was what made it easy for Ria and all of them to go to church.

Sophia barely picked at her food. Instead, she focused on her phone. Julie sighed, shoving down the annoyance she felt. She'd led Sophia to the empty end of a table so they could talk to each other rather than just to Julie's church friends.

Apparently, that wasn't happening. After a couple of leading questions brought just a half answer from Sophia, Julie leaned forward. "Why did you come, if you just want to be on your phone? You didn't have to."

Sophia looked up and smiled a little too wide. "I wanted to spend time with you, Grandma!"

The words didn't ring true, and suddenly Julie remembered the text she'd seen on Kaitlyn's phone that time she'd taken the girls to the beach. "Wait a minute," she said. "Did you pull Grandma duty today?"

"No!" But a telltale blush reddened Sophia's face.

Julie shook her head and patted Sophia's arm. "Honey, your mom means well, but you truly don't have to babysit me."

"We're not..." Sophia broke off and looked directly into Julie's eyes for the first time all day. "I guess we kinda are babysitting you."

"I have to find my own way, honey. When you three coddle me, it just makes me feel worse. Who are you texting with?"

"Abby and Katie. They're at the coffee shop."

Julie fumbled in her purse and pulled out a twenty. "Go get coffee with your friends." She handed over the money.

Sophia's eyes lit up. "Thanks, Grandma!" She started to stand up and then sat back down. "You're sure?"

"I'm sure. Go."

Sophia came around to her side of the table and gave her a quick hug. "Thanks, Grandma. You're cool." And she hurried off.

"Did I just hear a teenager call you cool?" Earl Greene stood by the spot on the picnic bench that Sophia had vacated, right across from Julie. "Are you too cool to let an old friend sit with you?"

"Sit down." She smiled to see his friendly face. They chatted and ate while conversations swirled around them.

Gradually, she noticed a couple of "shh" sounds and turned to glance in the direction of them. There was a circle of women, all leaning in toward Primrose Miller, the church organist and the biggest gossip in the community. Primrose was talking excitedly.

No big deal. Julie had ignored Primrose's tales ever since she'd come to the island and started attending church.

"I have to play for the ceremony," Primrose was saying, "but I don't have to approve of it."

Earl had stopped eating, and his forehead wrinkled. "We should go get some of that dessert while it's there. I hear that Amanda Jones made lemon meringue pie, and Mary brought a terrific fruit salad. What do you think—should we go up?"

Another line drifted over from Primrose's table. "I mean, he *has* to marry her. Honestly, at his age!"

"At least come up with me," Officer Greene said. He stood and held out a hand to her, waited courteously for her to head toward the line in front of him. He really was a sweetheart.

She surveyed the desserts and truly intended to concentrate on Mary's fruit salad, but she couldn't resist a sliver of lemon meringue. And then she saw the cupcakes—piled high with fudge frosting, Goody's specialty—and snagged one. Since she'd already blown her fast for the day, she might as well enjoy it. "I'll start my diet tomorrow," she said to Officer Greene.

"You're just right the way you are," he said.

What a loyal friend.

As they walked back to the table, she noticed the women at Primrose's table looking at her. When she caught the eye of Primrose herself, though, the woman looked away. She said something to the other women and they all leaned closer and lowered their voices.

"You know," Officer Greene said, "why don't we sit over on the other side? I think there's more of a breeze."

There was that fake sound in his voice, the same sound she'd heard in Sophia's. She looked at him. Then she looked at Primrose and her crowd.

She replayed their conversation in her mind. Primrose didn't want to play at someone's wedding.

They'd all been looking at her.

And Earl was acting weird. "Wait a minute," she said. "Whose wedding was Primrose talking about?"

"Oh, who knows with that woman." He took her elbow and urged her toward a seat at the opposite end of the picnic table from where they'd been. "Could be anyone."

She felt as if someone had slammed a sledgehammer into her chest. She sank onto the picnic table bench. "Is Melvin getting married?"

Earl got very focused on arranging his silverware and wiping off the table.

She reached out and put a hand over his, stilling them. "Earl. Tell me the truth."

He blew out a breath. "Yes, he is," he said as he sank onto the seat opposite her. "I don't approve of what he's doing. Not at all."

Pain radiated out from her heart. She'd been thinking this girlfriend was a temporary thing, an aberration. But if he was... Could it be...? Was he really *marrying* her?

In the church he'd been so reluctant to attend? Julie's church?

The words he'd kept repeating during their counseling sessions, during their predivorce discussion, echoed in her mind.

It's nothing about you. I just don't feel like being married.

Even through her anger and distress, that had been a balm to her. Melvin was like so many other middle-aged men. He was railing against the constraints, all constraints, of his life. He wanted the freedom he hadn't been able to experience as a younger man with a family to support.

But if he was marrying that girl...the *poor child*...

That meant it wasn't marriage he'd disliked, as he'd said; it was *her*.

Earl looked at his hands. He straightened and flexed his fingers. "I mean," he said, "a marriage under those circumstances is hardly going to last."

She looked at him. "Under what circumstances?"

His skin flushed darker. Now he was picking at a splinter of wood on the table. "Oh, you know. Just recently divorced, that sort of thing."

"No. Uh-uh. You meant something else."

"Now, Julie, don't read anything into what I said."

Again, there was that maddening tone: coddling her, babying her. She thought back to what she'd overheard from Primrose. "Wait a minute. Why does he *have* to marry her?"

"I'm not sure..." He looked up and met her eyes. Under her glare, he trailed off. Looked away.

"Tell me," she said as an ugly suspicion washed over her. No one really said it anymore, but when she was growing up, there had only been one reason people had to get married.

She looked into Earl's dark, concerned eyes. "Is she...?"

He blew out a sigh. "Yeah. She's pregnant."

Julie's eyes closed and her nails dug into her palms.

Melvin had gotten someone pregnant. Someone younger and prettier than Julie.

He was going to be a father again, the father of a baby.

That was something Julie, at her age, couldn't give him.

She thought of the young woman who'd come into the bookstore, the one who looked every bit of a temporary fling for an old guy.

But getting married to someone who was having your child wasn't temporary. It was awfully, horribly permanent.

Or, at least, permanent until he got tired of you.

"Julie," Officer Greene said. "I'm sorry. Like I said, I don't approve. He's lost his mind. I didn't want you to know."

"Don't you think I'd eventually hear about a baby?"

"Eventually, but not while you're so..." He trailed off.

She shoved her plate away and stood. "So what? So fragile? Listen, Earl, I'm not made of glass, despite what you and my daughter think."

Although it felt like she might shatter into a million pieces.

Or have a tantrum, or just fall down into a sobbing heap. And she didn't want to do that here.

"I'm leaving," she said as a dizzy, roaring feeling spun in her head.

"What are you going to do?" he asked as if from a great distance.

"I don't know yet," she said. "But it's going to be good. Or at least it's going to *feel* good."

THIS HAD TO WORK.

Monday morning, Erica took a huge gulp of bitter gas-station coffee and looked around at the grumpy kids who were picking up trash and pulling weeds on Sunset Street, the neighborhood of mostly older folks that adjoined the school.

If this service project went well, and if news of it got back to Principal O'Neil, it *might* make up for Friday night's bad scene.

Friday's bad scene with Trey, who was in the next yard over rebuilding a retaining wall and who seemed determined to ignore her.

Well, fine. She could ignore him, too. It was probably for the best so they didn't appear to be *in a relationship.*

"It's so hot," Venus complained, sitting back from the rocky garden she was weeding. "And it's only nine o'clock. *How* long are we doing this for?"

"And *why* are we doing it?" Shane used the hem of his T-shirt to wipe sweat from his face.

"Studies show that activities integrating troubled teens and disadvantaged elderly are beneficial to both," Rory said in his most pedantic voice. "I did some research before we walked over here."

"Who are you calling troubled?" one of the kids snarled, and a couple of others bristled. Rory, socially awkward, tended to say the wrong thing. Or, sometimes, the truth, but in a too-blunt way.

Erica sucked in a breath, bracing for a fight.

"Who are you calling elderly?" came a lazy, cultured voice from the porch next door. Bookstore owner Mary Rhoades stood on her front steps, graceful as always in skinny jeans and a button-down shirt, her little dog in her arms, her white-gray hair back in a loose ponytail. "Let alone disadvantaged," she added. "But I have to say that it would be *very* beneficial to me to have you young people tidy up my front gardens, whether you're troubled or not."

"No one would call *you* elderly," came a gravelly voice from the porch next door to Mary's. "They might call you gorgeous."

Mary ignored this remark except for a slight eye roll that made a couple of the kids chuckle.

The man's voice seemed familiar, and when a big, fit-looking older man with a bald head and piercing eyes leaned over his porch railing, Erica stared at him. "Kirk James?" she asked.

He tilted his head to one side. "And who might you be, pretty lady?"

"I'm Erica Rowe," she said slowly, "and I think you used to date my aunt Jane."

"He used to date three-quarters of the women in this town," Mary said dryly.

Kirk was frowning like he didn't remember Aunt Jane, which was pretty bad since Aunt Jane had been crazy about him. "Jane Newell?" Erica said to prompt his memory.

His face broke out into a wide smile. "Lovely,

lovely woman," he said, and then the corners of his mouth turned down. "Such a shame. She left us too young."

Erica swallowed an unexpected lump in her throat, thinking of the woman who'd been a second mother to her and Amber, inviting them for extended visits every summer right here in Pleasant Shores. "You're right—she did."

Once again, Mary seemed to know intuitively how to relieve an awkward moment. "Now that he's reached the *elderly* stage," she said, nodding at Kirk, "he's slowed down. His dating pool is only half what it used to be."

The two had both come down the steps and they met on the driveway between their houses. "I'd give them all up for you, Mary," Kirk said.

"No, please don't. But thank you for the offer." Mary continued out into the yard to walk her dog around. Kirk sat down on the rock ledge beside the driveway, staring moodily after her.

"That's kinda gross, old people dating," Shane muttered, but the rest of the kids seemed amused by the show.

Erica grabbed the opportunity to snap a few pictures of the kids, and then glanced over at Trey and caught his slight grin. Her mouth went dry as she tried and failed to look away from him. Patches of dark perspiration showed on his T-shirt, and he wiped his brow on his sleeve, and Erica tried to focus on that—he was so sweaty!—instead of his broad shoulders, strong biceps and slim hips.

He seemed to be studying her, too, and then he turned sharply away. "You kids need to get back to work," he ordered.

"But it's *hot*, and my back hurts," Shane complained. He picked up one small branch and carried it toward the trash bin.

"Yeah, it's hot, and it doesn't affect you near as much as it affects the folks who live in these houses. And your back might hurt, but I'll bet a nickel it's not as much as—" He broke off and slapped Shane's arm, gently. "Just get to work, kid. You're plenty strong enough to carry a bigger load."

Shane straightened and did as he was told.

A deep, happy sigh escaped Erica. Trey was so much better than he thought he was with these kids. And he worked hard despite his injury, which she could now see was bothering him—he was limping slightly and he winced as he bent over to pick up another pair of heavy rocks.

He'd mentioned working extra hard in a PT session when they'd seen each other in passing, over the weekend, each of them walking their dogs in carefully different directions. She'd been preoccupied with Amber, nursing her through a cold—at least, that had been her excuse for not stopping to talk.

Truthfully, she was too troubled by questions about what their relationship was and what it might mean to be able to be around him one-on-one.

"Hey! That's my flower bed!" The indignant, out-of-breath shout came from the house on the other side of Mary's, where some of the kids had gone to haul a stack of boards to the pickup in which Trey or Erica would drive them away. One of the kids had gotten careless, dragging a board through a struggling swatch of flowers.

Oh, great. It was Primrose Miller, the church organist and a notorious gossip, though from what Erica had seen, she didn't mean any harm.

"Be more careful," Erica ordered the kids. "Sorry, Primrose," she added. "We'll fix your flowers, and I'll keep a closer eye on them."

"Thank you, honey." Primrose worked her way across the porch—she wasn't using her wheelchair today—and sat down on a wide bench, breathing heavily. "Wish I could do it myself, but I can't, not anymore."

"'Cause she's too *fat*," one of the kids said from Mary's yard, low enough that Primrose couldn't hear. But Erica could. She spun around to confront the offender.

Venus was a step ahead of her. "You shut up," she scolded the kid who'd made the comment, her voice low and angry. "She's a lot like my grandma who died, and I never let anybody pick on Old Mama." The teenager continued lecturing, having more impact than Erica or any adult ever would, so Erica went over and sat down next to Primrose. Partly, she wanted to distract the older woman from the argument among the teens, but she also wanted to make sure she wasn't too upset about her flowers. It was important that whatever word got out about this project was positive, not negative.

The door to Kirk's house opened a few minutes later, and this time, a frail elderly man made his way out, using a three-pronged cane to steady himself as he came to the edge of the porch to survey the scene.

Trey, working right below him, looked up, then took a step back. "You're a World War II veteran?"

The old man smiled. "Hat gives it away every time," he said, indicating his ball cap. "Bob James."

"Trey Harrison. Pleased to meet you," Trey said, then added, "Thank you for your service."

"You're very welcome, young man."

Rory had been listening, and now he approached Trey and Mr. James. "Were you there on D-Day? We read about that in class."

Erica walked over, her teacher brain going into overdrive. If they could get Mr. James, who she guessed was Kirk's father, to visit, the kids could videotape his stories, fitting right into her co-teacher's unit on oral history.

More of the kids had drifted over while Trey, Rory and Mr. James continued talking. There was nothing but respect in their expressions and demeanor, and she was proud of them.

Behind her, voices rose, and she turned away reluctantly to troubleshoot. Kirk and Primrose were up on Primrose's porch, talking and gesticulating, and Shane and one of the teenagers had started weeding the flower bed below and were listening.

And looking ready to blow. Erica hurried over.

"It's the property value," Kirk was saying to Primrose. "It could be through the roof, but not with that school right here. Do you know how much we could sell these houses for if it weren't for those kids?"

"Oh, well, the school is part of the community," Primrose said. "They're not bad kids."

"They didn't used to be, but things are getting worse over there. Did you know one of them was arrested?"

"I did hear that," Primrose said, her voice troubled.

Shane stood up from where he'd been blocked from view, startling the elders. "These old shacks ain't worth anything anyway," he said. Then he deliberately kicked over the metal trash can they'd been throwing the weeds into, causing a loud clanking as the can rolled, spilling weeds along the way.

Unfortunately, the can was rolling toward a vintage car parked along the street. "Stop that can!" Erica yelled, and one of the kids ran gamely after it, but it was too late. The can crashed into the vehicle, and when it bounced back off, a dent was visible.

Kirk came down the steps double-time. "That's my father's car! You kids did that on purpose."

Shane looked shamefaced. "I'm sorry. I didn't mean to dent the car."

"Sorry doesn't fix a vintage vehicle," Kirk fumed.

"I'll pay for it," Shane said quickly. "I'm really sorry."

He sounded sincere and almost ready to cry, and Erica put an arm around his shoulders. "You have money?"

He nodded miserably. "From work last summer. I'm saving up for a car."

"Maybe when you own one, you'll have more respect for other people's property." Kirk was kneeling in front of the old car, examining the small dent. "This won't be cheap."

"Shane, you need to go apologize to Mr. James. The older one, over there." She pointed at the World War II veteran, sensing he'd be more forgiving than his son. Then she turned to Kirk. "We'll make sure it's paid for and fixed," Erica promised.

Unfortunately, she wasn't sure the damage this little incident had done to the program's reputation could be repaired as easily as a dent to an old car.

CHAPTER TEN

MONDAY MORNING, TREY was at the school supervising a small group of kids in putting together a Cinco de Mayo presentation board—which for whatever reason involved sawing and hot-glue gunning and therefore had to be done outside—when he heard shouting behind him.

Specifically, he heard someone shouting his name.

He turned. Leaning on the chain-link fence, fingers laced into it above his head, was Cochran.

His heart sank even as the sight of King's former new handler set off fireballs of anger in his head. Word of the episode with King had somehow gotten back to Earl Greene Friday night, but there had been no official report. Trey had hoped Cochran would make the right decision and let the whole matter go.

But it looked like a few days of stewing had made Cochran madder, not calmer, and Trey needed to contain this. "Keep working," he said to the kids, and jogged over. "Cochran. What do you want?"

"You're really asking me that?" Cochran looked just a little like Arnold Schwarzenegger in an old movie. "You took my dog."

"I took back *my* dog," Trey corrected, "because you were abusing him."

"I was *training* him. Since you didn't."

Anger burned in Trey's belly and heated fast, threatening to engulf him. All the hours he and King had spent in specialized trainings, search and rescue, drug detection, taking down a perp. King's multiple successes.

Not only had he been trained, he'd been well trained. "He's a very smart dog," he forced himself to say mildly. "He doesn't respond well to being screamed at and kicked."

There was a noise behind him, and he turned to see the kids he'd been working with in a small cluster. "You want us to get Miss Rowe?" Shane asked. "Or the principal?"

"Not the principal, idiot," Venus said. "Maybe Miss Rowe."

Nice that they had his back, and that some of them, at least, had some sense about who might be a help and who definitely wasn't. "No, that's okay. Mr. Cochran and I just need to have a conversation."

Cochran rattled the chain links. "You *need* to give me my dog back."

"Not happening."

"I have your chief, old Abe Lincoln, on speed dial."

Here was the consequence he didn't want to face. But for King's sake, he would. "Do what you want. I'm not giving you back my dog to mistreat."

"Your dog is vicious and needs to be taught a lesson. He bit me."

"After you provoked him. And that wasn't a bite. That was a warning. If he'd really bitten you, you'd have needed serious medical attention."

He heard the school's heavy doors clang and turned, and there was Erica—and, oh great, the principal—marching toward them.

"What is the meaning of this disturbance?" Principal O'Neil asked.

"What's going on, Trey?" Erica asked.

"Oh, so you work with your girlfriend?" Cochran sneered as he said it.

"She's not…" He stopped. It was true, she *wasn't* his girlfriend, but he didn't feel right denying it in front of her, because there was no doubt some feelings were growing between them.

"Don't try to cover it up. You were all over each other the other night at the beach."

Behind him, Erica sucked in her breath. The kids started murmuring and giggling.

"What?" Principal O'Neil barked out, so much indignation in his voice that they all turned to look at him, students included. O'Neil faced Erica. "I'll deal with what he's saying about your relationship later, but you, sir—" he punched a finger at Cochran "—you need to back away from school property."

"Fine," Cochran said, "if you don't mind that you're employing a thief and the owner of a dangerous animal."

"That's ridiculous," Erica said hotly, and Trey had

to love that she defended him even though he could tell it wasn't doing him—or her—any favors with O'Neil. "First of all, King isn't dangerous. You're the one who's dangerous. Trey did the only thing he could in taking him away from you."

"You admit he took him." Cochran's voice was rich with triumph.

Behind him, a squad car pulled up and stopped. Officer Greene got out. "I got a call that there was a problem here."

One of the kids must have called, and Trey didn't know whether that was good or bad.

"An accusation of theft has been made," the principal said.

Greene looked at all of them in turn. "Who made it?"

"I did," Cochran said.

"If you have a formal report to make," Greene said, "you'll need to come to the station. I can run you over there."

"I have my own car," Cochran said. "And I'm calling *your* chief." He pointed at Trey, sneered again and started toward a sports car parked on the street.

"I'll meet you there in ten." Greene waited until Cochran was out of earshot and then looked at the remaining three. "Anything else I can help you folks with?"

"We've got it under control," Trey said, although he didn't feel that was the case.

What kind of a report would Cochran file? What would his chief say when he knew?

"I can't say any of this surprises me," O'Neil said. "It's just another example of why I don't want this program here."

The kids started murmuring, and Erica's back stiffened. Trey shoved his hands in his pockets so the fact that they were clenched wouldn't register with the rest of them. What kind of a school administrator started adult arguments in front of the kids he was supposed to be in charge of?

"Are we going to have to go back to our own schools?" Rory asked. "Because…things weren't going too well for me there."

"Me, either," another kid said, and the rest of them started talking more loudly among themselves.

Erica looked stricken.

Shame licked at Trey's insides. He'd put the academy at risk. Just when he was starting to realize how great it was for the kids.

Not only that, but once Cochran had called his chief and put his slant on the story, Trey might not have a chance of being reinstated to the force.

King, either.

And worst case, they might take King away from him again.

He wouldn't allow the dog to be returned to Cochran, though. He'd go into hiding with King before he'd do that.

This day was a disaster. "I'm sorry," he muttered to Erica. "Come on, kids. Nothing more to see here."

They fell into place around him as if they were his rear guard. Which was sweet. If misguided. If ineffective.

It would take more than a bunch of ragtag kids to get him out of this mess.

"So O'Neil bawled him out? Is he gonna have to quit?" Hannah took another bite of burrito and leaned forward. "We saw it all through the window, and then we heard the other kids talking. They said the support program might be cut!"

Her niece's words slashed through Erica, opening up a vision of all the potential consequences. The kids would lose the program that was keeping them out of worse trouble. Erica would lose the only job that paid enough to cover the rent here in Pleasant Shores. They'd have to move, which meant that Hannah would have to change schools again. Worst of all, Amber would lose a lifelong dream.

But Erica couldn't let her anxiety show in front of her sister and niece. "The program's future has always been a little shaky," Erica said, "but what happened today with Trey isn't going to push it over the edge."

Hannah's face broke into a relieved smile, and then her phone buzzed. "Oops, there's my ride. See you guys tomorrow." She'd convinced Amber to let her sleep over at a new friend's house.

"It's still a school night," Amber reminded her. "Go to bed early. Brush your teeth and wear your retainer."

"Mom! I'm seventeen!" She rolled her eyes, but leaned down and gave her mom a quick hug, and then another to Erica.

As soon as Hannah and her friend had driven away, Amber stood and beckoned to Erica. "Come on, girl… We're going out!"

Erica raised an eyebrow. "We are?"

"We are." Amber couldn't suppress a wide smile. "Because I got some more good news today."

Erica jumped up and rounded the table. "Your doctor called?"

"Uh-huh. Scan results looked good."

"Oh, Amber, that's wonderful!" She wrapped her arms around her sister and held her, eyes closing, whispering a prayer of thanks.

Amber shook herself loose. "Put on your cutest skirt. I am. We're going to an actual, grown-up bar and celebrate like the young babes we are!"

An hour later, they were nursing margaritas on the deck of Pleasant Shores' sole waterfront bar that remained open year-round. A local guitarist picked out oldies and the crowd was mixed, from the group of twentysomethings holding up drinks while they danced to eighty-year-old Henry Higbottom holding court at one end of the bar.

Erica leaned back in her chair and regarded her sister, who had her feet propped up on another chair and was surveying the bar crowd, smiling. "So did the doctor say when you have to get another scan?"

Amber put both hands over her ears and shook her head back and forth rapidly. "This scan was good, and I'm not thinking about the next one," she said. "I'm here to have a good time."

"You're right," Erica said. She herself couldn't help thinking about the future, worrying and obsessing about it, but she didn't have to inflict her own anxieties on her sister, who was more carefree by personality. "You got a good report today, and that's what matters. And you look like your old self."

"Only better," Amber said. "I was never quite as skinny as I wanted to be. Now I'm a size four. And I for sure never had the long, curly red hair." She flipped back her curls.

"When did you get that wig?" Erica reached out and touched that natural-feeling hair. "It's gorgeous."

"This afternoon, after I met with my oncologist. I wanted to celebrate, and this is how I did it. At least, this was the first step. Next, I'm going to dance." She took a long draw on her margarita.

"Okay. If you're sure you're feeling up to it." Erica didn't like the part of herself that questioned Amber's good health and stamina, but she'd been around Amber too many bad mornings to feel comfortable with her sister having a wild night. "Remember, going to the ice cream parlor almost did you in."

"Stop being such a wet blanket." But Amber wasn't angry, not really, Erica could tell. "I feel great. And no matter what the future holds, I've realized I have to take advantage of every good hour. Every good *moment*."

"You're right. It's just the division of labor we've always had. You're the wild one, and I'm the responsible one."

"Yeah, and I'm paying the price." Amber's mouth tightened for a moment. "But just for tonight, I want to forget about all that."

Erica's heart lurched. "What do you mean, you're paying the price?"

"I should have gone to the doctor sooner. I should have drunk more green tea than wine coolers and eaten more vegetables than hamburgers. I should have read all the literature about cancer genetics the way you did."

Tears pushed at the backs of Erica's eyes and she blinked to keep them from forming and falling. "Honey, this cancer is not your fault. It's just a rotten twist of fate. Understand?"

Amber waved a hand. "Whatever. What's done is done."

Erica stood and motioned to the bartender. She held up two fingers for another round and then drew Amber to her feet. "Come on, sis," she said. "Let's dance."

For the length of two fast-paced country songs, they danced their hearts out, and it was like old times. Amber laughed and held her hands up and shook her hips with an abandon that Erica couldn't ever seem to find. More patrons joined them, and as the sun sank out of view, tiny lights came on all around the low wall that surrounded the bar area.

Finally, Erica and Amber headed back to the

table, arms around each other's shoulders, laughing. "Do you remember," Erica said, and stopped to catch her breath. "Do you remember when you went to prom with Nelson Anderson and made him the most popular boy in the school?"

"Aw, shucks," Amber said, grinning. "I didn't do that much, really."

"I think it was your acting ability. You made everyone think you were in love with him and that the two of you had been, well…"

They sank into their seats and Amber chugged some ice water and then pointed at Erica. "You are still such a prude," she said. "You can't even say it, can you?"

"Say what?" Erica said, even though she knew.

"Say how I improved Nelson's reputation as a stud," Amber said. "Although I will admit, I never said a lie in that whole episode. I'm just good at making people believe things they want to believe, anyway."

Erica took a long draw of her margarita and giggled. "I'm telling you, that boy had the best senior year because of you. I think he dated six different girls."

"He was a great kid, if you got past the high-waisted doofus pants and the acne. I just helped everyone else to see that. And look at him now. I think he's a neurologist or something."

"Probably with a beautiful wife and 2.6 kids," Erica said.

"Actually," Amber said, "I looked him up on social media. He's single."

"Is he, now?" She tilted her head, looking at Amber. "Just why were you looking up Nelson Anderson?"

"In case you didn't notice," Amber said, "I've had a lot of time on my hands lately. Hey, isn't that Trey?" She gestured toward the dance floor.

Erica looked, and her heart skipped a couple of beats. It *was* Trey, and he was dancing. His movements were sedate, probably due to his back issues, but his wide smile said he was having a blast. It was the last thing she would've expected after all that had gone down today at the school. "Who's that he's dancing with? I can't see her."

"Jealous?" Amber taunted.

Maybe it was the second margarita, but Erica nodded, admitting the truth. "Yeah, maybe I am." Because she'd have thought he would want to process, or forget about, the day with her, not with some other woman. It wasn't like they had an agreement between them, but she hadn't seen or heard of him dating anyone else.

Which was stupid of her. They weren't dating. She didn't date.

"Stop worrying," Amber said. "He's dancing with Julie White."

That was surprising enough that Erica half rose out of her chair to squint at the dance floor. Sure enough, Trey was rocking it out with Julie, who had to be almost twice his age. The woman definitely had some moves, though. As Erica watched, Trey took her hand and gave Julie a twirl, which she executed perfectly. He, on the other hand, winced a little, his hand going to his lower back.

As the song ended, both Julie and Trey were laughing, and Julie reached up, kissed his cheek and whispered something into his ear. Then she headed over to the bar where another woman was sitting. Trey grinned and headed toward a table, alone.

"I gotta admit, I like a guy who doesn't limit himself to women who are twenty years younger than he is," Erica said.

"Same." Amber nudged at her margarita, but took a big drink of ice water. "Why don't you invite him to come over here and sit with us?"

"No! I can't do that. I don't want him to get the wrong idea."

"Do you hear my eyes rolling?" Amber stood, stabilizing herself with a hand on the back of her chair. "Hey, Trey! Come here!"

Amber wavered a little bit, and Erica jumped to her feet to steady her. A moment later, Trey was there in front of them, gripping Amber's arm. "Everything okay, you two?" he asked.

"Think I'll sit down." Amber eased herself into her chair. Then she looked up at Erica and Trey and shook her finger. "No. Uh-uh. You're not allowed to worry about me. I'm fine, just a little out of shape." In her eyes was a plea: to be treated like a regular person, not a cancer patient.

And Erica would do pretty much whatever Amber

wanted, whatever made her happy. She sat down herself, patted her sister's shoulder and then looked at Trey. "Join us?" she asked, nodding toward the empty chair at the table.

"I'd be honored to sit with the two most beautiful women under fifty in the place," he said.

"Hey, that's a weird compliment... Oh, I get it," Amber said. "You're thinking about Julie."

"Gotta admit, I have a little bit of a crush on her. She's a lot of fun. Sympathetic about my aching back. *And* she works at a bookstore, which makes her even more cool." He smiled and spread his hands, palms up. "But she doesn't take me seriously. She's just hoping word will get back to her ex that she's out dancing."

"Makes a certain amount of sense." Erica met his gaze and looked away, not wanting him to see her relief. She wasn't jealous of Julie, not really, but you never knew. Plenty of women dated men a lot younger than they were these days.

"You like to read, do you?" Amber asked.

Trey nodded. "Picked up the habit as a kid and never stopped. Nothing like a good thriller to take you away from your troubles." He flushed, almost like he wasn't used to sharing that about himself. "It was you two that inspired us to dance," he said. "You guys were shaking it like it was going out of style."

"Lots to celebrate." Amber clinked her water glass with Trey's light beer. "Unfortunately, I don't have much stamina for celebration yet."

"Give it time," Trey said. "You look like a pro. I'm sure you'll get back to it just fine pretty soon here."

"From your lips to God's ears." Amber settled back in her chair, ice water in her hand.

"Hey, redhead. You with anybody?" A paunchy man in a cowboy hat had walked over toward the table, and now he knelt beside Amber. "Saw you dancing. You're real pretty."

"Why, thank you, cowboy," Amber said. "You're quite a looker yourself."

Erica raised an eyebrow at Trey as Amber and the cowboy continued flirting. "You see what I'm dealing with here."

He grinned. "All in good fun."

She leaned forward. "Truthfully, I thought you'd be hiding out and planning your defense," she said. "Any word about the whole King thing?"

Trey grimaced. "Don't remind me. I got an email from my chief. He wants to meet with me and Greene tomorrow."

"Are you worried?"

"I mean, yeah. I really want to get my old job back."

The thought of Trey leaving, going back to the city he came from, not being here on the shore anymore, not working with her... All of it made Erica feel a big sense of loss. Too big. She'd let herself get attached to someone who wasn't going to stay.

On the other hand, that was pretty much what she

had facing her. She could get attached to someone, if at all, only for a short time.

Suddenly, the music and laughter and happy, dancing people weren't lifting her spirits anymore.

Trey, of course, was oblivious to her inner thoughts. "I just don't know what else I could have done," he said. "When I saw him yelling at King, it was bad enough, but when he kicked him I couldn't just stand by."

"You couldn't have. You did the right thing." And she admired him for it, but she wasn't going to go all mushy on him. She didn't need to be showing him her softer feelings.

"And I know they're going to say I shouldn't have gone there, shouldn't have been spying on him, but I can't wish I didn't do it." Trey's jaw tightened. "If I hadn't, King would be there getting abused, still."

Just the memory of how King had been treated made Erica's stomach tighten. "How's he doing?"

"He's okay. Glad to be home. But a lot more jumpy than he was when he left."

"That only makes sense." And it was really, really sad. "I'm sure he'll get better with time."

"I hope so." Trey's voice was grim. Then he stretched and twisted his neck like he was consciously trying to relax. "Did O'Neil say anything to you?"

"Not yet, but I'm sure he will." Her chest felt suddenly heavy. If there was anything her status-conscious boss disliked, it was a public conflict at his school. "I'm afraid he'll use this as one more reason to recommend closing down our program, and I'll be out of a job."

"Look," Trey said, "if my presence is hurting the program, I'll step back."

"Your presence isn't hurting the program as far as the kids are concerned. They're really starting to care about you." As was Erica herself. But again, she didn't need to let him know that.

Erica felt a hand squeezing her arm and turned toward Amber. "Hey, you okay?" she asked. She'd gotten too caught up in her conversation with Trey, lost track of her sister.

"Help?" she asked, half laughing as she nodded sideways at the cowboy she'd been talking with.

"She *ish* gonna dance with me," the cowboy slurred, draping an arm around Amber.

"Whoa. That's her choice." Erica stood and gestured for Amber to scoot over to her chair, away from the guy. Then Erica took a step closer and loomed over him, trying to look intimidating. "I think she's had about enough of you."

"You volunteering for the job?" He reached a hand toward Erica's arm—at least, she hoped that was where he was aiming. She stepped back.

He stood and stepped forward.

"Not interested," Erica said, sidestepping away from him. "Amber, I'm thinking it's time for us to head home."

"Are you just stuck up?" the cowboy asked with a mean laugh. "Or don't you gals like men?"

"Oh, please," Amber said. "Don't you think there might be other reasons a woman wouldn't like you?"

"Yeah, because she's a—"

Before the word could come out of his mouth, Trey stood and bumped into the cowboy, hard, and then the man wasn't there anymore. Or at least he wasn't at eye level. He was sitting on the ground, looking confused about how he'd gotten there.

"My apologies." Trey reached out a hand and helped the man up. "I think the ladies would like to be left alone."

"Fine. I don't like them anyhow." The cowboy stomped away.

Amber chuckled. "I'd forgotten the downside of going to bars," she said. "I do think I've had about enough for tonight. Thanks for coming to my rescue, you two."

"Not a problem," Trey said. "Can I walk you ladies home?"

Erica hesitated. On the one hand, she would like nothing better. But on the other hand, she didn't want to give people the impression that she and Trey were dating, and she didn't want to rely on him any more than she already was. Plus, a glance at Amber told her that her sister could use her undivided attention tonight. "No, we can make it fine," she said.

Trey frowned, his eyes going from her to Amber. "I've got my car here. How about a ride? Those few blocks seem longer after a couple of drinks."

"That would be great," Amber said. "Truth is, I'm a little tired."

"My pleasure." He put out a hand to tug Amber to her feet and helped her with her sweater.

Then he turned to Erica. "Ready?" The look in his eyes left no doubt: he was interested in her.

Which both made her insides dance and made her mind swirl with worries. If only things could be simple.

TREY'S MEETING WITH the chief didn't go well.

"You hunted Cochran down and spied on him." The chief paced back and forth through the Pleasant Shores police station's small conference room. "I would never have had King placed so near if I had thought you would do something like this. How did you find him?"

"Word of mouth." The last thing he wanted to do was implicate Erica. "I knew it was against protocol, but I'd heard he was mistreating King. I found out the rumor was true. He was abusing a K-9. That's not acceptable."

"He denies it."

"I have a witness."

Lincoln spun to face him, hands on hips. "Yeah, about that. Erica Rowe is your contact in Healing Heroes. You work with her. Dating her wasn't in the job description."

"I'm not…" Trey trailed off and stared at that wooden table in front of him, marred with carvings and ink stains and what looked like a dab of ketchup. What could he say? He wasn't dating her, not technically, but apparently the fact that they had feelings for each other was pretty obvious to everyone. "I know the boundaries," he said finally.

"The fact that you're seeing each other negates her viability as a witness," the chief said.

He couldn't argue, so he moved on. "King can't go back to Cochran."

"No, he can't. I take your accusation seriously, and I don't want any canine abused. And after I discussed K-9 training techniques with Cochran, he decided he doesn't want him back. Says he's gotten vicious and out of control."

"Only when somebody's kicking him," Trey said, indignant on King's behalf. "He's a great dog, a great officer. You know how good he is at detecting drugs, and all the other jobs he's done."

The chief shook his head back and forth, slowly. "He can't work anymore."

Trey exploded to his feet. "That's not fair!"

"It may not be fair, but it's reality. I can't have a dog who can only work with one handler. I can't have a dog who's been threatening and out of control. You know perps hit and kick dogs all the time. They can't take things into their own hands." He half smiled. "Paws, whatever."

Trey stared at the table. "Can I keep him?"

"As a pet."

The very word made Trey cringe on King's behalf.

"And you may have to purchase him. I'll talk to city council, but the fact that he displayed undue aggression—"

"He was being attacked!"

Lincoln shook his head. "That's a matter of debate. I don't want you to be responsible for the cost of him, but council may see it differently."

Trey stared down at his hands, clenched too tight. "If I have to raise the money I'll do it." Somehow. He'd borrow it, work a second job, sell off his stuff.

"It's you I'm worried about. Not only with the physical rehab, but with your attitude. You're not exactly following the chain of command."

Trey's heart sank. "I want to come back to the force."

"I know that. I was hoping the chance to get away and do some community work would help you calm down and get your head back where it needs to be. But I don't see that happening."

"My physical therapy is going well," Trey protested. And it was, to a point. He didn't add that the trainer wasn't sure he would recover full range of motion or live without pain. He could do it. He could suck it up.

"I'm debating whether to recommend that you stay in Healing Heroes." The chief leaned back against the wall, crossed his arms over his chest and glared at Trey. "I hear there are two new candidates who are interested in participating, and they both fit the mission—K-9 officers, disabled, eager to work in the community as volunteers."

"You'd recommend that they replace me? Now?"

"Considering it. Considering it more after this blowup. It's not only about King. The principal of the school isn't happy with your performance. He doesn't like disruptions like what happened when Cochran came to the schoolyard yesterday." He sighed heavily. "I want this to work as much as you do, but we have to be realistic. It's not going well."

"I'll work on it, sir," Trey said, and held his breath. Would the chief kick him out right now?

He didn't want to leave Pleasant Shores, not yet. He was starting to care about the kids, to feel like there was more he could do with them. There was more he wanted to do with Erica, too.

The chief looked around the conference room. "You know, I started out in a small police department like this," he said. "There's a lot to be said for small-town police work."

"Why are you saying that?" Was Lincoln preparing him for a job hunt that was a step back, career wise?

"Because it's the truth. Do you know anything about it? Have you paid attention?"

"I... A little." Trey thought of Earl Greene. His initial impression had been negative. The guy wasn't in the best of shape, and his department was small, just three guys. As a result, the man always seemed to be working, despite the fact that there was no real crime around here. Greene did a lot in the community. Everybody knew him, and Trey was beginning to realize that everybody respected him, too. "I can see the appeal," he said.

"Good," said the chief, "because if your return to our force doesn't work out, there could be a middle ground. You could get a job in a place like this. Less stressful, less taxing physically."

"But—" Trey broke off, trying to figure out why the notion bothered him so much. "It's just… I'm a city cop."

"Do you have the discipline to be a city cop?" The chief frowned. "Do you have the physical ability? Look, I don't want to cut off your chances prematurely. I'm just telling you that the odds of your returning to the force aren't great. I want you to think about other possibilities."

Trey opened his mouth to argue and instead shut it again. Part of what was bothering the chief was his attitude, and part of the attitude problem was him forgetting about the chain of command and talking back. He knew better, had thought he had gotten that childish behavior under control after college and the police academy, but when Michelle had left, he'd regressed. "I'll think about what you said," Trey said. "But in the meantime, I'm hoping to be able to still have a chance at returning."

The chief studied him. "I like you. You're talented, and you've done good work for me. So I'm not closing that door. But what has happened in the last few days has had its impact. Don't let it happen again."

"I won't, sir," Trey said.

He wasn't lying. He was going to work harder at distancing himself from Erica, doing his job, keeping his head down. Put his extra energy into physical therapy. Try to adjust to the idea of King as a pet.

Out of all those, the hardest thing was going to be keeping his distance from Erica. But he was going to do it. Starting tomorrow, there would be some changes.

SATURDAY EVENING, JULIE walked through the bookstore at the end of her shift, inhaling the scent of books, straightening shelves and running a feather duster over the few high spots that might have collected cobwebs, checking in with the couple of customers who were still browsing.

She wished it wasn't almost time to close. She found Saturday nights to be downright lonesome. Yes, she could go out, and she'd tried dancing with a couple of guys at the bar, even been asked for her phone number, but it didn't fill the void.

Mary had driven to a restaurant up the shore with a friend. Ria and the girls were undoubtedly busy, and anyway, Julie didn't want to impose on them. None of them wanted to spend time with her outside of their scheduled shifts.

Stop feeling sorry for yourself. She had a great job, a place to live, a daughter and two granddaughters who loved her. In fact, she had plans with Ria and her granddaughters to do mani-pedis tomorrow for Mother's Day.

Lots of women didn't have it so good.

Decisively, she flipped the switch to turn off the soft jazz they always played in the background.

"Oh, you're closing! I'm sorry!" Erica Rowe

emerged from the mystery section with a book in her hand. "Do you still have time to ring this up?"

"No problem. I'm in no hurry." She took Erica's book and went behind the counter. "Oh, this is a good one." She rang up the book and ran Erica's credit card. "You'll be really surprised at the end, unless you're a smarter reader than I am."

"I'm not. I never try to guess the ending of mystery novels. I just like how everything turns out so neat and perfect."

"Unlike life." Julie slid the book and receipt into a Lighthouse Lit bag.

"My mom and I always read the same books and talked about them," Erica said, her voice wistful. "She loved to read. She even kept a list every year of all the books she'd read."

"That's a great idea." Julie studied Erica's sad face, and her heart went out to the younger woman. She didn't know Erica well, but she'd heard Erica and her sister didn't have much family. "Mother's Day weekend can be tough. Did you lose your mom recently?"

"Two years ago, and I miss her every day." Erica's eyes got a little shiny.

Julie brought the bag with the book around the counter and patted Erica's shoulders. "I'm sorry. Do you want to talk about her?"

Erica sniffed and smiled. "You're so sweet. Thanks, but no." She held up the bag. "I was just looking to find a distraction. My sister and her daughter went out to dinner and I just didn't feel like going home alone."

"I hear that," Julie said.

"What's new with you?" Erica seemed to want to change the subject, but also prolong the conversation.

Even though Julie didn't know Erica well, maybe because of that, she blurted out the truth: "I just found out my ex is getting married to his pregnant girlfriend. So you're not the only one looking for a distraction."

"Oh, I heard that, too," Erica said.

"You *did*?"

Erica clapped a hand over her mouth. "I'm sorry. You didn't want it confirmed, did you?"

Julie sighed. "I didn't want to know it was all over town. It's humiliating."

"I don't think it's all over town," Erica said. "She used to work at the school where I work, as an aide."

"So," Julie said, infinitely curious but keeping her voice neutral, "you know her?"

"A little. She's very shy, but she's about my age and we talked sometimes. She recently quit, but not because she was doing a bad job. I think she was fine."

Something twisted inside Julie. The *poor child* was a good worker? Shy? Nice enough that Erica had enjoyed talking with her?

The door jingled open. "Grandma!" Kaitlyn brayed. "You about ready?"

Ready for *what*?

"I'm sorry to keep you here talking," Erica said. "It's my fault, Kaitlyn. She hasn't had a chance to count the money or whatever it is you do when you're closing a store."

"This is the first thing." Kaitlyn flipped the sign from Open to Closed and turned the lock on the door.

Julie had actually already had the drawer counted, so it was just a matter of adjusting the numbers for Erica's purchase.

"Do you two have big plans for tonight?" Erica asked Kaitlyn.

"No. We're supposed to go out to dinner because Mom and Sophia are busy."

"We are?" Julie asked. "Wait—don't tell me it's your turn to babysit Grandma."

Kaitlyn flushed a deep, unattractive red that suggested it was, indeed, her given duty tonight.

Julie put the money into the cash bag and leaned on the counter, studying her granddaughter's face. Kaitlyn looked tired, overwhelmed.

The way she looked almost every day when she arrived home from school, but now the stress was bleeding over into Saturday. Not good.

And Julie didn't know if "time with Grandma" was a hurdle or a help. But God forgive her, she dreaded sitting across the table from her sullen granddaughter, watching her play games on her phone.

Inspiration struck. "Erica, would you like to join

"One Minute" Survey

You get up to **FOUR** books <u>and</u> Mystery Gifts...

YOU pick your books –
WE pay for everything.
You get up to FOUR new books and TWO Mystery Gifts.
absolutely FREE!
Total retail value: Over $20!

Dear Reader,

Your opinions are important to us. So if you'll participate in our fast and free "One Minute" Survey, **YOU** can pick up to four wonderful books that **WE** pay for!

As a leading publisher of women's fiction, we'd love to hear from you. That's why we promise to reward you for completing our survey.

IMPORTANT: Please complete the survey and return it. We'll send your Free Books and Free Mystery Gifts right away. **And we pay for shipping and handling too!** *We pay for EVERYTHING!*

Try **Essential Suspense** featuring spine-tingling suspense and psychological thrillers with many written by today's best-selling authors.

Try **Essential Romance** featuring compelling romance stories with many written by today's best-selling authors.

Or TRY BOTH!

Thank you again for participating in our "One Minute" Survey. It really takes just a minute (or less) to complete the survey… and your free books and gifts will be well worth it!

Sincerely,

Pam Powers
Pam Powers
for Reader Service

www.ReaderService.com

"One Minute" Survey

GET YOUR FREE BOOKS AND FREE GIFTS!

✓ Complete this Survey ✓ Return this survey

► DETACH AND MAIL CARD TODAY!

1 Do you try to find time to read every day?
☐ YES ☐ NO

2 Do you prefer stories with happy endings?
☐ YES ☐ NO

3 Do you enjoy having books delivered to your home?
☐ YES ☐ NO

4 Do you share your favorite books with friends?
☐ YES ☐ NO

YES! I have completed the above "One Minute" Survey. Please send me my Free Books and Free Mystery Gifts (worth over $20 retail). I understand that I am under no obligation to buy anything, as explained on the back of this card.

☐ I prefer
Essential Suspense
191/391 MDL GNRG

☐ I prefer
Essential Romance
194/394 MDL GNRG

☐ I prefer BOTH
191/391 & 194/394
MDL GNRS

FIRST NAME

LAST NAME

ADDRESS

APT.#

CITY

STATE/PROV.

ZIP/POSTAL CODE

us for dinner? We usually go to the Crab Shack or Elmo's Pizza."

Erica's face lit up. "I'd love to!" Then she glanced at Kaitlyn. "If it's okay with you, honey. I don't want to horn in on your time with your grandma."

Julie stifled a snort.

"It's fine," Kaitlyn said, sighing, "except I really don't want to go out at all. Can we just order pizza and take it home?"

And there went Julie's brief vision of a pleasant evening with a new potential friend. Except... somehow, she wasn't willing to give in to Kaitlyn's whim, because she knew what it would be like: Kaitlyn would grab pieces of pizza and disappear into her room, and Julie would be eating alone. "Tell you what," she said. "I'd like to get together with Erica and talk books. We could either go back to the motel, or the two of us could go out and you could have pizza on your own."

"I'll do that," Kaitlyn said instantly. "You go on out, Grandma."

Julie fumbled in her purse for some cash. "Call now, and Elmo's will have the pizza ready by the time you walk past."

"Can't you drive me?" Kaitlyn whined. "I don't want to walk home alone carrying a pizza on a Saturday night, like some loser."

"You're not a loser," Erica said. "But I get why you don't want to walk home alone. Julie, couldn't we drop Kaitlyn off on our way to the restaurant?

We could even hit the little Greek place up the highway, if you don't mind a drive."

"Perfect." Julie was happy. And it was because she wanted to get to know Erica better and offer some consolation on an evening when the younger woman was missing her mom.

It *wasn't* because she could learn more from Erica about Melvin's new squeeze. Not much, anyway.

TREY SPENT THE next week working hard at school and in PT and trying to keep a polite distance from Erica. But by Friday afternoon, he was struggling. How long could he stay aloof when she was so incredibly appealing?

He wasn't the only one who'd worked hard all week; so had Erica, and so had the kids, who were clearly worried about the possibility that the academy program might shut down.

Today, Erica had decided that the kids needed an art day, so she'd invited one of the local painters to come in and give a lesson. She and Trey had participated, trying to figure out how to paint a seascape. His own was pathetic, and Erica's wasn't much better, but a couple of the boys had shown real promise.

Now, having dismissed the kids to the school's main area, where they joined the rest of the students for their various buses, Trey and Erica were in the classroom cleaning out paintbrushes.

"You would think that a bunch of teenagers would

know better than to leave such a mess," Erica said, but she didn't sound really mad.

"Teenagers not leaving a mess? I think that's what would be out of character." His hands touched hers under the cold flowing water, and the temptation to grasp on was strong. So strong that he left her to the washing up and instead walked around the room, picking up newspaper and wiping down desks.

The trouble was, she kept tugging at his heart with her passion for her work and the kids. He'd never dated anyone who was that serious about something, that committed. Most of the women he'd known—his ex-wife included—had been mainly committed to having a good time.

In a way, that was what had drawn him to them. He was overly serious and he knew it. He thought of women as part of the fun side of life, helping a guy to lighten up and have a good time after work was done.

It had never occurred to him that a man and woman could share a passion for work. That was what was happening with Erica, and it was surprisingly satisfying. Her own strong desire to serve and help the teenagers had rubbed off on him, and he found himself more and more energized by the job.

"How did your meeting with your chief go?" Erica laid the paintbrushes out on paper towels to dry. She glanced over at him. "If you don't mind my asking. It's really none of my business."

"It's okay. I have no one else to talk to about it."

He'd lost himself in the classroom enough that he hadn't thought about it all day. Now, when he did, worry squeezed his stomach again, the way it had most of the week. "He doesn't think I'm going to be able to be reinstated," he said. "Among other things, he asked me how I felt about being a small-town police officer."

"Meaning what?"

"Meaning, if I don't get my old job back, maybe I could look for something less intense."

"How *do* you feel about that?" Erica asked.

He opened his mouth to say that it sounded way too low-key and boring, but he stopped. Was that even true anymore? Now that he was part of a small community for the first time in his life, he was starting to understand the nuances. He could see the benefits of knowing everyone you were working with, of having a small enough jurisdiction that you could keep up with people's histories, possibly prevent crime before it started.

So maybe he didn't know how he felt about being a small-town cop. "He said King can't do police work anymore."

"Oh, no!" Erica's eyes crinkled with immediate sympathy. "I thought he was so good at it, right?"

"Yes, but my chief thinks there's too much risk. Cochran did a bite report."

"Bite report?" Erica put her hands on her hips. "King didn't bite him. He may have snarled, defending himself, but Cochran is the one who should have a report against him."

Trey's good mood had dissolved. He might as well tell her all of it. "One of the other things he brought up is that I might not be able to continue as a volunteer myself. I'm in trouble for basically stalking Cochran."

"Oh, no, Trey. That was my fault!" Erica stepped closer and put a hand on his sleeve. "Can I tell him? Is there anything I can do?"

"No." Her touch felt warm, made him want her. Which sort of proved the chief's point.

"Why is he questioning whether you should continue?"

He smiled a little, gestured toward her hand.

"What?" She pulled it away.

"People think we're dating," he said.

A blush climbed her face. "What people?"

"Cochran. And your principal."

She stared at him. "O'Neil told your chief that? What does he know?"

Trey drew in a breath and let it out slowly. "Look, you and I both know that we're not dating. But..." He met her eyes and didn't look away. "I think we also both know that there are feelings between us. Feelings that are growing, at least on my side."

She bit her lip and then stared at the student desk they were standing by, automatically reaching down to straighten the book and ruler that were sitting atop it.

Was she going to say anything about the feelings on her side? Trey hadn't intended a discussion to go in this direction, but now that it had, he wanted to know. He reached out and touched her chin, causing her to look at him. "Am I misreading things here?"

Her tongue flicked across her lips and she took a step backward. Looked off to the side.

Great, so he *was* misreading things. Just like he had a habit of doing, just like he'd done with his wife. He'd thought she really cared about him when the truth was, he had just been a fling. He was the one who talked Michelle into getting married; she would never have done it without the pressure, because she really didn't want to *be* married.

"You didn't misread it," she said in a voice so low he had to lean closer, and even then, he wasn't sure whether he had heard her correctly.

He drew in a breath and, with it, the fragrance of her hair, clean and flowery. It woke him up in all kinds of ways. He almost forgot what they were talking about.

"But it's not a good idea." Her voice was husky and she was still looking off to the side.

"It's *not* a good idea." He let his thumb skim her cheek. So soft. He leaned closer, wanting to taste her lips. Just taste them, no more, just this once.

She lifted her hands and touched his face, both sides at once, and then her fingers tangled in his hair.

She stood on tiptoes, getting closer. Their faces were inches apart.

He knew he shouldn't. This was just what his

chief had been talking about, just what he'd pledged in his mind to avoid.

But there were some forces stronger than a human male could withstand. He pulled her close and kissed her.

CHAPTER ELEVEN

THE MOMENT TREY'S lips touched hers, all Erica's doubts and all of her sense of caution seemed to dissipate into the classroom's musty, paint-scented air. His lips were warm on hers, gentle, almost careful, but from the tension of his body she could tell he was holding back.

She appreciated that, because she had the feeling that Trey holding back was about the same as any other man at full throttle.

His hands cupped her face and then slid slowly down her neck to rest on her shoulders, making a pathway of fire.

She must have made some little noise because he lifted his head and opened his eyes and looked at her. "Are you okay? Is this okay?"

She felt so out of breath. "It's good," she said, and rose on her tiptoes to brush her lips against his again.

A sound came from him then, something like a growl, and his fingers threaded through her hair as he pulled her closer. Now his kiss was harder, deeper, and suddenly she felt like she had been running for a long time, she was that out of breath.

But she felt safe. His passion was obvious in the movement of his lips and the tightening of his hands, but he didn't go caveman on her, didn't push for more.

She was soaring inside, brought to flight not only by his touch, but by the emotion in his eyes, the gentle way he held her. The tenderness suggested a kind of caring she'd never felt before from a man. She liked it. A lot.

Then, suddenly, he was stepping away, straightening the neckline of her shirt, running his hands through his hair and taking deep breaths. She felt the lack of him, the loss, and then she heard something and realized why he had pulled away.

A deep voice, right outside the classroom door.

Principal O'Neil?

With a *baby*?

Sure enough, there was the sound of a baby's cry. Then a man's irritated voice. It sounded like O'Neil. She knew he had an infant, but bringing the child to school was the last thing she would've expected of him.

She fingered her hair back into place, fanned herself with her hands and turned to face the door as it opened. Behind her, she could hear Trey gathering the paintbrushes into a can.

Good. Nothing to see here.

"Erica." The principal walked in, an adorable baby clad in pink propped on his hip. The same baby, she realized, that his wife had been holding that night at the fair.

"Well, now, who is this?" she cooed, drawn to the baby as any reasonable woman, any reasonable person, would be. The little girl had blond curls clustered around her face and the most adorable rosebud lips.

"I guess you've never met baby Brittany," he said, his voice going gentle, undeniable fatherly pride in the way he looked at the baby.

"Can I hold her?"

He handed the baby over readily, then looked at Trey and nodded. "Harrison," he said.

Erica turned to make sure Trey's face didn't betray anything, and it didn't. It was fixed on the little girl, lit up in a way she'd never seen it before. He strode over, held up his hands and swept the child out of Erica's arms. He lifted her high, making her chortle.

Erica felt slammed and she didn't even know why. She looked at the principal. She was expecting him to look upset that Trey had taken over his baby, but he didn't. Instead, he was nodding and smiling. "Good," he said to Erica. "I came to your classroom hoping you could take care of her for an hour while I have a meeting."

Didn't that just figure, Erica thought. He was looking for a babysitter, not reaching out to make a connection with one of his teachers.

"You're a lucky man," Trey said.

Principal O'Neil smiled a little. "I guess I am."

"We'd be glad to watch out for this little sweetheart," Trey said. "You have a diaper bag? Maybe we'll take her for a little stroll."

"In my office. Stop by." Now that he had taken care of business, the principal was turning away, intent on his next professional activity.

Erica couldn't focus on her annoyance, though, because she couldn't take her eyes off Trey.

"You're a natural," she said.

"I love babies," he said. "Always hoped for three or four of them of my own. Maybe more."

His words brought reality slamming back into Erica. He kissed her like he meant it, but he didn't know the truth about her. That she was flawed, sterile, not a whole woman.

A wave of the old familiar sense of inadequacy swept over her. Being a mother was the highest calling a woman could aspire to, and it was one that her medical problems had taken away from Erica.

Oh, in her head she knew that there were many ways to be worthwhile. She'd known many women who did amazing things in the world even though they had never borne children. She knew wonderful adoptive parents.

And that was all fine for other people, but she'd grown up hearing about that intense mother-child bond, how it was different from anything anyone else ever sensed, how it was special, spiritual, irreplaceable. A part of what it meant to be a woman.

She didn't have that.

She wasn't what Trey needed.

Not only that, but the man had faced a lot of

losses. He'd come here desolate from his divorce and from his injury, and it had taken a while, but Pleasant Shores had worked its magic. He was improving, doing better.

The last thing he needed was a woman who not only couldn't have children, but who might face serious medical challenges in the future.

No, the kindest thing she could do for Trey was to keep her distance.

She turned to tell him she had somewhere to go, somewhere to be, that he should take care of the baby alone. But the sight of him gently bouncing her in his arms simply took her breath away.

There was something about a big, muscular man and a baby that went straight to her heart.

"What should we do with her?" Trey asked. Gone was the businesslike police officer, the capable volunteer. Trey with a baby looked more like a delighted little boy.

That shouldn't have been a surprise, since she'd seen his fondness for kids that evening at Goody's. If things had been different, she would have loved it. "Well, I guess we should get the diaper bag if we're going to take her somewhere," she said. Because even though Trey looked comfortable and seemed happy, who knew if he was able to take care of a baby, and she didn't want Principal O'Neil to have something else to hold against them.

In fact, she was amazed that O'Neil had even allowed Trey to hold his child, but then again, he probably didn't see childcare as a valuable, important activity. He just wanted to get back to business himself. His wife must've dumped the baby on him and he'd hurried to find a teacher to dump the baby on in turn.

"She looks tired." Trey shifted her expertly and studied her sweet little face. "Let's just get her things and a blanket and go sit under the apple tree at the side of the school. It will be quiet, and she can nap."

"Okay." So he did know how to take care of a baby. Even more torturous.

They went outside with little Brittany, grabbing the diaper bag on the way. Trey got a blanket from the back of his car and they lay on it, the baby in between.

Could Erica be blamed for pretending, just a little, that the baby was hers? Hers and Trey's?

But she knew the answer to that. Even though it made sense that she'd think that way, she shouldn't. Shouldn't let herself imagine it, even for a minute. "When did you learn how to take care of babies?" she asked him.

Trey lay on his side, dangling a plush toy in front of the sweet child. "I was the oldest in the foster family I lived with some of the time. I did a lot of babysitting."

"Nice."

"It was." He sighed and looked away. "Until they got taken away to be adopted or sent back to their parents. Broke my heart every time, so I want to do it differently myself. Just have our own babies to raise, rather than someone else's who get taken away."

That was a lot to process. "Our own babies, huh?"

He actually blushed. "I mean...that's all theoretical. I don't know if I'll even get to that point. I rushed into it with my marriage and that was a mistake."

She nodded, unable to speak.

She wouldn't be bearing Trey's children. If she did want to be a mother, it would no doubt be through the foster care system. The couple of adoption agencies she'd contacted had expressed doubts about potential parents with serious health issues in their backgrounds.

And if they were okay with it, one of the adoption counselors had explained, the birth parents usually weren't. Why should they be, when there were way more people wanting to adopt infants than there were infants to adopt?

Thinking about it made her throat tighten. She needed to get out of here. "Look," she said, "would you be comfortable taking care of the baby until Principal O'Neil is done with his meeting? I have..." She was really choking up now. "I have to get some things done, and I'm not feeling well."

"No problem, if you think he'll be okay with it." He dug around in the diaper bag, found a pacifier and popped it into the baby's mouth. "Listen, this isn't because of what happened before, is it?"

"What? Oh..." He must mean the kiss, and that made her cheeks feel hot. "No, no, that's not it. Although…" She hesitated, thinking about kisses and babies and lost opportunities, then plunged ahead. "I think we both know we don't want to go there, so we should probably avoid any more opportunities to, you know, be too close. In the future."

He was looking at her with his forehead wrinkled, like he was trying to figure out what she was saying. "We don't want to go there," he echoed.

"Right, for all the reasons…" She trailed off, because she didn't want to tell him her real reason and experience his pity. "You know, like how O'Neil wouldn't like it. And how it would hurt your career. How you want to try to get back on the force and…and leave."

"Right." He nodded, looked out across the field for a minute and then sat up. And didn't meet her eyes. "It's fine. I'll take care of the baby. See you tomorrow."

CHAPTER TWELVE

POUND. POUND. POUND.

It was Saturday morning, and Trey might have had one more beer than he should've the night before, but surely that wasn't enough to create this severe pounding in his head.

Or...maybe it wasn't in his head. He sat up on the couch of the Healing Heroes cottage where he'd fallen asleep and looked blankly at the still-on TV and the bright sunshine coming through the windows.

"Harrison! Are ya in there?"

The pounding recommenced, accompanied by a child's loud shouting: "Uncle Trey! Wake up, Uncle Trey!"

At which point Trey realized who was at the door.

Denny. Coming to spend the weekend, along with his kid and his pregnant wife.

Trey *really* wished he hadn't agreed to this. But Denny wanted to take his family on a weekend getaway, and Trey owed the man, so he'd suggested they come for a visit.

And here they were, bright and early. Trey ran a hand through his hair and went to the door. "Come in. Make yourselves at home while I get cleaned up. Hey, Laura." He kissed her cheek, shook Denny's hand and swung Milo up and around until the boy was giggling uncontrollably. And then he escaped to the bathroom. When he looked in the mirror, he understood why both Denny and Laura had looked at him funny.

Bleary eyes, dark circles under them, hair on end. The same paint-spattered T-shirt he'd worn yesterday. Yesterday, when he'd kissed Erica and she'd kissed him back like she meant it, and then promptly thought better of it and pushed him away.

"Make your wife some coffee," he yelled down the hall to Denny, and then stepped into the shower.

Twenty minutes later, he found Denny, Laura and Milo out on the cottage's back deck. Denny and Laura were sitting down, their chairs pressed close together, drinking coffee while Milo rolled around with an ecstatic King.

"Get yourself some coffee, dude. But you should know it's decaf."

"Decaf?" Trey stared. "I don't even have decaf coffee."

"Which is why we brought our own." Laura patted her slightly rounded belly. "Baby doesn't like caffeine, and Denny actually quit it, too, just to keep me company." She grinned over at her husband. "Or wasn't I supposed to tell him that? He might think you've wimped out."

"He wimped out a long time ago." Trey went inside and made himself a cup of dark roast, then returned to the deck.

The morning sun was halfway up the sky already, warm on his shoulders as he leaned against the deck rail and surveyed his friend.

Denny looked…just plain happy. He'd settled into marriage as if he'd never been a discontent womanizer. Laura had come along, swept him off his feet with her beauty and brains, and held him to a higher standard of behavior than he'd needed to use before.

Now Denny was building a family.

Trey was happy for his friend, but that didn't stop the jealousy from eating at him. He'd always loved babies, always wanted kids. When his foster mom had brought home a new baby, he'd been the first to offer to feed it, hold it, play with it. To the point where the other boys in the family had laughed at him, but he hadn't minded. He'd been plenty rough and tumble throughout most of his boyhood, but a baby was something precious.

He could still remember the heartache when a foster baby had to leave.

Denny leaned close and whispered something into his wife's ear, and she put her hand on her belly and smiled.

What would Erica look like if she were pregnant? Would she love it, glow with it, as Laura seemed to be doing?

That wasn't something he was destined to know, because right after they'd kissed, she'd said it was a bad idea and backed off. As soon as she'd been able, she'd run away.

But why? He tried to think of whether he'd done something wrong during the kiss or right after, but he couldn't think of anything.

King whined a little from behind them, and Trey saw that Milo was trying to ride him. "Hey, buddy," Trey said, going to rescue his dog, "you can pat him, but no riding. Let's give him a break. Want to look at my phone?"

"Yeah!" Milo grabbed the forbidden item while Laura rolled her eyes at Trey.

King sniffed at Denny and wagged his tail, and Laura fawned over him until he rolled onto his back for a belly rub.

"How's King taking the time off?" Denny asked.

Trey hesitated, not sure whether he should give his friend the whole story.

But Denny had known him forever. "What's wrong?" he asked. "Did something happen?"

So he explained about how King had been re-assigned and mistreated, and how he'd found the dog and brought him back. Laura gasped indignantly and rubbed King's belly some more, and Denny shook his head. "I know Cochran a little, through mutual friends. He seems like a jerk."

"Yeah. Unfortunately, that's not a measurable offense."

"Can't believe he made K-9." He mock-glared up at Trey. "Course, can't believe you made it, either."

There was teasing but no malice in Denny's

words, even though he'd tried for K-9 himself and hadn't made it.

"Milo and I could use some exercise," Laura said after they'd chatted awhile longer. "Mind if we take King for a walk?"

"Go for it. Want company?" Trey pushed himself away from the deck railing.

Laura waved a hand. "No, you two have plenty to talk about. Man talk. Denny would probably like some real coffee or a beer, too." She snapped a leash onto King's collar and trotted with him down the deck stairs to the beach, Milo running ahead of them.

"Great girl," Trey said.

"She is." Denny watched her walk across the sand toward the water and then looked up at Trey. "So how's the rehab going?"

He shrugged. "Lots of core work, heat and cold packs, stretching."

Denny grimaced. "Sounds boring. Is it helping?"

"A little." Seemed like way too little, most of the time, but that was the way healing went.

"Rough." Denny looked out at the water and then back at Trey. "You think you're gonna come back?"

"I don't know." He paused. "I want to, but even if my back heals, without King…"

"Won't be the same. I get it." Denny blew out a breath. "Man, thought you made it out of the Heights mind-set, but…" He trailed off.

Denny's words stung. "I did make it out."

"Yeah, you did, but this kind of thing…losing

jobs, getting divorced...seems like you're walking in your old man's footsteps." He waved a hand. "Not that he was a bad guy."

"I know." Trey breathed out a sigh as the unwanted memories assailed him. His dad had tried to raise him after his mom had left, but it hadn't been in the cards. He'd loved Trey, for sure; he just couldn't give up his roaming and women long enough to take care of a child. Periodically, he'd resolved to do better and managed to get Trey out of foster care, but it had never lasted more than six months, and then Trey would be back in the Heights with the same patient, decent foster family, including Denny, who'd ended up being adopted by them.

It made sense that they'd adopted Denny and not Trey. Denny had an upbeat personality and did well in school, whereas Trey...didn't. Trey had gotten in fights, messed up in school, all due to a lack of impulse control. His foster family had worked with him on it, but the lessons hadn't stuck, not back then at least.

Now he needed to do better.

"Hey, don't worry about it. I'm sure it'll work out. It's just...you competed forever to get that K-9 certification. Everybody in the Heights was so proud."

Trey didn't want to hear it, so he went inside, grabbed a basketball and brought it back out onto the deck. One of the great things about the beach cottage was that there was a basketball hoop down on the driveway. "Are you still as bad at this as you used to be?" He threw the basketball straight at Denny.

"Fighting words." Denny threw the basketball back and they trotted together down the stairs.

They had grown up playing ball together in the Heights, and they shared a rough style of play. When they got down to the driveway, though, Denny held on to the ball and looked at Trey. "You sure you're up for this, man?" he asked.

"Way more up for it than you are," Trey said.

"You sure? Even with your back?"

"Forget about my back." Trey held out his hands. "You going to play or just stand there like a fool?"

Denny dribbled the ball and tossed it, and Trey went for it. Denny tried to get it away from him, but Trey could tell he was going easy on him. He took a couple of shots and taunted his friend.

"Look, I'm not that same guy who's going to win at all costs," Denny said. "Becoming a father tends to change you some."

Trey rolled his eyes and continued dribbling and tossing. But it was true—his back *was* hurting. And his heart was, too.

Would he ever get the chance to become a father? Would anyone ever choose him the way Laura had chosen Denny?

If anyone asked his ex-wife, she'd have said no, said that Trey was no good at marriage and that he wouldn't be a good father, not that she wanted kids anyway.

Would Erica choose him? It didn't look that way. Looked like she had chosen not to be with him.

He thought back on kissing her. Her lips had

been soft, so soft. Her body petite, thin, tiny in his arms. But he'd felt the strength of the muscles along her spine. She was a strong woman, a very strong woman.

A woman who could be strong and soft. That was what he wanted. And that was what Erica was. But unfortunately, she didn't want him.

Denny snatched the ball away from him and made an easy basket. "You're losing it, old man," he said. Teasing, because Trey actually was just two days older than Denny.

Trey tried to joke along, but he wasn't feeling it. So after a few more minutes of play, he admitted that his back was hurting, and they went back up on the deck.

Moments later, they heard barking—not King—and then the click of dog toenails on the stairs. Ziggy burst onto the deck and jumped up, first onto Trey, then onto Denny.

"Whoa. Who's this?" Denny laughed and pounded Ziggy's sides. The doodle's big fluffy tail wagged.

Trey's heart beat faster and he looked over the railing for Erica.

But Hannah's voice, and then Hannah herself, came up the stairs. "I'm sorry! He pulled the leash out of my hands. Ziggy!"

"Where's Erica?" He looked behind Hannah, on down the stairs.

"She, uh, didn't feel well." Hannah looked uncomfortable.

Had Erica asked the teen to lie for her? No, she

wouldn't have done that. So Hannah must have made an excuse for her on her own initiative.

"She said you're supposed to train him this morning?" Hannah looked at him with a nervous expression—was it pity, a desire not to be questioned about Erica? Had the teenager sensed something wrong between them, or had Erica told her she wanted to keep her distance?

"That's right. I'm training him today," he said. Never mind that Erica normally wanted to be involved in the training. Since training was more about owners than dogs, it was actually crucial.

But he wasn't going to beg.

"Thanks," he said, giving the teen a smile. "I'll bring him back over after his lesson."

"No, that's okay. I'll stop back and get him."

As soon as Hannah left, Denny turned to Trey. "Who's Erica?"

"Her aunt." Trey nodded in the direction Hannah had gone.

"Something going on with her?"

Trey opened his mouth to deny it and then looked at Denny's knowing expression and didn't even bother. Denny knew him too well. "I work with her at the school."

"And?"

Trey sighed. "I like her."

Denny squinted at him. "You like her, okay. Why? Is she different from your wife? You liked her, too."

"Yeah," he said, "but this is different."

"Different how?"

"She's better. A better person."

"Uh-huh." Denny leaned forward. "Just a word to the wise. Some of us aren't the best at choosing women."

"I know." Trey thought about his wife and the dreams he'd had. All completely unrealistic, he saw now.

"I got lucky," Denny said. "But we didn't see a lot of good examples back in the Heights. Might be you'd want to be cautious. Hate to see you get hurt again."

For Denny to be that expressive meant he was really concerned, and that didn't sit well with Trey. If Denny was concerned, there was a reason for it.

Trey was bad at relationships, and his best friend knew it. So where did he go from here?

On Monday morning, Erica kept so busy that she barely had time to talk to Trey.

And, yeah, that was on purpose.

She hurried the kids in and got them into their seats. "Listen up, everyone," she said. "Since we just have two weeks of school left, I really want to make them count. So we're doing something different. We're starting a new interdisciplinary unit today, and it's going to be a lot of fun."

Trey was leaning against the wall in the back of the room, and she couldn't resist sneaking a glance at him. But his face was impassive.

So very different from how it had been when they'd kissed, right here in this classroom.

"Interdisciplinary how?" Rory asked.

She cleared her throat. "It's all about one topic. We do math, science, English, social studies, history, even service learning, all focused on one thing." She looked around to make sure she had their attention. "And our topic is… Who wants to guess?"

Venus raised her hand. "Dogs?"

"Summer vacation," Shane called out.

"Quadratic equations." That was Rory, and a couple of the other kids groaned.

"No, none of you guessed it. It's…hurricanes!"

No one jumped up and down, and there were very few murmurs of interest, but that was just teenagers trying to be cool. At least, she hoped so.

She'd thrown herself into class planning this weekend to avoid thinking about Trey, and it had worked…somewhat. She'd only spent short periods of time remembering the feel of his lips, the warmth of his embrace, the caring in his eyes.

Too much of that type of thinking would derail her, she knew. She'd already learned that ruminating about what she'd lost—the opportunity to have kids, the likelihood of a long and healthy life—could send her into a spiral of sadness. Good old-fashioned hard work was a solace. So she'd spent hours putting this unit together, and in the gaps she'd cleaned the entire house and fixed a gourmet dinner Saturday night and a superhealthy brunch Sunday morning.

It was almost enough to chase away the taste of Trey's kiss, but not quite.

"So, um, what's the first step?" Trey asked. His question brought her out of her reverie and she realized she'd been staring into space. The kids were losing focus.

"Sorry," she said, her face heating. "Our first step is to hear from some local hurricane survivors about what it can be like around here in a big storm. In fact—" she looked at the clock "—they should be here any minute."

As if on cue, there was a knock on the door. Lindy Neuhaus, a seventysomething woman who owned the gas station on the road to the next town, came in, accompanied by old Mr. James and his son, Kirk.

Erica ushered them in and quickly arranged several desks in a row where they could sit as a panel. When Trey saw what she was doing, he helped, but his expression was guarded.

She probably should have run this whole idea by him, since he would be involved. Whoops. But after all, she was the teacher, and he was just the volunteer.

No need to think about the fact that he'd become far more than a volunteer.

She introduced the panel and asked them to describe their experience with hurricanes on the Eastern Shore. The kids were surprised to learn that there even were hurricanes here, as there hadn't been a serious one in several years.

"I'm telling you, Hurricane Agnes was every bit as bad up here as what you may have heard about down south," Lindy said. "Lots of property damage, and thirty-seven deaths along the coast."

"That wasn't a hurricane by the time it reached here," Kirk scoffed. "We've never had a hurricane make landfall here."

"If you'd been here instead of running around all over the country," old Mr. James said, "you'd know that there were hurricane-level winds. For all intents and purposes, it was a hurricane."

That piqued the kids' interest and they started asking questions. The older two panelists had been through that storm, and they described making preparations to the houses, and who had evacuated versus who had stayed back.

"I was smart and got out," Lindy said. "But this one…" She pointed at Mr. James. "He stayed put."

"You should always evacuate when ordered to," Mr. James said to the kids, "but…I didn't."

"Why not?" Erica asked.

"Because he's a stubborn fool," his son said.

"Because I loved my dogs. They weren't letting you take them to the hurricane shelters. I didn't have anywhere else to go and I didn't want to leave them to drown or be hurt."

"I wouldn't, either," Venus said. "That's cruel to ask you to leave them behind."

"What was it like in the storm?" Rory asked.

The kids were leaning forward, engaged, and Erica felt a rush of satisfaction inside. She had debated whether to have them do book research first, but had decided that having real individuals talk about their experiences would give them more enthusiasm to do research. She'd even invited Principal O'Neil to stop in if he had time, hoping that if he saw the community members connecting with the kids, it would improve his attitude toward the behavior support program.

She couldn't help glancing at Trey to see how this activity was going over with him. He was watching the kids, and then he glanced over at her and gave a nod, as if to show approval of her strategy.

Of course she felt warmed by his approval. Just because she had decided not to respond to her feelings didn't mean she didn't have them.

Before she could get too far into mooning about Trey, the conversation took a turn. "The wealthy new folks have overrun the island," Mr. James said, "and their houses are pretty near stormproof. Ours aren't. But back in the day, we all helped each other. Had to, because nobody had much."

"Those were good times," Lindy said. "But I know for a fact that my gas station wouldn't make it with just the old residents. It's the new folks and the tourists who give me the most business."

"The same people that built the giant houses that block our view," Kirk muttered. "Used to be able to see the bay from my place, but no more."

Mr. James nodded, the corners of his mouth turning down. "That part's a shame. I always did love looking out at the bay."

"That's not fair for them to do that," Shane said indignantly, and the rest of the students quickly agreed.

"Just because they're rich," Rory added, "that doesn't give them the right to block your view."

"We should do something about it," Venus said.

Erica glanced over at Trey and saw on his face the same mixture of pride and amusement that she felt. It was no surprise to most adults that people with money had more power in the world, but it was news to a lot of children and teens. That their kids' first response was indignation—and a desire to change things—was sweet, impressive, given their backgrounds.

A throat cleared in the back of the room. Erica hadn't noticed that Principal O'Neil had come in. Now he was frowning, and it wasn't hard to guess why. He was always kowtowing to the new residents, trying to get them to send their kids to his school.

The last thing he would want was for the old residents to talk about how things had been better before the wealthy people had moved in, let alone have the kids get an attitude about the wealthier locals.

She wanted to keep the students engaged, doing positive things, understanding about and helping the community. That was the true basis of the hurricane unit. The fact that it had helped her distract herself from Trey's kisses had been an added plus, but not the core reason.

Despite her motivations, though, if Principal

O'Neil used the unit as evidence against the program, her preparations had backfired.

There was a knock on the door, and Erica hurried to open it, racking her brain to remember if someone else she'd invited to present had agreed to come at the last minute. She'd thought the other two elders had sent their regrets, but she could have missed an email.

She opened the door, her mouth open to apologize. And snapped it shut again.

There was an older man outside the door, all right. A long-haired, beard-stubbled, very handsome man, looking at her with Trey's eyes. "Heard I might find my son here, sweetheart," he said in a husky voice. "You know a guy by the name of Trey Harrison?"

CHAPTER THIRTEEN

TREY GOT HIS father away from the school as fast as possible, ignoring stares from O'Neil, the kids and Erica.

It felt familiar. He remembered many occasions when his father had shown up out of the blue: when Trey was in class, or trying out for the baseball team, or running an errand for his foster mother. Chaos usually accompanied his arrival.

Dad didn't have a car—he'd hitchhiked here—so they ambled down toward the water. Trey turned them away from town, knowing what his father liked. And maybe, a little bit, trying not to contaminate his own image in Pleasant Shores. He wasn't proud of that motivation, but he recognized it from long experience. They headed toward the docks where the crabbers came in. There was a cheap little bar down there, of the sort his father liked.

"Not a cop anymore, huh?" Dad said.

The mixed feelings in his father's voice reminded Trey how Dad had always been intimidated by him being a cop and, in equal parts, proud of it. "Not for now," he said, "but I'll probably go back to it."

His father stopped walking to stare at him. "Back to Philly? Don't you like it here?"

Trey shrugged. "It's more of a family place, this town," he said.

His father studied him. "There's all kind of families." He kicked a stone and started walking again. "Ours wasn't the best. But I always loved you."

The outright expression of emotion surprised Trey, and he studied his father. It had been more than a year since he'd seen the man, and maybe something was wrong. "Are you sick? Dying?"

Dad let out a laugh, big and loud. "No, I just wanted to see my boy." He patted Trey's shoulder. "Called your buddy Denny last night and found out that you were here, so I made a little detour this way. Not for long, though. Heading south. Think I have a job on an oil rig."

"Glad you came." And Trey was. As troubled as their relationship was, he, too, loved his father.

And he was also aware of what his father usually wanted. "How are you doing really? Need anything?"

Dad glanced over at him, then looked off toward the bay. "Lost my job, but I've about got that straightened up. There was a woman... She's not around anymore." He shrugged. "Happens."

In the forced carelessness of his father's tone, Trey heard himself. Like his dad, he sort of wanted to run free without attachments, but sort of regretted the loss. In Trey, there was definitely a longing for more.

They were coming close to the docks, and noise

came from the little bar. It looked utterly unappealing to Trey, and on impulse he decided he wasn't doing that. Not here, not in Pleasant Shores. "Let's turn around," he said. "I'll buy you lunch at a place called Goody's."

"I'm hungry and thirsty both," Dad said, mild protest in his voice. He wasn't exactly an alcoholic, but on days he wasn't working, he usually started drinking by noon.

"I'm just hungry. Let's get lunch. Goody's has ice cream that will knock your socks off. And then I can set you up with some money." Not that he had that much, but this was his father.

His father glanced sideways at him. "You were always better than me, son. Even when you were a boy."

"I got in plenty of trouble."

"Yeah, a little, like most kids. But you were always responsible. Always tried to make me eat a good meal before I went out drinking. Told me when you sensed something bad about a woman."

A smile quirked Trey's mouth as he remembered a few of those choice conversations. "Seems to me you didn't listen real often."

"Not your fault." They walked into Goody's, and Trey placed an order: crab cake sandwiches, fries, coleslaw. While they waited, they scanned the ice cream bins, talking about the past. "Your foster family always thought the world of you." Dad smiled and nodded. "Yeah, you caused a little trouble, but they said you had a heart of gold. They wanted to adopt you, but I said no. I was wrong."

"They wanted to adopt me?" Trey was shocked. "I never heard a word about that."

His father shrugged. "Most likely, they didn't bring it up because they wanted to be supportive of the biological family. That's what foster families were told to do."

"You mean...me and you?" Trey had never looked at himself and his father as a family. More like a couple of wandering troublemakers.

"Yeah, but I couldn't give you up." His father looked down at his well-worn work boots. "I was selfish."

Trey thought about that while they picked up their lunches and sat down at one of the little tables to eat. He'd always thought of himself as unwanted, but here Dad was making it sound like he was wanted by both his own father and his foster family. That was a different take on his childhood.

After they'd eaten, Dad claimed to be too full for ice cream, said he needed to go. They walked together to the cash machine and Trey got out a couple hundred bucks for his father. Not much, but it was all he could spare right now. And he was fairly sure his father wouldn't use the money wisely.

"Not sure when I'll see you again." Dad gave him a little hug, thumped his back.

"This isn't a bad town, if you're looking to settle for a while," Trey heard himself say.

His father looked up at him, his weathered face

crinkling into a big smile. "Not now, but...thanks.
You're a good son." He patted Trey's shoulder awkwardly and walked off down the street.

Trey thought about calling after him, asking him
how he was going to get down south, but Dad always had it covered. He'd hitchhike, or meet a lady,
or figure out a way to ride a train. He wasn't going
to change.

But as Trey watched his father disappear, he found
his throat tightening up. Blood was blood. And being
here in Pleasant Shores, feeling a part of the community, must have softened him some, made him
emotional.

Plus, his father had given him something to think
about, a revised view of the past. He still wasn't sure
he'd had a heart of gold, back then, but maybe he
hadn't been as unlovable as he'd always thought.

ON WEDNESDAY MORNING, Julie groaned as she rolled
up her yoga mat and pushed herself to her feet to
join Erica and her sister, Amber. Yoga in the Park
might have been a mistake.

She felt stretched and sore and out of shape, and
there was something weird going on with the muscles in the back of her left leg.

Still, the sun was bright and the greenery soothed
her soul and continued to make her feel relaxed.
Looking around at the fifteen or so women who
were stretching or gathering their things or standing in little clusters, talking, she noticed that their
expressions were happier now, their voices calmer

than they'd been before class. Julie felt better mentally, too.

She put her bag over her shoulder and a little spasm crossed her back, making her wince.

"What do you think?" Erica laughed as she studied Julie's face. "Wait—don't answer that. And don't be mad at me for inviting you."

Julie stretched her neck and twisted it from side to side, turtle-like. "I'm glad you invited me. I'm just in a little pain."

"You're not the only one." Amber tossed the words over her shoulder as she headed for a stone bench. "I thought yoga was supposed to be easy and relaxing. My sister lied."

"You both did great." Erica started toward the bench and then turned to wait for Julie. "Come on. Let's sit for a few."

Julie followed Erica toward her sister, studying the two girls. No mistaking their family resemblance. Both were thin, with classic bone structure and wide, full mouths. But Amber sported a sleeve of tattoos and a nose piercing and was wearing a Harley-Davidson T-shirt with her tight black leggings. Erica's classic yoga cover-up and capris were a soft pink and she had no piercings that Julie could see.

The more striking difference, of course, was that Amber wore a head scarf and had the trademark lack of eyelashes that marked a tough round of chemo. She looked like she'd been through a battle, and according to the little Erica had told Julie, she had. Ovarian cancer, stage III. Poor kid.

A breeze cooled the back of Julie's neck and she lifted her hair off it. The time for her haircut had come and gone, twice, but she hadn't made an appointment. The first time, she'd been too depressed to bother. The second time, she'd decided longer hair would better disguise her chubby cheeks.

Today, she just wanted to cut it all off.

"It's so hot!" Erica said as she reached the bench and sank down beside her sister.

"I know. I'm dying." Amber fanned herself with her hand.

Julie sat beside the pair. "You young girls don't have a clue what it means to be hot. Wait until you hit menopause."

The sisters glanced at each other as if debating whether to say something. "We're not all that young," Amber said finally.

"You don't look old enough to have a daughter in high school. You look great." Julie reached across Erica to pat Amber's hand. Amber's situation broke her heart. "It's sweet that you two invited me, considering that I'm more your mother's age than your own."

"I'm glad we're getting to be friends," Erica said. "You know, we miss our mom every day. You're a little bit like her."

They sat back and watched the rest of the class packing up to leave. Most of the attendees were younger than Julie was, and almost all of them were thinner. But they'd been pleasant, friendly. She hadn't been the only one to struggle with some of the poses. The instructor had shown variations on each one and urged everyone to take things at their own pace, depending on their fitness level.

"Listen to your body," she'd encouraged repeatedly in her gentle voice.

God willing, Julie's body would soon be singing a fitter and leaner tune.

One of their classmates, clearly a yoga expert and also clearly pregnant, had been doing extra stretches on her mat. Now she shaded her eyes to look across the parking lot. Then she rolled up her mat, rose effortlessly to her feet and hurried across the sand. A good-looking man and a little boy were waiting for her, and she kissed the man's cheek and wrapped her arms around the child before they all headed off, talking in an animated fashion.

"I remember those days, being pregnant, then a young mom," Julie said dreamily. "Best thing I ever did."

And now Melvin's giving that same experience to another woman. He was probably taking care of her, lifting things, opening doors. Going out for ice cream or sour-cream-and-onion potato chips in the middle of the night, just as he'd done for Julie when she'd been carrying Ria.

She fought off the image in her mind and willed herself to stay in the moment. But when she looked at her companions, she realized that Erica was staring down at the ground, lines creasing her forehead, while Amber had put an arm around her and was patting her shoulder.

"What is it, honey?" Julie asked.

"It's okay," Erica said, the tiny waver in her voice belying her words. "I'm fine."

Amber looked across Erica's slumped shoulders. "It's the motherhood thing. I mean, we were raised to think it's the highest calling. Even though I had Hannah unplanned, as a single mom, she's been the best thing in my life. But no more kids for me. The cancer." She glanced at Erica.

A terrible feeling rose in Julie. "You don't have cancer, too, do you?" she asked Erica.

"No. No, I don't. But..." She drew in a deep breath. "I have a genetic mutation that makes it likely I'll get it, though, so..."

"Oh, no."

Erica nodded. "I had a hysterectomy." She drew in another breath. "Which is the best way to stay safe, but..."

Amber pulled her closer. "I helped talk her into it," she said. "Me and Hannah. No way do I want my little sis going through what I'm going through, and if something happens to me..."

Julie leaned over and hugged Erica. "That's so sad," she said. "I'm sorry for your loss."

"Thank you." Erica's voice was muffled.

"But there are lots of ways Erica can mother children," Amber said, giving Julie a stern glance.

"Yes, of course!" Just like there were lots of ways Julie could contribute even if her time as an active mother was over. "I'm sure you're a terrific aunt, and there's foster care, adoption…and you're a wonderful teacher. Everyone says so."

She was blathering, and she snapped her mouth shut. There could be no easy way around a hugely disappointing loss like that.

She'd sort of thought she was helping these girls who'd lost their mother, being an older, reassuring force in their lives. But now she felt awkward for saying the wrong thing.

The yoga instructor walked over at the same time Earl Greene did.

"Hey, no loitering," Earl said, joking.

"Sorry!" Julie stood and smiled at him. Normally, she'd have felt funny in front of a man in the old sweats that were her version of yoga gear. Earl, though, had seen her at her worst, during the days he and his wife had been couple friends with her and Melvin.

The two Rowe girls stood and greeted Earl, and introduced him to the yoga instructor.

"We've got to get you out on the yoga mats next time," the instructor said.

"I could use the exercise." He patted his rounded belly. "Unfortunately, the classes happen when I'm on duty. And I can't even touch my toes, so I don't think I could do yoga."

Across the street, Melvin's new squeeze walked by, her slight baby bump visible from this angle. Julie's stomach clenched, her good mood fleeing.

"Hey," the yoga instructor said, "isn't that Ashley Corrigan? I didn't know she was pregnant."

Earl cleared his throat. "No, no, I don't think that's her."

"I'm sure it is," the instructor went on chattily. "I used to see her with an older dude. Like, a couple years ago."

Julie's heart rate quickened. Did Ashley have a thing for older men? Or… "What did he look like?" she asked the instructor, trying for a carefree tone.

"He was a tall, thin guy. Brown hair going gray. I didn't get what she saw in him." She shrugged. "Hope she found someone better looking!"

As the instructor walked away, understanding Julie didn't want to have was pushing into her awareness. She looked at Earl. "Melvin couldn't have been seeing this Ashley girl for a couple of years. Could he?"

Earl didn't answer. His face flushed darker.

Julie's stomach clenched into a tight knot as a slideshow of her last years of marriage passed through her memory. Melvin working late. Melvin not liking her cooking, not wanting to talk, not wanting to take a vacation together. But he'd often come home in a passionate mood, and their love life had gotten quite creative for a while. But that could be because… "He *was* seeing her." She stared at Earl. "And you knew."

"Julie, I—"

"I have to go," she choked out, and hurried to her car so she wouldn't break down in front of an audience.

FRIDAY WAS AN early dismissal day, and just as well, Trey thought as he steered his truck through driving rain. Memorial Day weekend was here and the kids had been restless. But the weather was anything but summery. This rain didn't look like it would let up anytime soon, if those low-hanging clouds were anything to judge by.

Trey was restless, too—maybe because his back was finally feeling better—and so was King. And that was why he'd decided, on the spur of the moment, to take a drive up to the Eastern Shore service dog training center.

Why Erica was in the passenger seat beside him he couldn't quite figure out.

He hadn't intended to invite her to come. He'd resolved to keep his distance from her outside of work. But they'd gotten to talking with some of the kids, who had asked him what was going on with his police dog. In that conversation, one of the kids had brought up the training center and suggested that King could go there to learn a new kind of work. Erica had been nearby and expressed interest and enthusiasm for the idea.

Some part of him—not his brain—had invited her to come along.

"Can you talk, or do you need to focus on driving?" she asked now. "It's really bad out."

"Doesn't bother me. I can talk." He turned down the radio. What did she want to talk about? They'd never cleared the air about that kiss and her subsequent rejection of him. Maybe she was going to share something about that.

She glanced into the back seat and then settled

back to look at Trey. "I just wondered what King's status was. Is he back with you for good?"

"He is," Trey said. "Which is great, except it's because he's out as a police dog."

"It's final now? Oh, Trey, I'm sorry." Unlike some people, she didn't sound fake when she said it. "I know how much you've put into him working."

That was true, even though he hadn't quite thought about it that way. "Thanks," he said, then added slowly, "A lot of my free time has been working with him. I'm mostly sad for him, but I guess... I'm sad for me, too."

She reached over and squeezed his upper arm.

Everything in his body tightened. And that wasn't about King at all.

She pulled her knees up and wrapped her arms around them. "What about you? Did the chief talk about your future on the force?"

He looked away from those long, slim legs. "He did. He warned me this incident was against me, but he's still supportive about my coming back."

Funny, the thought of going back to Philly and living the workaholic police life suddenly didn't seem as compelling as it had before. But maybe he was just sad at the prospect of doing it without King.

Or maybe seeing his dad had gotten him rethinking his life, at least a little.

They pulled into the center. Trey left Erica and King at the door and drove off to park the truck. He trusted her with his dog, surprisingly enough. Even though she didn't have the authoritative attitude and tone of voice needed to work with a dog like King, the big shepherd was docile and well behaved around her, as if he knew better than to act up.

They went inside an immaculate reception area, and a smiling woman looked up from her desk. "Can I help you? Who's this?" She smiled at King and then came around the desk and knelt to pet him.

"King. Say hello."

King barked once and held up a paw.

"Awww," the woman and Erica said simultaneously.

Trey grinned. Yeah, he had been a little bored, and he'd been teaching King some new stuff. He'd enjoyed it. It had nothing to do with police work, more just crowd-pleasing tricks. This was the first time he'd unveiled any of them in public, and it looked like King-the-trick-dog was going to be a hit with the ladies.

"Are you Trey Harrison, then?" The woman rose and went back behind the desk to check her computer.

"Yes. I called a couple of hours ago to see if I could talk to a trainer."

"Right this way." She led them past a kennel and a couple of meeting rooms, and into a small training area set up with agility equipment and dog toys.

King looked around, mouth open, tongue out, panting in that smiling way of his. Obviously, he understood that this was for him.

"Cheyenne, one of our trainers, will be right with you," the receptionist said, and left them in the area.

"Are you nervous?" Erica asked.

"A little. I really want this to work." Trey knelt beside his dog, scratching his ears. He felt responsible for causing the end of King's police career. King was still a high-energy dog and he needed to feel useful, needed something to do.

"If he's trained as a therapy dog, he could probably come to the school on a regular basis," Erica said. Then she bit her lip. "Of course, who knows how long you guys will be here."

"Right." He had the strangest desire to ask her if it mattered, if she'd miss him when he left.

"Hey, folks, I'm Cheyenne!" A curvy blonde woman came in, bouncing on the balls of her feet, dressed in a tight T-shirt and shorts. "You must be Trey," she said, holding out a hand to him. She looked at Erica. "And you're…the wife?"

She shook her head. "Just a…a coworker. Had the afternoon off and rode along."

"Terrific!"

Maybe Cheyenne thought Erica's quick disassociation from him was terrific, but it left Trey feeling let down.

The trainer knelt in front of King. "Hi, big boy! So you want to be a service dog, do you?"

"Say hello, King," Trey commanded, and King did the same bark-and-paw greeting he'd done before, earning a smile from the trainer. "He's through with police dog work," he added, "but he needs to do something, and I think he'd be good as a service dog."

"What are you thinking," she asked, "training him to be a companion, say for a veteran or child with disabilities?"

"No!" He realized he'd sounded too vehement and smiled sheepishly. "I want to keep him living with me. Aren't there service dogs that do visits to schools and hospitals?"

"There were some that visited the cancer ward when Amber was there," Erica offered.

"You guys are talking about therapy dogs, then, not service dogs."

"I'm sorry. Do you still train those?"

She gave him a big smile and took a half step closer. "No, but for you, I'll make an exception."

He blinked. "No need to do that."

"Yes, there is, because it takes two to train a therapy dog. He needs to get used to hospital equipment and the like." She stepped closer still. "I'd enjoy working with you."

Was she hitting on him? Seriously? He gave Erica a look, trying to communicate, *Help!*

"I can help you train him, if you want," Erica offered, and Trey smiled his gratitude.

Cheyenne frowned. "You won't have the right equipment. You need to get a therapy dog comfortable in all kinds of environments and around medical equipment. It would be better if he worked with me."

"Actually," Erica said, "I have a wheelchair and canes and even a hospital bed at my house. It won't be a problem."

"But—"

"That's great," Trey interrupted. Was this what women felt like when men got pushy? "I'm sorry we wasted your time, Cheyenne."

"Not a problem. Do you have a business card? I can give you a call to check in."

"I'll be in touch if I need help," Trey said. "Come on, King."

"Here's my card," she said. She reached out and put it into his pants pocket.

Whoa! Trey's face heated and he backed away. There had been a time when he'd have enjoyed such a forward, pretty lady. Not anymore. "Let's go!" he said to Erica.

They hightailed it out of the building and ran across the parking lot through the rain, King at their side. Once inside the truck, Erica looked over at him, dimples in her cheeks. "Your face when she put her card in your pocket…"

Trey wiped sweat off his forehead. "Close call. She was pretty insistent."

"Well, you're a good-looking guy." Then she blushed adorably.

His own cheeks heated and he looked away. "I think she was interested in King. Right, buddy?" He turned around and reached behind the seat for a towel, then rubbed it across King's wet fur. "Sorry, he smells like a wet dog."

"He *is* a wet dog. It's fine." Erica's phone buzzed, and she clicked into the call. "Hey, Hannah, what's up?" She listened, her eyes widening. "Is she able to walk?"

Trey had been starting the vehicle but he stopped and turned, watching Erica's face grow more and more concerned.

"Call 911," she said into the phone, "and tell them what you told me." She listened. "You already did? Good girl. Wait with your mom and keep her calm. We'll be home in half an hour." She looked inquiringly at Trey.

"Less." He put the car in gear and squealed out of the parking lot, listening as Erica continued talking to her niece.

"If they take her to the hospital," she said into the phone, "see if you can ride along. Keep us posted because we could meet you there instead." She listened, and Trey could hear Hannah's loud, upset voice.

"Plug in a heating pad and get an ice pack, too. Offer her both, and sips of water if she wants." She swallowed hard and dropped her forehead into her hand, but her voice stayed steady. "It's going to be okay, Hannah. She's going to be okay."

She listened for another minute, offered more reassurances and then ended the call.

"What's wrong?" he asked without glancing over, focused on driving as fast as he safely could.

"Amber..." Her voice choked up and she drew in a deep shaky breath. "She woke up with a lot of pain in her leg and abdomen. I didn't say this to Hannah, but the doctor warned us that recurrence is likely and that it would probably manifest as abdominal pain. Oh, Trey, I'm so worried. Can you drive faster?"

He nodded and stepped on the gas, glad he could do something, anything, to help this woman he'd come to care for so much, almost against his will.

CHAPTER FOURTEEN

IT WAS ERICA'S worst nightmare.

As soon as Trey dropped her off at the Bay Coast Hospital's ER, she was directed to a cubicle. There she found Hannah, crying.

Amber wasn't there.

Erica took deep breaths to calm herself and then knelt in front of her niece. "Honey, I'm here."

Hannah leaned forward into Erica's embrace and sobbed.

After a minute, Erica pulled a chair next to her and just held her. Meanwhile, her own mind was racing. What had happened to Amber? Trey had driven like a maniac, but had he gotten here in time? "Honey, where is your mom?"

"Sh-she's having tests."

Tests were good, right? Better than emergency surgery. "Tell me what happened."

In response, Hannah gave a rambling tale of swollen legs and Amber crying out in pain, of the EMTs' fast action, of riding to the hospital. "They said it might just be something minor, or it could be, like, a deep vein thrombosis, whatever that is. They said it could kill her!"

"It's okay. It *didn't* kill her, and we're in the right place." Erica found a water bottle and got Hannah to wipe her tears and take a drink. Initial terrors calmed for both of them, Erica went outside of the cubicle and found a nurse. "Hi, I'm Amber Rowe's sister. She just came in a little bit ago?"

"Oh, good. There's a lot of paperwork to be done."

Of course. "It will get done, but first I need to know how my sister is doing and where she is."

The nurse's lips tightened. "You'll find that out in due time."

Erica's heart rate escalated. Did the nurse's reticence mean something awful was happening to Amber? "Please, I need to check on her now. I'm her closest relative, besides her daughter, and we're really worried."

The woman's jaw tightened and she glanced back at the nursing station, where two buzzers were beeping. Erica knew nurses were overworked and underpaid, but it was still hard to be patient when her sister was somewhere in this hospital, all alone. Hannah was letting loose with occasional sobs in the next room. Erica blinked back tears herself. "Please, is she going to be okay?"

The nurse sucked in a breath and let it out. "Look," she said, "I'm not allowed to give diagnostic information, and I don't know enough about her condition to do that anyway. But I'll tell you that she was joking with the orderlies while they wheeled her up for her tests. Her color was good, and the doctor took her time about writing up the test orders."

Not an emergency, then. Erica went limp with relief. "Thank you," she said.

"Hey, I'm here." Trey rushed into the corridor.

"Immediate family members only," the nurse snapped, back to business.

"I won't stay." Trey gave the nurse one of his amazing smiles, but it didn't seem to work on her.

"The tests will take several hours. We can't have you hanging around the ER until then. You'll need to go back out into the waiting room." She looked at Erica. "Now, you, as her sister, you might be able to wait upstairs and talk to her doctors there."

"Perfect. I will," Erica said. "I don't want her to be alone."

Trey patted her arm as another buzzer sounded in the nurses' station and the nurse hurried off to answer. "Maybe Hannah and I could take King home and we could pick up some stuff for the two of you. Would that help?"

"It would help a lot. Hannah will know what's needed." And it would do her niece a world of good to get away from this hospital and the impersonal tones of the medical professionals. It would also be better for her to know she was doing something to help her mom instead of just sitting there.

Within minutes, Trey had gotten Hannah to agree to come help them gather things for Erica and Amber. The two of them left, Hannah much calmer.

As she watched him open the exit doors and step

back for Hannah to go first—treating a young teenager like the lady she was—she thought again that
he was an amazing man. Any woman would be
lucky to have him in her life.

Unwanted, another thought pushed its way past
her worries. Most women would be able to give him
what he wanted: children. It was only Erica who
couldn't. She had no right to keep that from him.

She shook her head to banish the notion. It was
time to focus on Amber, not herself.

Half an hour of red tape later, Erica got the message that Amber had been admitted to a room. She
bypassed the elevators and hurried up the stairs, ar-
riving at the designated room just as a nurse was set-
tling Amber in and checking her vitals. Erica waited
until the nurse was finished and then went to her
sister and took her hand. "How are you feeling?"

Amber grimaced. "Not the best, but I'm getting
better. They wanted to finish the tests before they
gave me any pain meds, so I just got them. They'll
kick in soon."

"What's the pain about? Do you have an idea
yet?"

She shrugged, then bit her lip and looked away.

Erica sat on the side of the bed. "Tell me."

Amber sucked in a breath and turned her head
back to look at Erica. "No, I don't know. They named
all kinds of possibilities, but one of them is…" She
swallowed. "A recurrence. One or more tumors pushing on something."

Tears sprang to Erica's eyes. *Please, God. Not that.*

"I thought I was ready for that. We knew it could happen. But when I saw Hannah's face—" Her voice choked and her eyes filled. "She's still too young. She needs me."

"I know." Erica swallowed hard and stroked her sister's arm, carefully avoiding the IV. "So do I. So does this world. You have a lot still to contribute."

"Where is she?"

"Trey took her with him. They're dropping King off and gathering some stuff for you. Can you think of anything you need?"

"Some gym shorts so my rear end's not hanging out for all the world to see." Amber's lips twisted into a wry smile. "And a phone charger."

"I'll text her." Erica did, including the message that Amber was in the room and chatty. She didn't want to give Hannah false hope, but a hedge against despair, maybe.

When she finished the text and looked up at her sister, Amber grasped her hand. "Hey. I want you to know, I'm grateful for everything you're doing for us."

Erica tilted her head to one side. "I don't know what you're talking about. I'm doing what any sister would do."

"You're making it possible for us to have a home here, in this beautiful place." Amber waved an arm at the window. Beyond the parking lot and a row of houses, the bay shone like it was foiled with gold. "If this turns out to be bad—if it's a recurrence—I'm just so grateful I got to live here. All those af-

ternoons when you and Hannah are at school, I sit
on the porch and look out over the water. And I'm
at peace."

Erica leaned down and hugged her, carefully.
"I'm so glad. I love living here with you and Hannah."

But as Amber drifted off to sleep, lulled by the
pain pills, Erica thought about keeping her sister
here and what it meant.

For Amber to have peace and a good time, a
dream come true, with her daughter—well, that
meant everything.

And having a relationship with a man who
planned to leave was unthinkable. Having the
academy program's funding withdrawn at the end
of the year was unthinkable. More than ever, after
this scare, she wasn't willing to give up her sister's
dream.

She had to find more ways to convince O'Neil,
and the community, that the kids in the behavior
support program were a strength to the school, not
a weakness.

TUESDAY MORNING, TREY wasn't sure whether he'd
see Erica at school or not. She'd been staying inside
her cottage with her sister, who'd come home from
the hospital yesterday. Only Hannah had made a
brief appearance, heading to the waterfront shops for
pizza and funnel cakes with her friends from school.

Cloaked in silence in their cottage throughout
Memorial Day weekend, the sisters hadn't come out

at all, not even for the town's cookout on the beach or the fireworks.

And Trey, who'd welcomed feeling useful when Amber had first gotten sick, was left as much in the dark as any random neighbor.

He didn't like it.

Loud voices in the hallway snapped him back to the school day. The kids crowded in, dressed in work clothes, some of them carrying tools. They were supposed to do a service project in the neighborhood where they'd done the previous cleanup, this one helping elderly residents prepare for any seasonal storms.

Could he take them out on his own? He knew the basic itinerary. But he wasn't a certified teacher, and he didn't want to raise O'Neil's hackles. The principal being who he was, he'd undoubtedly stop by the site to check on them.

It was hard to believe Erica would miss a day so close to the end of school, but if her sister needed her, she might.

He was about to seek out the other teacher of the support group when Erica rushed in, dressed in jeans and a T-shirt. "Sorry, everyone! Sorry I'm late. Let's go ahead and get going. We only have a small window before it starts raining again."

So they walked from the school to Sunset Lane. The sun peeked out, then ducked behind clouds, and the breeze off the bay was brisk. Jacket weather.

He fell into step beside Erica. "How's your sister doing?"

"Pretty well. So far, her tests haven't revealed anything serious, but we're waiting for a few more results to come in."

"Is she feeling okay?"

"She's tired, but other than that she's okay. No more pain."

There was the sound of running feet behind them, a boy's voice. "Hey, I'm here. Sorry I'm late."

Trey was surprised to see the teenager who had been carrying the drugs when he first arrived.

Erica reached out a hand and patted the kid's shoulder. "I'm so glad you're back." She looked at Trey. "I'm sure you remember LJ," she said.

Trey held out a hand to the kid. "Welcome back."

For a moment, it seemed as though the kid wasn't going to shake hands, but slowly, reluctantly, he did.

LJ was suspicious of him, obviously, and Trey knew enough about teenagers now to grab the bull by the horns. "Look, I can't deny I'll keep my eye on you, but I keep my eye on all the kids."

"Right." LJ looked away.

Trey opened his mouth to scold the kid and then shut it again. He could hardly blame LJ, and he remembered all too well the feeling of not trusting an adult. Only consistent action and patience would convince LJ that Trey was on his side. "Clean slate from my end," he said, and walked faster to catch up with the other kids.

Behind him, he heard Erica talking to LJ. Her voice was warm, but casual. By the time they reached the house they were to work on, she'd even gotten him to laugh.

The sound warmed Trey's heart. Erica was really good with the kids.

They reached the James house, where they were scheduled to work first. Erica, petite as she was, capably lifted boards and showed the students how to stack them up where they could readily be nailed across windows. Then she showed them the hurricane shutters that protected the bigger windows, gave a demonstration about how to check that they were working. "It's not hurricane season yet, but technically, it starts June 1. Which is next week. So we want everyone to be prepared."

"Prepared for school to be out," one of the boys yelled, and a couple of others chimed in. But it wasn't bad-natured. Trey wouldn't be surprised if the kids would miss the academy once the school year ended.

Maybe, the idea flashed into his mind, he and Erica could even do something with the kids in the summer.

Not that he was planning to stay for the summer, of course.

The James men had a dilapidated shed where they kept their hurricane supplies. Erica talked the kids through how to fix it up, making everything easily accessible, and soon they were all working hard with the hammers, nails and small saws donated by the hardware store. Trey had never been much of a handyman, so he didn't try to take charge; he just followed Erica's leadership and did what the students were doing. The good news was that his back felt so much better. Just as the physical therapist had hoped, time and being faithful about the exercises had helped a lot.

After an hour of work, they were close enough to done that he took a break and approached Erica. "Anything you want me to do?"

"Just keep an eye on everybody. You're doing fine, for a guy that barely knows how to hold a hammer." She softened the words with a smile.

He grinned ruefully. "You noticed."

"I noticed." She threw back her shoulders. "Because I'm talented at this stuff."

Her cocky comment amused him. "Why don't you show me how it's done, then?"

"You want me to give you lessons?" She lifted an eyebrow.

"Yeah." He felt the side of his mouth perk up into a smile. "I'm putting myself entirely into your hands."

She bit her lip, and boy, did he want to kiss her right there.

Her eyes were pinned on his, and pretty pink color rose into her cheeks. Their eyes held for too long.

She sucked in a breath. "Well, okay, then! Here's how you hold the hammer. As you put the nail in with the other hand and tap. Gently, because you don't want to knock the nail off center or hit your thumb."

He laughed at her elementary lesson and knelt

to do as she'd done on the other side of the window. Once he had the nail positioned, he looked back over his shoulder at her. "Like this?"

"Yeah." She said it in a sigh, and she seemed to be looking not at the hammer and nail, but at his arms and shoulders. And he couldn't deny that made him feel good. Since his divorce, and even more since his injury, he hadn't exactly felt appealing as a man.

A throat cleared behind them. They both jumped as if they'd been doing something wrong.

It was Earl Greene. "Everything going okay here?"

"Yes, perfect!" Erica turned away from Trey and waved a hand at the side of the house where most of the kids were working. "They're having fun, but I think they're really helping Mr. James get his house ready."

"Any particular concerns, sir?" Trey asked, because he could tell Earl had something on his mind.

"Actually, yes." The man frowned. "I'm wondering how LJ is doing."

"He seems to be fitting back in just fine, Officer, from what I've been able to see." Erica blushed a little, and Trey could guess why.

Neither of them had been paying a lick of attention to LJ.

"Should we walk over there and take a look, see how he's doing?" Trey was pretty sure that was all that would satisfy the officer.

"That would be just fine." Greene turned and led the way.

When they reached the other side of the house, Trey's gut tightened.

There was Principal O'Neil, hands on hips, arguing with a couple of the girls.

"But this is how Erica told us to do it," one of the girls was saying.

"Your teacher happens to be wrong," O'Neil said. He looked up just as Trey, Erica and Earl Greene walked closer. "Oh, hello, there," he said. "Just checking out the kids' work."

"They're doing a nice job," Trey said, to give the girls a little positive reinforcement. They looked upset after O'Neil's correction of their technique.

"Any problems here, Officer?" O'Neil asked Officer Greene.

"Just checking on LJ Jones," Greene said. He was looking around. "Any idea where he is?"

"No, because I didn't realize he was coming back today," Principal O'Neil said. He frowned at Erica. "You need to keep me informed about that sort of thing."

"A kid's absence and return?" She said it mildly, but still managed to imply that O'Neil was nitpicking.

"One with a criminal background, yes." He crossed his arms over his chest. "That's exactly the sort of thing some of the parents dislike about our program. I should have been consulted before he was allowed to return."

"If the board of directors objects, I'll take the heat," Erica said, obviously trying to calm O'Neil down.

"Not to interrupt your discussion of protocol," Officer Greene said, "but where *is* the kid?"

Trey scanned the group. Sure enough, LJ was nowhere to be seen. He walked to the other side of the house where two of the kids were shoring up the little shed.

No LJ.

"He's run away! Should have known." O'Neil frowned and so did Earl Greene.

"Let's not jump to conclusions," Erica said. She turned to the kids who were obviously listening. "Have any of you seen LJ?"

"He was here a minute ago," one of the girls said.

Trey was kicking himself. He was the officer on the scene, and he hadn't kept track of the new return, the delinquent.

Erica's forehead wrinkled. She looked panicky, and understandably so. She probably thought it was her fault, but Trey disagreed. LJ's arrest history made it his responsibility.

He felt a raindrop on his arm and looked up at the roiling gray clouds in the sky. Looked like they would need to pack it in soon, but not before they found their missing kid.

The front door of the house opened, and LJ came out.

"What were you doing in there?" Principal O'Neil strode up to LJ and grabbed his shoulder, none too gently.

LJ wrenched away. "Let go of me, man," he said.

"Were you stealing in there?"

"No!" LJ looked around at his audience and muttered, "I was using the bathroom. Old dude asked me to help him with something."

A car pulled up: Kirk James, whom Trey had already identified as a bit of a blowhard. The older man pushed himself out quickly and strode toward the small group. "What's going on? Is Dad okay?"

Officer Greene climbed the porch steps with surprising speed—maybe he actually wasn't completely out of shape—and tapped on the door. When the older Mr. James appeared, Earl greeted him, then asked: "Did you have one of the boys in there helping you with something?"

"I surely did. Is that against the rules?"

"Not at all. Just checking." Greene went on talking to the older man.

"This is what can happen," O'Neil sputtered, face red. "I don't like it. No one likes it."

"No one likes what?" Trey tried to make the question sound respectful, but from the snicker of a couple of kids, he realized he hadn't succeeded.

"No one likes criminals in their homes!"

LJ's shoulders slumped, and Trey remembered what it felt like to be thought of as a bad seed when you'd done nothing wrong.

"The young man who helped me move my table is a criminal?" Mr. James frowned.

"Erica, could you kindly explain this young man's background?" Now O'Neil was in damage control mode.

"LJ got into some trouble a while back," she said,

putting an arm around the boy, "but he's faced the consequences and done what was legally required. Now he's back with us. He's an important part of the group." She looked steadily from one adult face to another, as if defying any of them to break the connection she had with the child or put him down.

"You had the kid who was arrested working on our house? Inside it?" Kirk clapped his hands on his hips.

"Son!" It was old Mr. James, and though his voice was raspy with age, Kirk's mouth snapped shut. "We aren't the kind of people who refuse to give others a second chance. After all, both you and I have needed a few of those in our lives."

Kirk opened his mouth as if to disagree and then shut it again and ducked his head. "I guess."

"Looks like everything is under control here," Officer Greene said to Trey. "You make sure it stays that way, understand?"

"Yes, sir." But he wasn't looking at Greene; he was looking at Erica. She was talking rapidly to Mr. James, her back toward the rest of them. Maybe she was trying to avoid getting O'Neil involved in the conversation.

She definitely had a balancing act there, and Trey knew how important the program was to her. The final decision about whether to keep the behavior support program going was coming up soon. He wished again that he hadn't let LJ out of his sight.

As Officer Greene walked away, Trey surveyed the low-hanging clouds. He was no weatherman, but it looked like there was going to be a storm. More fat drops of rain were falling.

"Put the tools away," he ordered the rest of the kids. Work on Mary's house, and Primrose Miller's, would have to wait until another day.

LJ sidled toward the back of the house, so Trey strolled after him.

The boy didn't stop where a couple of other kids were gathering supplies, but kept walking toward the alley behind the house. He was looking side to side.

He was going to run away. Trey recognized the signs because he'd done the same himself.

He speed-walked toward LJ, ignoring the twinges in his back. "It stinks when someone makes assumptions about you, doesn't it?"

LJ looked back at him, fear on his face. "I wasn't doing anything."

"I could see that. And I think Erica and Officer Greene could, as well."

"Principal's never going to trust me."

"You're probably right. Are you going to let him define you?"

LJ shot him a resentful look and didn't answer.

They were walking down the alley now, but Trey stopped moving and gestured for LJ to turn back. "Head back with me. What I mean is, are you going to let the fact that the principal thinks you're a bad seed actually make you a bad seed?"

LJ stood still.

"Look, you have a chance to make a fresh start.

I'm not accusing you of anything, and neither is Erica nor local police. But it's your choice. You can let your life take another downturn, live up to the principal's expectations, if you want."

"It's not my choice. You're not going to let me run away."

"Well, you do have to follow the laws of the land. In this case, that means when you come to school, you have to stay at school and do what your class-mates are doing, not follow your every impulse. You're not some special exception to the rules every-one has to follow."

LJ's mouth twisted, but he did start walking back toward the house with Trey.

"Believe me," Trey said, "I know something about making mistakes because of not thinking things through. You can come back from that. I did."

"Huh." LJ's grunt wasn't hostile, which was about the best you could expect of a teenage boy.

Their conversation got more general, but at least the kid was talking. That made Trey feel good. Like he could maybe do something helpful around here.

But that wasn't in the cards for him. Yeah, he'd felt good vibes with some kids and a woman in a sleepy small town. And, yeah, his impulse was to pay attention to that, see where it would lead.

It was just that his impulses had gotten him into trouble before. When he was a kid, when he'd jumped into marriage with Michelle and when he'd started taking too many chances at work after his marriage had broken up.

Including the meth lab fiasco that had led to his back injury.

Now he didn't trust his impulses. Didn't trust himself.

But maybe, a small inner voice said, he was wrong about that. Maybe his impulses were getting better.

His father's description of Trey's childhood flashed into his head. Dad hadn't seen him as a bad kid, and apparently his foster family hadn't, either. So maybe Trey had been too hard on himself for a while now.

Maybe, in addition to having something to offer the teenagers, he had something to offer a woman like Erica.

And just like that, he made a decision. He was going to take her out on a nice date, as soon as school was out so they wouldn't be breaking any rules. Get to know her softer side a little better. See where that connection that kept sparking between them might go.

CHAPTER FIFTEEN

SUNDAY AFTERNOON, JUST like she'd started doing almost every week, Julie worked the front desk of the Chesapeake Motor Lodge. Mary's suggestion had been a good one; it was a help to Ria, and it made Julie feel like she was earning her keep in the little suite she occupied. Most of Ria's customers were by the week, so business was brisk. Ria herself was busy supervising the cleaning staff as they got the rooms and suites ready for the next set of customers.

Julie had mostly gotten past the pain of realizing that Melvin had been having an affair during the last years of their marriage. Partly because she'd half known it already.

What she hadn't gotten past was her anger at Earl. He'd known, and hadn't told her.

"This place is adorable!" The squeals from a couple of new teenage guests were a welcome surprise. A lot of the younger customers weren't too sure about the humble, retro motel Ria had taken over when its ninetysomething owner had retired at the same time Ria had gotten divorced. She'd done a little updating when she could, but not much; the place was a throwback to the 1950s.

Julie hummed along to "Love Me Tender" as she filed receipts in the old-fashioned filing cabinet. She'd taken a long walk before church this morning, had been doing it most mornings, and her jeans were feeling significantly looser. Over the weekend, she'd gone out with Mary and they'd run into Earl Greene, who had complimented her on her new, colorful dress. She'd snubbed him, of course—he was just kissing up to try to redeem himself for keeping the truth from her—but the admiration in his eyes had still given her a little lift. The self-help book she was reading and the meditative yoga she'd been practicing seemed to be helping her to calm down and relax.

Life was getting better. It was almost good.

A throat cleared behind her, the sound rocking her with its familiarity, and she turned to see Melvin standing at the desk. Heat swept through her, just as it always did when she saw him—some mix of anger and embarrassment and remembered passion. "What are you doing here?"

"Ria's giving me a free room for the week."

"Really? Why?" She went to the computer and scrolled through their reservations, taking deep breaths in an effort to regain her composure. Melvin was staying here? Would his girlfriend be joining him?

"I'm working on a project here in town," he said, sounding peevish. "Besides, it's too expensive living up in Saint Michaels. And Ria is my daughter, too."

She lifted her hands, palms out. "Of course she is.

I'm not criticizing." Even as she said it, she remembered Melvin's annoying habit of taking everything she said as a criticism. Between him and her temperamental teen granddaughters, she'd been walking on eggshells for the past few years. No wonder she'd felt stressed and in need of comfort eating!

"If you don't mind, I'm in a hurry." He held out his hand for the key.

She lifted an eyebrow at him. "You're seriously telling me to hustle faster serving you?"

"Don't get nasty. We're going to have to get along if we're both staying here."

His words made her feel the ramifications of his checking in. It was true; they'd be in each other's faces every time they exited their rooms, because they were right across the parking lot from each other.

"Or I should say, we're *all* staying here. Ashley will be joining me."

"Is that so." She leaned forward, elbows on the counter, and glared at him. "Let's just hope your project goes quickly."

"We're cleaning out Ashley's place. She's…she's going to move in with me." He puffed out his chest and lifted his chin, at the same time looking a little scared around the eyes.

"Isn't that sweet," she said.

His face flushed red. "I used to think you were a reasonable person."

No, you never really did. But you did used to love me.

Someone else came into the lobby then, mom in designer duds, dad in golf clothes and a pair of adorable twins who looked like they could be in a magazine. The little girls ran immediately to the large, old-fashioned dollhouse Ria had set up on one end of the lobby.

Rich people—and just as Julie predicted inside, Melvin stopped being a jerk. "Cute kids," he said with a wide smile to the man. "I'm just finishing up here."

"No hurry, no hurry."

He smiled at the couple, ducked his head at the husband and left.

Julie watched him go. So handsome. So confused.

The truth settled into her very bones: she was better off without him. Her days were easier, less fraught. She could move comfortably through her own life.

The awareness nudged at her while she checked the next couple of families in and described the nearby attractions and restaurants.

She didn't want him back, even though the idea of him having a young, pregnant live-in girlfriend— actually, wife, once he got around to marrying the poor child—scratched at her like an itchy tag in a new shirt.

Mostly, she realized, that had to do with what people would think. They'd think Melvin had dumped her for a newer model, which in essence he had, despite his initial vague claims about not wanting to be married. Part of her effort to get him back had been about saving face. She wanted to be the one to leave him, not the reverse.

She blew out a breath. Even though she was moving on in her life now, was happier than she'd been in a long time, it wouldn't be easy to have her ex-husband staying at the same motel as she was. *With* his new squeeze.

She was going to be facing that reality all day, every day.

As Erica and Trey pulled up to the nicest restaurant in Pleasant Shores, Erica sucked in a breath.

She was on an actual date with Trey. Wow.

She was dressed up, wearing a floral summery dress with a full skirt that swirled around her knees, and high-heeled sandals that made her as tall as Trey's chin.

All the better to kiss him.

No. This date wasn't about kissing. She'd agreed to come so that she could tell him the truth about herself. It was high time, since his stint in the Healing Heroes program wouldn't go on much longer. She had to do it, had to see how he reacted. Had to give a stab at opening herself up to love.

He'd been so, so good lately. When Amber had gotten sick, he'd acted like a boyfriend, like it was his job and his duty to help, and he'd brushed off her thanks. Then he'd been so helpful with the kids, especially with LJ. The boy might have run away, and certainly would have had a harder time reintegrating with the group, without Trey. When the school year had ended on Monday, all of the kids had said goodbye to Trey with what looked like real respect, and LJ had lingered behind for a few minutes to talk, almost missing his bus.

Now Trey jumped out of the car, opened her door and held it, his eyes dark with appreciation. "Did I tell you how pretty you look?"

"A couple of times." She felt her lips curve into a smile.

"Sorry, but it bears repeating. You should wear dresses more often." He closed the car door and offered her his arm as they approached the restaurant. "Have you been here before?"

She shook her head. "Couldn't afford it. I feel funny about having you take me here. If you need me to help with the check—"

He turned to her, reached up to put a finger ever so gently at her lips. It was a featherlight touch, but it made her suck in a breath and stop walking.

He stopped, too, facing her. "I've got this," he said, and put a hand on her shoulder. He pulled her ever so slightly closer. "I asked you out. I'm paying."

"O-o-okay." She could barely breathe. He was going to kiss her.

She was going to let him.

Something hit her neck. A fat raindrop. Then another on her arm. She looked up.

He tugged her closer to the building, under a small awning, and wrapped his arms around her.

He wanted to hold her. Pure happiness. She snuggled in and, at that point, the hard angles of his body stole her breath. She looked up at him.

"Kiss me?" he asked with a crooked smile and raised eyebrow. He was asking permission, and how many men were gentlemen enough to do that in this day and age?

In answer, she stood on tiptoes and brushed her lips against his. But when she was going to leave it at that, out of nervousness, he caught her chin in his hand and tightened his other arm around her. He made a sound almost like a growl and deepened the kiss.

Her heart felt like it was going to explode from pounding so fast. His touch was authoritative, his kiss masterful. He knew what he was doing. She didn't, and she clung to his muscular back, trusting him not to take her anywhere she wasn't ready to go.

A huge gust of wind blew over a parking sign beside them. But she didn't want to stop kissing him.

He broke off the kiss, looked into her eyes for just a second. "We should go in."

"We should." Her voice sounded breathless. Another gust of wind knocked over a trash can.

"Come on. It's gonna pour!" He took her elbow and they ran together to the restaurant's door as the skies let loose.

"So much for good hair," she murmured as he held the door for her.

He gave his name to the hostess and then turned back to her, tucking a lock of wet hair behind her ear. "You know what I'm going to say. You look pretty. Including your hair."

"Thanks." Again, she felt breathless.

"This way," the hostess said, and Erica followed her as she led them to a table overlooking the bay. The clouds were thick overhead and the water choppy, but as they approached the table, a ray of light broke through the clouds near the horizon, illuminating the sky and bay and shining golden on Trey's face. She sucked in her breath, and a moment later the golden light dimmed. He pulled out her chair for her.

When she sat down, she leaned forward. "This is going to sound like a weird compliment, but you have the best manners. Where did you learn them?"

"Not exactly what you'd expect from a guy with my background, huh?"

"Not what I'd expect from any guy our age. That gentlemanly stuff is a lost art. Most men don't even learn to hold a door for a woman, let alone pull out a chair. I just wondered who taught you so well."

His face relaxed into a smile. "That would be my dad. He wasn't the best at taking responsibility, taking care of a kid, but he was a big charmer. Always had a lady friend, and he taught me that manners make the world go around. And make the girls *come* around." He flashed a look at her that was almost shy. "Is it working?"

She nodded slowly. "Yeah," she said. "Yeah, it is."

And then their eyes met and held and they just

stared at each other like smiling fools until the waiter came to take their drink order.

"Sorry," Trey said, "we haven't even looked at the wine list." He looked at Erica. "Do you have a preference? I'll order a bottle."

"No, really. I'll have one glass at the most. Your house white," she added to the waiter. Certainly, she didn't want Trey to spend the kind of money a bottle of wine would cost here.

More than that, she didn't trust herself to stick to her plan of being honest with him about her situation if she had a couple of glasses of wine inside her.

"You're sure?" Trey asked, and when she nodded, he grinned up at the waiter. "I'm really more of a beer man, myself. What do you have on draft?"

That made the waiter smile, and he named off the beers and discussed their merits with Trey. As they spoke, Erica looked out the window, needing to get a little distance from Trey. Talk about charm!

Lightning flashed across the sky and she winced.

"Storm warnings are coming true," the waiter remarked. "It's a big one moving up the coast, but it's not going to hit here. Supposed to make land-fall up north. So it just adds to the romantic ambience," he added with a smile. "Here, let me light your lantern." He produced a long lighter and the small storm globe at their table came to life.

That brought them closer, somehow; they both leaned in. There were other couples in the restau-rant, and one big family group, but everyone's conversation was muted. Erica and Trey seemed to be in their own little world.

And it was too romantic. Erica cast about for a nonpersonal topic, hesitant to possibly ruin the evening by bringing up her real agenda right away. "So O'Neil is even more determined to end our program," she told Trey.

"Because of LJ?"

"That's his latest excuse."

"What's really behind his dislike of the kids?"

"Mostly," she said, "it's that he wants to recruit more of the wealthy students who can pay full tuition. That's what he was hired to do, when the school expanded."

"Is there more?"

She frowned. "He likes to be in control, and he likes to look good. Our program threatens both of those goals. Because he's not technically in charge of it, and because he doesn't know anything about working with troubled kids."

"Why did he even agree to it?"

"He didn't," she said. "It's been part of the school for ages, certainly since I was a kid spending vacations and summers here. That was before all the tourists came. We're privately run, and we were the place all the local districts sent their problem kids."

"What happened?"

She propped her chin on her hands. "When the wealthier residents started building here, they liked the idea of a school right in town—well, on the edge of town—in walking distance of their homes. The academy was struggling, so we became just a small part of a mainstream private school. Which is nice in a way, because it helps the support kids integrate into the community, but…" She shrugged.

"But at what cost?" He frowned.

"Right. If the focus is going entirely toward the mainstream kids, then our program goes. So it's at the cost of the kids," she said, then added, "and of my job."

He reached out and put his hand over hers, like he knew what that meant to her. "How's Amber doing?"

She lowered her gaze, her shoulders slumping a little. "They're still trying to figure out the source of her abdominal pain," she said. "She's on some strong painkillers right now." Her voice choked on the last words and she pressed her lips together. The painkillers were taking her sister—the sharp, witty, edgy sister she knew and loved—away from her.

He squeezed her hand. "That's got to be tough."

She nodded, not trusting her voice.

A group emerged from a private room at the back of the restaurant, and Erica waved when she saw Mary. Then she realized that Kirk was there, as well, and a couple of her fellow teachers, and Principal O'Neil… Oh. It was the school's board of directors.

And they were arguing as they walked out.

"What's wrong?" Trey asked.

"Well…the board just saw us out on a date, for one thing. Not that we're breaking rules, not now, but… Wow. I wonder if they were meeting to talk about the fate of our program." She bit her lip, watching the group leave the restaurant. "Could this be the last meeting before they vote? Or did they just now vote?"

"Hey," Trey said. "Don't worry about what you can't control. You've done terrific things at the academy. Take a break tonight."

She inhaled and let out her breath and smiled at him. "Good advice," she said.

Their drinks came then, and they ordered food, Trey urging her to get an expensive seafood dish rather than the pasta she'd initially ordered. And he was right; she'd only ordered it because it was the cheapest item on the menu, and she really did want to try out one of their seafood specialties, so she finally agreed.

He was taking care of her, and it had been so long since someone had done that. Not since her mother had gotten sick and she'd become the caregiver, first of her mother, then of Amber. Even when she'd had her own surgery, she'd gotten by with the bare minimum of help from Hannah and then sent her away, hobbling around her apartment, fixing food and washing dishes when she absolutely had to.

To have someone look at her needs first, try to help her rather than asking her to help them, was not just a big relief; it was intoxicating. If only she could be open to it, revel in it, enjoy it.

But the cost was being close to Trey, and that wouldn't work. Not for long; not in the end.

Would it?

Trey seemed to sense that her mood was slipping

again and began to talk about lighter subjects, asking her about her childhood spending time here at the shore, about her mother, about how she'd gotten into teaching. Then they talked about his father, how Trey didn't see him much anymore, since he loved to travel, finding jobs where he could, living a carefree and pretty wild lifestyle. He dropped by to see Trey every now and then. His last visit, when he'd come to the school, had been a good one.

Watching his face, Erica was impressed that he didn't seem to be bitter about his father's failings, but accepted him as he was.

The restaurant was quieter now, and the storm outside made their little circle of light seem warmer, more protected.

Their meals came, and Erica reveled in the buttery explosion of taste that was the Maryland rockfish topped with some kind of delicious crabmeat mixture. They enjoyed their food in companionable silence, watching the clouds thicken and the rain wax and wane.

When Trey insisted that they share a chocolate dessert, Erica didn't even protest. She just savored the velvety sensuousness of the chocolate decadence cake, melting on her tongue, and smiled at him when he play-fought her with his fork for the last bite.

When he smiled back, he was so handsome that her mouth went dry.

Once they'd finished, Trey pushed the dish out of the way and reached forward to take both of her hands. "I have some dreams," he said. "Do you mind if I share them with you?"

Erica's heart began a steady, dull pounding, because of the way he was looking at her. "What kind of dreams?" she managed to ask.

"I really want to marry and start a family," he said. "I want a do-over on my childhood. A couple of kids at least."

What was he saying? Was he actually asking her to…? And then the meaning of his words slammed into Erica. Children were the one thing she couldn't give him.

"I know," he said with a smile and a squeeze of the hands he still held. "You're probably thinking that I tried that before, and I did. I got married and hoped to start a family, but I didn't have my head on straight. I didn't know what I wanted. Didn't know how to choose. I've learned a lot in the past year and a half since Michelle and I split."

Her mouth was bone-dry. She couldn't have spoken if someone had held a gun to her head.

"Erica," he said, "what would you think about taking our relationship deeper?" He put up a hand. "I don't mean physically. I mean thinking about whether we could make a go of it…together."

She bit her lip as her eyes filled with tears. What kind of a dream come true was this? For a wonderful man like Trey to want her, to say he'd chosen her… She couldn't speak, couldn't break the illusion that this was real and it was for her.

"I know it's early times," he said. "But I want to

take this further. To explore the possibilities with you."

Yes! Yes, I want that, too.

But she couldn't have it. Not now, not ever.

A new sense of all she was losing flooded her. Not just her inability to have kids; that was awful enough, but she'd dealt with it, figured it out with her therapist. In teaching, she'd found a way to connect with young people that, while it wasn't anything like being a parent, still offered solace and helped fill the hole in her heart.

But this, the loss of a good man because he wanted to be a father—and what an awesome desire that was!—and a man who wanted to do that with her... That was a fresh, sharp pain.

He was looking at her with all the tenderness in the world, and she had to protect her heart. Being with Trey wouldn't work in the end, especially since she couldn't bear his children. And it was all well and good to think about adoption, but the fact remained that she was an unlikely candidate.

"I can't," she forced out.

"Uh-uh." He leaned closer, studying her face. "You backed off before. Why? What's wrong? Is it something about me?"

She studied his blue eyes, knowing they wouldn't look at her with this caring for much longer. Because Trey was sensitive, beneath the macho exterior. She'd figured that out.

Maybe she could say it without hurting him. She

cleared her throat. "It's me, Trey. I can't be what you need."

He scooted back a little, his eyes cooling, and even though she'd been expecting it, the change hurt. "It's not you, it's me?" he asked. "That's a pretty old line."

So maybe he wasn't going to take it well. Best to get it all out at once. "And…I won't be having kids."

"No kids," he said, his voice curiously flat. He looked out the window, where the bay was barely visible through the sheets of rain. Then he looked back at her, studied her face for a moment and then said the most devastating thing he could say: "That's a deal breaker for me."

Her stomach tightened and quick tears rushed to her eyes. She realized how much she'd been hoping he would understand. "I'm sorry," she said, biting her lip hard to keep from crying. When she could speak without her voice shaking, she added, "It's complicated, the reason why."

"Sure it is. It always is." He looked around and gestured to their waiter, obviously wanting to go.

He didn't get it. But did that matter? Her revelation had obviously closed a door between them.

The restaurant staff stood conferring in a group, and now their waiter and another man came over to the table. "I'm sorry, but we're closing," he said, handing Trey the check. "Gale-force winds. We're getting that tropical storm after all, at least the edges of it. It took a turn."

"Here in Pleasant Shores? It's here?"

"I'm afraid so. We're boarding up the windows and heading home, all of us." And indeed, even as he spoke, a cook and a busboy closed hurricane shutters across the large plate-glass windows.

Trey counted bills off a big wad, and Erica stood and grabbed her purse. "I have to get to Amber and Hannah," she said. "They don't know what to do, and Amber can't…" The thought of her heavily medicated sister trying to manage in a bad storm made her stomach clench. "Hurry, Trey."

"Here," he said, thrusting the money into the waiter's hands. "Keep the change. Come on," he added to Erica, and strode out toward the truck.

It was hard to even push open the door of the restaurant, and outside, the wind raged. Panic had her gasping for air as she tried to protect her face and head from the blowing objects.

"Careful," he said, putting an arm around her and guiding her across the parking lot. "We'll get there."

It was crazy that even with what had happened between them, even with the storm, she still liked his touch. Which made it even harder to do the right thing and push him away.

CHAPTER SIXTEEN

TREY DROVE THROUGH the storm. No matter how wild and rough it was outside, it couldn't match the turmoil in his heart.

What was wrong with him?

He was surprised and he shouldn't have been. Giving in to his impulses never worked. Why had he expected that Erica would fall into his arms just for the asking?

Because of how she was looking at him, maybe? Because of her response to his touch, her warm conversation, her apparent joy at being with him? The romance of the setting had helped, too, pushed him into declaring himself earlier than he'd planned.

But better to know now that she didn't want him, not seriously and long-term, and didn't want the kind of life he did. He was surprised, but then, he'd been surprised about his wife, too.

He was a rotten judge of women, that was all.

"Look out!" she cried, and he swerved to avoid a fallen tree limb. There were electrical wires down, too, a couple of them sparking. He saw a bedraggled group of kids standing too close to one such wire and hit the brakes, but a woman in a slicker reached them before he could and shepherded them away.

Erica was punching numbers into her phone. But from her frustrated sigh, he guessed that there was no response. "Cell service could be out," he said so her mind wouldn't go to a worse place, a place where Amber and Hannah were hurt.

Then again, why did he care where her mind was when it had so definitely rejected him?

Of course, he did care. He glanced over and saw the wrinkles across her forehead, the shaking of her hands. "Amber's sensible," he said. "She's not going to go out in this."

"Normally, yeah, but she's on those painkillers," she said. "Come on, Hannah. Why aren't you answering?"

"Try Julie," he suggested.

She punched into her phone. "A text got through!" she cried, but then, as she waited, it was apparent that there was no answer back. Undoubtedly, they were up to their ears in worried hotel guests needing reassurance. So far, it didn't look like any structures were down, but there were tree limbs and shingles aplenty.

"I'm so worried," she said, leaning forward, hands on knees, peering through the rain-pelted windshield. "Can you drive any faster?"

"Not without putting us at risk," he said tersely as the truck plowed through a midroad river, eight or ten inches deep. Truthfully, he welcomed the focus, the chance to help people. It was what he did best, and it might chase away the pain in his heart. He'd drop Erica off and then see what else he could do. The police and fire departments had to be swamped.

When they got closer to the cottages, though, that plan changed because the road was entirely underwater and live wires were thick on the ground. The wind shrieked, and he had to yell over it. "We can't drive any farther!" he yelled to Erica. "Stay there. I'll come around!"

She didn't listen, of course. By the time he'd made his way around the truck to her side, she had the door open and was clinging to the jamb with both hands, her face wet in the rain, hair soaked and blown back.

Was it sick that he wanted to kiss her?

Yes, for sure. He was one sick dude.

"Hold on to my arm," he ordered, "and keep your head down." And they fought their way through the wind and rain. Once, a child's wagon flew in front of them, and he jerked Erica out of its path just in time.

If this wasn't a hurricane, it was about as close as you could get. He'd never seen worse.

As they reached Erica's cottage, he could hear King howling next door. Not because he was scared, most likely, but because he wanted to be out with Trey, working and helping. "Get you in a minute, bud," he muttered as they climbed the steps to Erica's cottage.

Funny, he didn't hear Ziggy. If any dog would be freaking out in the storm, he'd have expected it to be the giant, goofy goldendoodle.

The awning of the cottage hung down precariously, swinging back and forth in the wind. Trey grabbed it and held it safely away from Erica while she forced the door open.

"Hannah?" came a rough voice from inside. Amber.

"It's me, honey. Are you okay?" Erica ran to her sister.

Amber leaned against the wall, wearing flannels and a T-shirt, huge circles beneath her eyes. "I'm fine. Waiting for Hannah to come back."

Trey's heart sank. "Where did she go?"

Amber shook her head, rapid little movements as if she were trying to shake the cobwebs off. "I think she went out after Ziggy. She wasn't supposed to be gone long."

"She just left you here?" Erica asked.

Amber waved her hand. "I'm fine. Ziggy, though…" She put her back against the wall and slid down to the floor, knees upraised. "Ziggy went nuts. And Hannah opened the door to see what was going on and he ran out. I told her to go get him, that I was fine." She frowned. "But it's been too long. I don't know where she is."

Trey thought of the flying wagon, the blowing awning, the pools of water. His gut tightened. "We'll find her," he promised Amber.

"I'll come, too." She tried to push herself to her feet and then stumbled back down, barely catching herself on her arm. "Wretched pain pills."

Erica hurried to help her, easing her into a chair. Amber's frustration was palpable, and Trey knelt in front of her. "Do you have something Hannah wore recently? It wouldn't hurt to have King sniff it." King wasn't highly trained in search and rescue, but he had a good nose and was smart.

"Just take him up to her bedroom." Amber laughed shakily. "I'm sure there are clothes all over the floor."

So Trey ran next door and brought King back to the women's cottage.

"Top of the stairs, first door on the left," Erica directed, and he and King trotted up.

"Get something of Ziggy's for him to sniff, too," Trey called over his shoulder.

When he came back down, Erica was holding a flat pillow. "Ziggy sleeps on this every night," she said.

Trey took it and held it to King's nose, and the dog sniffed for a few minutes and then looked up inquiringly at Trey.

"Okay," he said to Erica. "You stay here with your sister. King and I will find Hannah and Ziggy. I promise."

He turned and then paused in the doorway. "Search, King," he ordered, and dived out into the storm again, hoping that, with King's help, he'd be able to keep his promise.

"Just get inside, Mom!"

From the middle of the motel parking lot, Julie heard Ria's shout behind her and turned back into the wind, rain slapping her face and eyes. "I'll check the guests over here," she called, gesturing to the far wing of the motel.

Ria ran toward her, her feet splashing through puddles. "It's too risky! Get inside!"

What was it that kept adult children from seeing that their parents were still competent adults? "Go on. Do what you need to do. I promise, I'm fine."

Ria threw up her hands and then, at a shout from in front of the motel office, she rushed back in that direction.

Julie headed back toward the far wing, realizing only belatedly that this was where Melvin and Ashley were staying. Ugh.

Despite the Melvin factor, things were getting better for her. Life was okay. Just within the past week, she'd realized how far she'd come out of the post-divorce slump. Giving up the cottage and seeing it used in a positive way had helped, as had moving into Ria's motel. As annoying as her granddaughters could be at times, Julie loved them madly. As for Ria, she was a wonderful daughter, the child of Julie's heart, and it was good to be so close to her.

She rounded the corner of the building and looked down the row. All the doors were closed except for one, and she squinted to see who was out in the storm.

It was a child, about eight, standing in the door and crying. Behind him, two more children cried.

"What happened?" she asked as she hurried toward them. "Step back. You're getting soaked."

"Mama!" The little boy pointed.

Julie squinted through the driving rain. It was as if nightfall had come early, everything was so dark, but she dimly saw a figure on the other side of the fenced-in pool. "Is that your mom?" she asked.

"Yes. She went to check on our car and she can't get back."

Indeed, the parking lot between here and the pool was a river. The woman on the other side was pointing and crying. "My children!"

"Go back in and stay inside," Julie told the kids. She braced herself and started toward the woman, grabbing a stick to steady herself.

"Grandma!" It was Kaitlyn calling out, and when Julie turned back to look, she realized that Sophia was there, too. "Mom told us to come get you," she shouted.

She braced herself on her stick. "Go help the kids," she ordered, pointing toward the open hotel room door.

"Help them how?" Sophia shouted.

Good heavens, didn't they know anything? "Keep them inside and get them warm. Tell them their mama will be fine."

The girls turned toward the kids, and Julie headed for their mother, but now the storm was even worse. The wind whipped at her as she made her way as close as she could get to the woman.

The woman pointed at the rushing water between them. "It's deep! Don't try to go through it!"

The wind blew harder and the woman turned, and suddenly she was falling into the flooded, racing river of water between them.

Julie stuck out her stick and braced herself. "Grab on!"

The woman grabbed for the stick, but missed it and fell backward into the water again, briefly going under. When she came up, gasping, Julie screamed at her. "Grab on and hold tight. I'll get you to your kids!"

"Yes, yes!" The woman caught the stick and this time grasped it tightly with both hands. Struggling mightily, Julie pulled her to the motel side of the flooded parking lot. A huge gust of wind blew a couple of branches their way, and Julie helped the young mother to her feet and tugged her into a sheltered area beside a storage shed.

"You're freezing," she said. She stripped off her own warm rain jacket and wrapped it around the shivering woman.

"My babies, my babies," the woman moaned, and despite Julie's reassurances that Sophia and Kaitlyn were with them, she couldn't calm down, couldn't even catch her breath. She was panicking.

Julie was a mother and she understood. At the next break in the gusty wind, she put an arm around the woman's back. "Come on. Let's get you back to your kids."

They struggled across the parking lot together, sloshing through ankle-deep water and squinting through the driving rain. As they reached the building, Melvin came out of his room two doors down. "Julie!" He sounded shocked and he was staring at her. "Cover up!"

She glanced down at herself and realized she might possibly win a wet T-shirt contest, if there were one for older, curvier ladies.

If she'd had a dream of looking good for Melvin, it washed away with the pouring rain.

And she didn't care in the least. Ignoring Melvin, she pounded on the door of the woman's room, and Kaitlyn opened it. "Grandma!"

"Mommy!" the older boy yelled, and threw himself into his mother's arms.

Julie steadied her, and then all the kids were hugging her.

"You're rocking the T-shirt, Grandma, but it's not the time or the place." Kaitlyn was actually smiling.

"It's not intentional, believe me." She indicated the jacket the young mother was wearing.

Kaitlyn slipped off her hoodie and helped Julie pull it over her head.

"Come on," Sophia said. "Let's go or Mom will kill us. We're supposed to watch out for you."

"You know what," Julie said. "I'm fine. You girls can go back to your mom and report or you can help me check on people. Your call."

The oldest of the woman's three kids threw his arms around Julie. "Thank you for saving our mama."

"They weren't very nice," the middle-size boy said, pointing at Kaitlyn and Sophia. "They wouldn't let us come outside."

"They were right. They were keeping you safe," the mama scolded. She gave Kaitlyn and Sophia quick hugs. "Thank you so, so much for helping my kids."

"Come on," Julie said to them. "Let's go." And as she led her granddaughters through the storm, checking doorways and windows on the way, she felt her shoulders square up, her spine straighten.

She'd done something good today, and she was going to see how else she could help. Because it didn't matter that she was no spring chicken, and it didn't matter how she looked to Melvin, her granddaughters or anyone else.

All that mattered was what she could do, how she could help. There was a role for her to play in this world, and she was going to play it, not from the sidelines, but from center stage.

CHAPTER SEVENTEEN

MOMENTS AFTER ERICA plunged out into the storm, despite her boots and rain gear, she was soaked. She put her head down and fought her way through the water flooding the street, the force of the wind pushing her, slowing her legs.

She tensed her muscles for balance and looked back at the cottage. Through the dense rain she saw Amber illuminated in the light of the front window. Erica had left her wrapped in a blanket and fortified by black coffee. She'd hated to do it, but when Trey hadn't come back, Amber had begged her to go, to search for Hannah.

She sloshed through puddles, squinting against the needles of rain that struck her face and eyes. Hannah had to be out here somewhere. Probably at risk and afraid.

And Ziggy. Ziggy couldn't understand weather. He had to be terrified, and the thought of him running around in the storm, frantic and barking, looking for his humans, broke her heart.

Trey had gone to find them. But where was he?

Trey could take care of himself and she could guarantee he wasn't frightened. But she could also guarantee that he'd put himself at risk to save Hannah or even Ziggy. That was who he was. He'd sacrifice himself in a heartbeat, and what if he'd done so?

What would the world be to her without him in it?

Her chest ached at the very thought. She stopped dead still, water washing around her ankles, rain plastering her hair to her head.

She loved him.

She'd gone and fallen in love with him and it stunned her. Oh, she'd known her heart was going in that direction, that she felt drawn to him, that the fact that her infertility meant she couldn't be with him had become not just sad, but crushing.

But love?

She'd never even dated much, let alone fallen in love, so these feelings had crept up on her and she had no framework to understand them.

She wanted his arms around her. Wanted his touch, his kiss. Wanted to talk to him, explain more fully why she couldn't be with him, reassure him that it was nothing unlovable about him.

Maybe even to try to find a way to make it work despite all the obstacles.

Right now, she just wanted to find him, see him and make sure that he was safe. Because of who Trey was, she was pretty sure that finding Trey would mean finding Hannah and Ziggy.

She passed the motel and saw Julie standing under an awning, arm around an older woman, pointing out into the parking lot where cars were axle-deep in water. She ran toward them.

"Have you seen Hannah, or Trey, or Ziggy?"

"They haven't been by here," Julie said. "Oh, honey, are they missing? How can I help? I can't leave the motel, I'm needed here, but I can ask around."

"Ask if anyone's seen a big white dog," she said. "He'd be the most noticeable, and he's the one Hannah would be following. And Trey went out to find them."

"I saw a big white dog running around," the elderly woman said unexpectedly. "Looked like a giant drowned rat."

"What direction did he go?"

She gestured vaguely toward the waterfront. "That way, but it's been a while."

Of course Ziggy would head for the water. Exactly where you weren't supposed to go during a bad storm. A cold hand seemed to squeeze her stomach. "Thank you. I'm going to go look for him. For them."

She left the hotel and now she ran, rather than walked, toward the beach. Water splashed up as she stomped and skidded through the puddles, and rain lashed at her face. As she got closer to the beach, road signs rattled on their poles with the force of the oncoming wind. The noise made it hard to think. She shivered in her soaked clothes.

Beside the road, a tree rocked and swayed and suddenly uprooted. She backed away, panting, and it crashed down directly in front of her.

Her heart pumped double-time. She could have

been killed! But there wasn't time for maybes or even prayers of thanks; she had to keep going.

Thinking of Ziggy and Hannah out in this storm stole her breath.

At the beach, the water was pure chop and the waves splashed up as high as the pier. Someone had put caution tape across the beach access, but it had blown partly down and was flapping wildly.

As she reached the row of Sunset Lane houses they'd worked on, she felt a flash of relief that the shutters were closed and the roofs and boards seemed to have held.

The argument between the elder and younger James men flashed into her memory.

"It's too early in the season," Kirk had said, and, "Hurricanes don't make landfall here."

Old Mr. James was right, she said in her head.

"I was right!"

Her head whipped around toward the James house. Had she really heard a voice in all this wind and rain?

IN PRIMROSE MILLER'S HOUSE, Trey knelt beside Ziggy, who'd stood up and was pacing restlessly. "Hey, buddy, it's okay."

Ziggy gave his face a distracted lick and then walked over to the window and put his big paws up, standing like a person, much to the delight of Venus, who started snapping pictures with her phone.

Trey was proud of the little group of local teenagers, mostly the support kids but a few from the main school, as well. They'd assured him that their

parents knew where they were and had given them
permission to come to Sunset Lane when the storm
had worsened. He didn't know how they'd convinced
their parents to let them leave home in a dangerous
storm, but apparently one of the students' fathers
had driven his SUV around picking them up and
brought them here. They'd wanted to make sure the
older folks were okay and to help get the plywood
up over windows. King had led Trey that way, too,
somehow tracing the scent of Hannah and Ziggy
despite the storm.

Trey had seen LJ first, and stopped to yell a
greeting on his hunt for Hannah; then the girl herself had burst out of Primrose's house and shouted
to him. Ziggy had rushed toward him and King,
stopped only by Hannah setting her heels and holding tightly to his leash.

Cell phone service wasn't working, so there was
no way to let Amber and Erica know that Hannah
was safe. Trey figured to send someone back to the
house as soon as they got all the Sunset Lane residents settled and secure.

Primrose, navigating her home in a wheelchair
after some recent surgery, was fretting that her garden would be ruined. Ziggy paused in his pacing to
nudge his big head under Primrose's hand.

"You smell like a wet dog," Primrose said, but a
shaky smile crossed her face.

Ziggy leaned against her leg, looking up at her
with a doggy smile. Then he stood and trotted to
the window again.

What was bothering him?

Maybe just the storm, because King was pacing restlessly, too.

"Over here, Mr. Harrison," LJ yelled from the James place, and after ascertaining that two of the teens would stay to keep an eye on Ziggy and Primrose, he hurried next door. The wind had died down a little, and the rain might have let up a tiny bit.

A tree limb had fallen onto the corner of the house, cracking a window through which the rain was coming in. Working quickly with duct tape and garbage bags, they created a makeshift patch.

Trey went next to look in on Mary, who was hunkered down in her house, comforting Baby-the-Maltipoo and seeming perfectly self-sufficient. Moments later, Hannah came rushing over and pounded on Mary's door. "Come on back to Primrose's," she said to Trey. "My cell phone worked for a little over there, and I got a text to Mom. Erica's not there. Mom says she came out looking for us!"

Erica was out in this storm? Anxiety gripped at him as he followed Hannah back to Primrose's house, yelling for those at the James place to come along.

Just as they trooped in Primrose's front door, Ziggy started barking and jumping madly and scratching at the back door, and understanding dawned. Trey hurried to open the door, hoping against hope, and...

There was Erica. She stood, soaked to the skin, breathing hard, staring at him.

Before he could think or react, Ziggy and then Hannah flung themselves on her.

Incredible relief and wild joy danced inside him, and he wanted to wrap his arms around her and never let go. Held tight on to a kitchen chair so he wouldn't do it.

He couldn't follow his impulses, because they'd been proved not just wrong, but downright destructive. Now the storm had boiled things down to elementals and he knew one truth: he couldn't survive if he let her keep on breaking his heart. "Glad you're okay," he said, and turned away.

She broke away from Hannah and Ziggy, walked across the room and gripped his arm. "Trey, I... Can we talk?"

He wanted to. Oh, how he wanted to.

Pulling away from her was the hardest thing he'd ever done, but he set his jaw and did it. "Why put ourselves through it? We both know it's not going to work."

He turned away quickly, because she was softhearted and his words, though true, might make her cry. And he couldn't watch that happen without throwing all good sense aside and taking her into his arms.

CHAPTER EIGHTEEN

ERICA WANTED TO go collapse in a ball and cry, and she did slip away into Primrose's bedroom for a miserable half hour and did just that. Soon enough, though, the rain ended and there was work to do. She helped a couple of the kids gather Mr. James's bent and broken lawn ornaments and store them in the shed behind his house to repair later. Then they lifted the awning that had fallen and moved it to the side, weighting it down with concrete blocks.

The physical work almost drove away the pain of Trey's rejection. Almost, but not quite. She'd had the crazy hope that, after all they'd been through together, he would have been willing to talk about what she'd said at the restaurant. Maybe they could figure out a way to try.

But apparently it was too late. He'd given up, said it wasn't going to work, wasn't worth bothering about.

Ziggy and Primrose came out to join them. Primrose eased her way carefully down her wheelchair ramp, Ziggy walking slowly beside her. When they got to the bottom, she leaned over and dried him off with a towel she'd been carrying in her lap, and he not only allowed it, but gave her a quick lick on the cheek.

"Ziggy's been so great," Hannah said. "He's like a different dog. I guess it's Trey's training, that or the fact that he knows people are upset."

Trey's training. That probably wouldn't happen anymore, since the school year had ended. He was surely making plans to leave forever.

The thought of him leaving made her want to double up with pain. Only with an effort could she hold herself together. She sucked in a breath and pinched the skin between her thumb and forefinger, willing herself not to cry. "What happened that you and Ziggy even went outside?" she asked Hannah.

"It was my fault he got out," Hannah said. "I'm so sorry. I opened the door to see what was going on, how bad the storm was. And you know how he is—he pushed past me. I felt terrible that he was out in the rain, so upset, so Mom let me go out looking for him."

Mr. James chimed in then. "I didn't know what to think when this crazy dog came running down the street with the girl behind him. Me, I was out in the yard trying to get some of the plants and lawn chairs inside."

"Which you shouldn't have been doing," Kirk said. "I was going to get to that, just as soon as I'd checked on a couple of folks down the street."

"Women," Primrose mouthed to Erica with a knowing nod. "He had to check on his lady friends."

Old Mr. James ignored his son and Primrose.

"Anyway, I saw them coming and I just opened our gate and called to the dog. He came running in and I shut the gate and he was caught." Mr. James looked proud of himself. "Then this young lady comes in and thanks me and starts helping me gather up my lawn chairs and get those hurricane shutters closed. And soon enough another kid showed up, and then another."

"I was watching out the window, and at first I thought they might be coming to loot us," Primrose admitted, "but they've been real sweet."

"I got stuck helping Mary with her generator," Kirk said. "I was worried about Dad, but when I checked on him, he said everything was fine, the kids were helping." He looked steadily from one to the next. "I've misjudged you. I'm truly grateful for what you did for Dad."

Some part of Erica felt good about the kids, the same part that put her arm around Hannah and gave LJ a pat on the back. It was as if she was reaching out from beneath a coating of cotton to interact with the world.

This is what you have, the kids. This has to be enough.

But it wasn't enough.

She felt Ziggy beside her pressing against her leg. Hannah was right: he was much calmer than what she'd expected.

The storm was abating now and Primrose invited them all to stay awhile. She'd collected rations and had candles and a lamp, and they all gathered around and ate cookies.

Even Trey stayed, at the kids' urging. And sat as far away from Erica as was possible.

He didn't meet her eyes.

They sat talking for another half hour while the rain came and went. Erica wanted to go home, to lick her wounds in private, but she just didn't have the energy.

Finally, there was a pounding on the door. "Police!"

It wasn't Earl Greene, but another of his officers. As she checked with everyone, making sure there were no injuries, Principal O'Neil pushed into the room.

"There you are!" he scolded when he saw a couple of the kids from the mainstream school there. "Your parents have been worried sick about you because they couldn't reach you on your phones. They called me on my landline because they knew the school might be used as a shelter. And then I heard from another parent that you were here."

"Why were our parents upset?" one of the kids asked. "I left a note about where I was and that I was safe." He gave the principal a skeptical look, as if he didn't believe his parents were really worried.

Erica wouldn't put it past O'Neil to exaggerate for effect.

"I texted my folks," another said, "although cell service hasn't been good."

"Leaving a note or texting isn't the same as getting permission." He frowned at Erica and then at Trey. "It's just like the parents on the board have been saying—those support kids are having too much of an influence on the rest of the students. I'd like to speak with the two of you."

It was the only thing that would put them within arm's length of each other. Numb, not looking at Trey, Erica followed the principal into Primrose's kitchen.

O'Neil turned to face them both. "We had a meeting tonight, as I'm sure the two of you saw on your little date."

Just the thought of that date was enough to make Erica's chest ache.

"The parents on the board are very concerned that the support kids are leading the rest of the students into poor behavior."

Trey spoke up. "Helping older people in need is bad behavior? How do you figure that?"

"Going out at night, in a storm, without permission—yes, it's a problem, though I wouldn't expect you to see that." He frowned at them severely. "I've been thinking about what recommendation to make about the group, and this is the last straw. The program just isn't going to work. I'm recommending we close it down."

It wasn't going to work. Just like she and Trey weren't going to work.

She knew she should argue but she didn't have the strength. She couldn't help what was happening with the kids, couldn't save it. She'd done her best and it was all just a disaster.

Losing her job meant she couldn't keep Hannah and Amber at the beach.

"So there won't be a behavior support program next year." Trey said it with some kind of emotion in his voice, but she couldn't pull herself together enough to analyze it.

Dimly, she realized that Trey was arguing a little, challenging O'Neil's decision. But, of course, it didn't help. The program was going to end, and that was all she needed to know.

They'd failed. She'd failed.

Tears welled, and she couldn't let them fall in front of her boss and Trey. She cleared her throat. "If you're taking over with the kids, I'll go." She snapped her fingers to get Ziggy's attention and picked up the leash he was dragging.

The teenagers were all talking energetically, high on the adrenaline of the storm, unaware that their program was about to end. Let O'Neil be the one to tell them. Him, or Trey. She didn't have the stomach for it. She opened the door, slipped out quietly and slunk home to reassure Amber that Hannah was safe.

Then she climbed the stairs to her bedroom and wept.

THE NEXT DAY, when Erica dragged herself outside—because Ziggy had to be walked, no matter how Erica was feeling—the rain had stopped entirely and the air was already humid as the sun beat down. Tree limbs lined the road, fences were flattened and electric lines were down. People walked around their yards assessing the damage, with lots of conversations and greetings. There'd be plenty of hard work to get the town in shape by the time the high season started in just a couple of weeks.

The good news was, no loss of life, no serious injury and only a couple of structures had been badly damaged by the storm.

As she trudged down the street behind Ziggy, someone who was grilling burgers called out an invitation. Ziggy strained toward the scent, but she waved and shook her head and pulled the dog back onto course. She wasn't hungry and she couldn't face anyone.

Last night, she'd seen finality in two men's eyes.

O'Neil was firm in his decision that the program had to end. And sure, she could blame Trey for letting the kids all stay on Sunset Lane and work together during the storm, but there was nothing wrong with what he'd done. He'd found Hannah, and the other kids had found their way to the same place, and they'd all helped the elders of Sunset Lane. They'd done the right thing, and she was proud of them.

Proud of them, and filled with admiration for Trey.

He was a good man. He'd come to Pleasant Shores with a bad back and a lost job, and he still had those things, but rather than letting that define him, he'd moved forward to help the kids. He'd changed so much since his initial reluctant presentation in the classroom. He'd grown, or maybe just let a side of himself come out that hadn't been apparent at first.

He was a good man, and last night—was it only last night?—he'd said he wanted to explore a relationship with her.

She'd had to turn him down, but doing that had just about done her in. She didn't feel like she could ever say life was unfair, not when she looked at all Amber had gone through, but she did wish something could be easy for her for once.

Or not even easy—she didn't care about that. What she wished for was Trey.

Instead, she'd lost him and she'd lost the job that was the linchpin of her and Amber and Hannah staying here. She'd totally failed.

Ziggy looked up at her and whined, and she rubbed his big head as they trudged past the motel, headed back toward home. Or, at least, what was home for now. It couldn't be for long, because they couldn't afford to stay here once Erica's paychecks stopped coming.

She'd have to tell Amber, but she couldn't face doing that yet. Which meant she couldn't go home yet, because her sister knew her too well not to ask her what was wrong, and then what could she say?

A piece of a sign had blown into the driveway in front of the church, jagged and dangerous. She veered over to tug it off the driveway, but it was heavier than she'd expected. She tugged and tugged and then, suddenly, it was easier, and she realized that someone was there to help her. She looked over: Julie.

"I was just on my way to do that when you got there first," Julie said. "Are you guys okay at your place? Need anything?"

We need everything. But nothing that Julie could provide. "Thanks, but things turned out fine. We found Hannah and Ziggy over on Sunset Lane."

Julie tilted her head to one side. "Why there?"

"Mr. James caught Ziggy, and Hannah started helping him with the storm damage, and then some of our kids from the academy came over to add their efforts. We'd been working with the folks there as a service project," she clarified at Julie's puzzled expression, "and the kids got worried about how they were managing the storm." She felt a sad surge of pride. Those teenagers had so much to offer the world.

"Impressive," Julie said with a nod and a lift of her eyebrows. "You've done a lot with those kids."

"Yeah. They're great." She choked the words out, and then she couldn't hold back a few tears that welled up out of her eyes. "Sorry."

Julie put an arm around Erica. "It's been a rough couple of days for you. You're entitled to break down." She patted Erica's back. "You're okay."

It was what Erica's mother had always said, and it was the last straw, and she really did break down, and Julie pulled her into a full-on hug. "It's okay to cry," she said.

"They're going to cut my program," Erica blub-bered into Julie's shoulder.

Julie went still, then pulled back and held her by the shoulders to look at her face. "Who's cutting the program?"

"Principal O'Neil," she said, and wiped her nose on her sleeve. "He's been gunning for us forever, and it's gotten worse since Trey came, and now he plans to make a recommendation to the board. To close us down." She couldn't speak anymore.

"Okay. Okay. Maybe there's something that can be done, but not today." Julie put an arm around her and walked her toward the street. "Today, you need to go home and take a nice warm bath and relax."

"Thanks," she said, meaning it. Julie's motherly, caring nature was a balm to her spirits. "I'll be fine."

Someone called to Julie from the other side of the fence that separated the hotel from the church. "Grandma! We need you!"

Erica stepped out of Julie's hug and gave her a little push. "Go on."

Julie looked at her doubtfully and opened her mouth to speak.

"I'm fine, really." Erica forced a smile to give credence to the words. "You go help your grand-daughters. I'm just a hop from home."

But once Julie was out of sight, Erica turned away from the street and back toward the church. She couldn't face Amber like this. Amber had enough to deal with.

There was a little courtyard that the church

used for early summer services. She made her way around the building to it, Ziggy at her side. Sticks and a few shingles littered the grass, but the stone altar was intact.

She cleaned up the courtyard, letting Ziggy run free. She was comfortable now that he wouldn't leave her side and she was right. After she'd put the debris in a neat stack beside the trash can, she walked slowly into the church, with some idea of finding comfort there. Ziggy looked up at her inquiringly.

"Come on. It's okay," she said, putting her hand down to rest on his head. Normally, of course, she wouldn't bring her dog into the church, but there didn't seem to be anyone here, and he was behaving so well.

He nuzzled her hand and then trotted along beside her, down the hall.

If she'd thought that coming into the church would chase away the anguish she felt, she was wrong. Her thoughts wouldn't let up.

The situation she was in, losing her job and the kids' special classes, wasn't solvable or fixable. She knew that because she'd done her best for several months to convince Principal O'Neil to support it and she'd failed.

And she'd tried to tell Trey the truth, but the hard look in his eyes as he blocked it out, reinforced by his anger after the storm, let her know their relationship couldn't be fixed, either.

With God all things are possible. It was what her

mother had said when she'd gotten discouraged as a kid. Her mother had been a woman of faith, more so as she'd gotten sicker.

But she was wrong about all things being possible with God. Getting well hadn't been possible for Mom, even though she'd had plenty of people praying for her.

Mom had maintained that there was a reason she was being taken so young. Maybe it would make Amber and Erica's bond stronger. For sure, it had nudged them into genetic and medical testing, which had led to Amber's cancer being found early. Not early enough, but early.

Those were silver linings, sure, but they didn't nearly make up for losing Mom. Nothing could make up for that. And now that Erica's life and her dreams were skidding into a train wreck, she missed her mother so much that her whole chest ached.

She stumbled a little and looked up through tears only to discover that she'd come to the worst possible place for her mood: the church nursery. And maybe she just wanted to punish herself, but she couldn't resist pushing open the door.

The three cribs along the wall, the sweet-sour smell of babies, the colorful toys piled in a bin— all of it hit Erica harder than the storm had, so hard that she doubled over and sank into a rocking chair, burying her face on her knees.

She'd never be the frazzled mom bringing her baby here, the happy, refreshed mom greeting the caregivers after church, the cranky mom complaining about breastfeeding and messy diapers and lack of sleep. She'd never be a mom, never be one of the moms.

She'd thought she was done with crying, but now the tears came again, harder than ever. Ziggy leaned against her leg, watching her with what looked like worry on his face.

Her own mother had talked so much about the joy of bearing children, the sweetness of babies, the soul-growing challenges of raising kids. "It's not going to happen," she whispered, maybe to herself, maybe to her mother's spirit, maybe to God. "It's never going to happen."

Trey had rejected her for that. Maybe Mom would've, too.

No.

She breathed in deeply, let her breath out slowly. A deep certainty came over her, even as she wiped tears.

No one who loved her would blame her for this wretched medical situation. Mom wouldn't. Amber, Hannah and her friends obviously didn't.

She wouldn't blame her own friends if something similar had happened to them.

She kept breathing deeply, and the tears slowed down, then stopped. She picked up a small quilted bear lying beside her rocking chair and studied it. Then she stood, grabbed a handful of tissues and wiped her eyes.

It was sad she couldn't have children. So, so sad.

But everyone had some sadness in their lives, some disappointments.

Being infertile didn't mean something was wrong with her. Didn't mean she was bad. Didn't mean she was less of a woman.

She ran a hand along the rail of an empty crib, leaned over and looked into it. A few more tears fell.

But her sadness felt just a little cleaner now, simpler. It was just sadness. She'd make it through, just as she'd made it through losing Mom.

The sun peeked out from behind a cloud, sending golden light through the suncatchers in the nursery's window. She and Amber had always loved the suncatchers Mom had put up first, every place they'd lived.

And she remembered what her mother had said to her and Amber, during those dark final days. *Always remember you have each other. Lean on each other.*

She needed to go home, needed to talk to her big sister. Needed, for once, to let go of being the strong one and let Amber's love and wisdom give her the strength to go on.

When she stood, she realized that every muscle ached from all the running and work she'd done yesterday. She had a cut on one shin and a bruise on the other.

But they'd made it through the storm. And as she thought about what the kids had done, how they'd helped the elders, a fierce pride rose inside her.

Yes, they'd gotten in trouble for it, pushing the support program over the edge of the cliff into ruin.

But that would have happened anyway. The teens' actions during the storm were just another brick in the wall O'Neil was building to shut them down.

It didn't mean she couldn't feel pride in what they'd done. She'd helped, and Trey had helped, and the kids had reached inside and shown their core of steel.

She wouldn't change a thing about the program or about them. She straightened her spine, clicked her tongue to Ziggy, and headed out of the church and home to her sister.

CHAPTER NINETEEN

TREY WORKED WITH the cleanup crews all morning, dealing with fallen branches and downed electric lines. It was odd to see the sun out after yesterday's thick clouds and high winds.

Denny drove down to join in and help, and they ran a chain saw together, cutting up a tree that had fallen across a road and shoveling mud out of someone's basement. The smell of damp earth was starting to rise, but since it wasn't too hot and the floodwaters had receded quickly, it wasn't unbearable.

What *was* unbearable, to Trey, was thinking about Erica, especially how upset she'd looked after Principal O'Neil's visit. He'd like to slug the man, because he knew the kids' actions during the hurricane were only an excuse. In fact, he thought it likely that O'Neil had already been recommending that the program be terminated earlier that evening, when the board had met.

Whenever he'd made his final decision, O'Neil had the power to destroy the academy program apparently, and he was doing it.

While Trey and Denny worked, going from one

small job to the next, they talked. Denny was all caught up in the soon-to-be birth of his second child, wondering how it would go, worrying about whether there was enough money to pay for another baby's needs. Trey listened and made a few suggestions— very few, because what did he know about father- hood?—and reassured Denny that he'd be fine, that he'd done it once before, that it was going to be the best experience of his life.

King kept pace beside them. Trey told Denny about how King had helped to find Hannah and Ziggy.

"Have you thought about volunteering him for search-and-rescue work?" Denny asked. "He'd be great at it."

Trey looked down at King thoughtfully. It didn't matter to a dog whether his work was volunteer or paid. He just wanted to work.

People called out to Trey and greeted him, thank- ing him for his help, during the storm as well as today.

"Different rep than what you had in the Heights," Denny said. "Although, even back there, you were always lending a hand."

Trey thought about that while they hauled more downed tree branches to the curb. He liked to think that he'd changed in Pleasant Shores, but maybe part of it was more central to his personality. Maybe he'd always had something to offer, even when he'd barely known it himself.

His father thought so, apparently.

Halfway through the morning, Trey's phone buzzed, and his heart turned over as he pulled it out. He really, really hoped it was Erica, against his better judgment.

But it wasn't Erica. It was the chief. "Great work with the academy program," he said. "You've really turned it around. Got it some excellent publicity and our department's name is all over it."

"What's that?" Trey was kneeling to examine a piece of siding that had come loose from Mr. James's house. "What good publicity?"

"Look online. There was a local spotlight on the way your teenagers were helping senior citizens and it went viral, sort of. It's a feel-good piece." He paused. "I'm finally seeing the results I was hoping for from your participation in Healing Heroes. It looks like you're getting your head in the right place."

"I guess I am," Trey said, surprised to realize that it was true.

It looked like Healing Heroes wasn't just a place to wait for disability benefits. If the chief was right, it had actually changed Trey for the better.

"If everything continues good with your physical therapy, seems like you're ready to rejoin the force."

The chief's words hit Trey like a gust of hurricane-level wind. "No desk job?" he managed to ask.

"Nope. I want you out in the community, working."

Trey barely maintained his end of the short remaining conversation. When he clicked out of the call, both Denny and Mr. James were looking at him with obvious curiosity.

"I've got my old job back if I want it," he said slowly. "In Philly."

"Dude, that's great!" Denny pounded him on the back, making Trey wince.

"Easy, man. I'm still healing."

"I saw you carry those branches. You can't use that excuse much longer." He paused. "Seriously, bro, I'm happy for you. I know how much you wanted this."

He wanted it desperately...didn't he? Why didn't he feel the rush of joy he would have expected? "The chief was happy about the way the kids and I were helping folks during the storm. I wonder how they found out."

Mr. James's face crinkled into a million-wrinkle smile. "A few of us made some phone calls," he said, "and Kirk used his influence with the veterans' organizations to talk about how the kids saved a WWII vet, and the kids put it on those social media sites. We didn't think it was going to get any press, but all of a sudden, the internet got it lots of attention."

Denny was scrolling through his phone. "Look, here it is," he said, and clicked on a video.

It was short, but showed Trey and several of the kids wading through floodwater, carrying lawn ornaments and tree branches, King running alongside them. Both the academy and Trey's department were named.

He didn't know who had taken it, but he vaguely

remembered seeing several of the kids holding up their phones to photograph things at different points during the storm.

"If it got you your job back, and that's what you want, I'm glad," Mr. James said. "But we sure will miss you around here."

That got Trey's attention. He couldn't really say that the folks on the force in Philly missed him. Well, maybe Denny, and a couple of the dispatchers. But they didn't miss him much. He was interchangeable with any other big-city cop.

Here, he was known. To the kids, but also to the community at large. Julie and Mary at the bookstore, where he went to buy the thrillers and military history books he loved. Earl Greene, whom he was helping to computerize some forms and apply for a grant to expand programming for youth. The folks on Sunset Lane.

And, of course, Erica.

But he wasn't staying here. He was going back to the city, back to a job that he loved. Well, liked at least.

King could do search and rescue in Philly. Maybe.

Trey had been dumped by Erica, yeah, and that still stung. But he'd dumped her back, pushed her away. He should feel better about that.

Mr. James went inside, and Trey and Denny took a break and walked with King down to the waterfront. They sat down on a long stone bench, looking out at the water.

"Hard to believe there was that big of a storm yesterday," Denny said.

"Until you look at that." Trey waved an arm toward a pile of twisted metal and tree limbs stacked beside the road for trash pickup.

"True." Denny reached down for a handful of sand and let it fall between his fingers. "So you're not happy about getting your job back?"

"I'm happy about it," Trey said automatically.

"You sure?"

Trey looked out at the water, watching the whitecaps play on the waves. "I like it here better than I expected."

"It's nice," Denny said doubtfully. "Kind of slow-paced."

"I'm liking slow," Trey said.

"What else are you liking?" Denny glanced sideways at him. "Or who?"

Trey blew out a sigh. He and Denny had been through a lot together, and reading people was a key cop skill. No use trying to hide it. "There's this woman."

"That teacher you're working with," Denny said. "I figured. After my wife put the idea in my head. Women always know."

"It's not gonna work, though," Trey said. And then he thought about staying here without Erica.

She'd said if her program ended, she'd probably have to move.

And Pleasant Shores without Erica would feel… empty. Meaningless.

The kids would disband and Erica, Amber and Hannah would be gone, and what would there be for him here?

Come to think of it, he couldn't get excited about being *anywhere* without Erica.

He shook off that gloomy and self-pitying thought and stood to stretch his back. Then he heard a familiar bark. King started to whine.

A giant white soaked creature galloped toward them, a fish from the bay in his mouth. King barked an excited greeting.

Hope and happiness blossomed inside Trey's chest. He looked around for Erica.

But she wasn't there. Hannah was running toward them, leash flapping out beside her. "Ziggy! Drop that fish! Don't jump!"

Trey automatically uttered a sharp command and the wet dog stopped and sat. Another command, and he put down the smelly dead fish, which Denny grabbed and threw into a nearby trash can.

"I'm helping Erica out, exercising Ziggy," she said. "She's gathering boxes to pack up the classroom, since the school year's over and so is the program. And she's lining up job interviews." She talked to them a few more minutes and then jogged on with Ziggy.

And Trey realized none of it was any good without Erica. He wanted to share the news about the program's viral video with her, so she'd at least know the program had made a difference. Wanted to talk with her about what the chief had said, get her perspective on whether he should take the job.

But if she said he should, what then?

"You going to do anything about Erica, man?" Denny asked.

"Like what?"

He shrugged. "Talk to her? Apologize?"

He'd like nothing better, but he'd pushed her away pretty hard. He wasn't sure she'd even be willing to talk to him.

And what could he say? She'd made it clear that she didn't want kids, didn't want him. That desolate expression on her face when she'd walked away might have had little or nothing to do with him. It could have been all about the academy.

"Whatever you do," Denny said, "don't give up. A good woman…" He shrugged, his face reddening. "She's worth the work, man. Believe me."

That was what Trey's every impulse said.

His impulses had gotten him in trouble before. Making him jump into a doomed marriage, telling him to run into a meth lab without backup.

Maybe now, though, he'd grown. Changed. The chief seemed to think so.

Maybe his impulses weren't so bad after all.

Or maybe loving Erica was a whole lot more than an impulse. And maybe they could talk through the kids issue, figure out why she was resistant, see if they could come to a compromise.

He cared about her. Cared about her enough that it was worth a try.

Denny was right—a good woman was worth any amount of work. He needed to apologize and he needed to persist, but a simple little "I'm sorry" wasn't enough. And Erica wasn't the type to be influenced by diamonds and roses.

He needed to do something meaningful. Something big.

CHAPTER TWENTY

"MAYBE THIS WASN'T such a good idea."

Stirring a huge pot of chili to serve with hot dogs, Julie heard her daughter's words behind her and laughed a little. Ria could be such a worrier. "What's not a good idea, hon?"

"Having a picnic so soon after the storm. We're still cleaning up."

"Don't be negative, Mom," Sophia said, surprising Julie. "Everyone was so happy to get invited to a motel picnic. It'll be fun. Although," she added, peering into the chili pot, "that looks disgusting."

"No, it doesn't," Kaitlyn said from behind a tall stack of napkins and plasticware she was rolling up together. "Grandma's chili is really good. Everyone will love it." She stuck out her tongue at her sister, who responded in kind.

"It'll be fine, you'll see," Julie said to Ria, patting her shoulder as she walked past her to check on the mac and cheese. "We're doing our part to help the community come together, and as a bonus, it'll be good for business."

The only dark spot on the picnic horizon was that Melvin might come with his young fiancée. In the adrenaline rush of the storm, Julie hadn't minded that they'd seen her looking like a wet rat. But thinking about it later had made her cringe.

The church and the motel had shared a lawn for years, complete with barbecue grills and picnic tables. Since the church had a large kitchen, it had made sense to do the cooking there. The timing made sense, too: they'd serve the meal right after late-morning services let out.

The courtyard was pretty well cleaned up by now, and the workers had started on the adjoining lots and yards. Most of the hotel guests were participating, as were a number of members of the congregation. Debris was stacked in messy piles along the highway to be picked up as soon as cleanup crews got to this point on their priority list.

"It's looking good around here, for so soon after a big storm," Julie said as she held the door open for Ria to carry out a huge basket of sandwich rolls. The sky was blue, the breeze from the bay cool and pleasant and strong enough to blow away the faint swampy odor from the flooded areas.

Ria nodded, biting her lip.

"What's eating you, honey?"

"I just had so much to do, I feel like I didn't put enough into preparing for this party. And now I just want to keep working to get back to normal."

"Hello, Mom, you're getting the motel property cleaned off for free." Sophia nudged her mother. "Just chill, would you?"

"That was never your mother's strength, chilling out," Julie said. She looked at Ria and it was as if she saw a fast-forward movie of her through the years: a five-year-old chewing her lip at the thought of going to kindergarten, a high school senior wondering if she'd be asked to prom, a college student calling home at midnight, afraid she'd fail an important midterm.

A bride, wondering if she'd made the right choice. And a newly divorced single mom, upset that she hadn't.

Mostly, Julie was glad she'd encouraged Ria to go for it, not to worry, that things would be okay. She felt a little guilty pooh-poohing the marital cold feet, but she'd truly thought Ria and her husband were right for each other. Still thought so, if the truth be told, but something had gone wrong between them that they hadn't been able to fix.

The fact that Ria hadn't shown any interest in other men, the slightly wistful way she talked about her ex, Drew, after he'd come to take the girls for a weekend…all of it made Julie think Ria still held a candle for Drew.

When she'd hinted at it, though, Ria had gotten red-faced, angry and teary. "No way. Subject closed."

People were starting to arrive and mill around, and Sophia shot a video and shared it on her social media. "Good PR," she said. "It gets the name of the motel out there."

What it really got out there, though, was the fact that there was free food at the Chesapeake Motor

Lodge, and within an hour, twenty high school kids had shown up.

Ria panicked about the extra guests and Sophia apologized, but Julie took it all in stride. All those years of volunteering for the soup kitchen and entertaining Melvin's business colleagues stood her in good stead, and she'd bought way too much food anyway. The smell of barbecued chicken filled the air. Mary brought over a huge tray of crab cakes, and a couple of people brought desserts, cookies and brownies. The family she'd helped during the storm brought a big pan full of hush puppies, fragrant and sweet.

"Everything's going well," Mary said, taking the cover off her crab cakes. "People are having a good time."

"They are." Julie looked around at the clusters of people talking, the tables full of people eating, the sound of happy voices. "I never had any doubts." And she hadn't, she realized. She'd known it would go well, because this kind of thing was what she did.

"Grandma's good at this stuff," Sophia said. "Right, Kait?" She nudged her sister.

"Sure." Kaitlyn barely looked up from her phone, but she did somehow notice the brownies enough to grab a couple.

A small group of teens about Kaitlyn's age stood nearby, and they were looking at Kaitlyn and laughing.

Kaitlyn ignored them, but a blush crept up her neck.

"What's that about?" Julie asked Sophia. If Kaitlyn was being bullied…

"Oh, just kids being dumb. I'll talk to them." She marched over and soon dispersed the group.

Ria, looking a bit more relaxed, came over and gave her a side-arm hug. "Mom, you're the absolute best and I'm so glad you're staying here with us," she said. "I don't know what I would've done without you."

Mary grinned at Julie and headed off toward a group of bookstore regulars.

Erica arrived and started talking to some of the schoolkids. She didn't look great, and Julie figured it had to do with the demise of the academy's program. Which she'd like to fight; she just hadn't figured out how.

Music blared out from one of the kids' phones, an explicit set of lyrics in the chorus raising the older guests' eyebrows, and Erica stood and shook her head and pointed at the offender, who quickly shut the music off. But not before Trey appeared out of the crowd, walking toward them. As soon as it was obvious Erica had the situation under control, he veered off in another direction.

"Did they have a falling-out?" she asked Ria, who was watching, too.

"I don't know. I heard a rumor they were dating, but it sure doesn't seem that way now." Suddenly, she tensed. "Uh-oh."

"What's wrong?" Ria was so high-strung.

"Dad's here," she said. "With Ashley. Do you want me to try to make him leave?"

"No, no need for that," Julie said. "It's fine. No big deal." Slowly, she turned to look in the same direction Ria was looking. There was Melvin, handsome Melvin, *her* Melvin, with his arm around his much younger fiancée. Currently, he was smiling and shaking hands with the mayor and introducing Ashley.

Julie remembered when she had been the wife he proudly had on his arm. She remembered how he'd like to show her off, had said she was an asset to his business.

Nostalgia nudged its way in, but Mary marched over and grabbed her with a clawlike hand. "Don't you go wishing for the past," she said. "I remember how much you hated going to events with Melvin. He's awkward and he's always trying to curry favor with the wealthy."

Julie looked at her friend and the past readjusted in her head. Of course what Mary said was true. If she were being realistic, she didn't want to be on Melvin's arm.

As a matter of fact, the new girlfriend didn't look particularly happy to be there, either. She was at that awkward stage of pregnancy where it was unclear whether you were expecting or had just gained weight. Her face was puffy, and as she shifted from foot to foot in her loose dress, Julie couldn't help but notice her swollen ankles.

She felt a quick, not-very-nice rush of satisfaction. Despite his fiancée's age, Julie looked better than she did. It served Ashley right for having an affair with a married man.

"You look a lot better than she does," Mary said, echoing her thoughts.

Hearing it from Mary's mouth, Julie felt ashamed of herself. Ashley was just a young woman who didn't know any better, and now she was stuck with Melvin.

She remembered then how absent Melvin had been as a father. How difficult it had been to raise her daughter basically as a single mother, but not really linked into the single mother network because she was technically married.

She also remembered feeling fat and ugly during pregnancy.

Yes, despite how wonderful motherhood had been, she was glad to be done with that part of it. Having an adult daughter and teenage granddaughters was pretty awesome.

Earl Greene was talking to Melvin and Ashley now, but the sight didn't stir Julie's anger as much as she would have expected. In keeping Melvin's affair to himself, Earl had been doing what he thought was right. Melvin hadn't—he'd definitely done her wrong—but suddenly she didn't feel so much like judging him. Not when things had turned out pretty well for her.

She didn't feel like sitting around waiting for Melvin to see her, wondering if he and Ashley would talk to her or not. So she strode over to Melvin, Earl and Ashley. "Hi, welcome," she said brightly.

All three looked at her with similar wary expressions.

"Come eat," she said. "There's barbecued chicken and some great pie."

Earl's eyes lit up, as she had known they would. Melvin's did, too, briefly, and then he shook his head. "I'd better not," he said, and patted his ever-so-slight paunch.

Trying to look good for his young girlfriend, she supposed. She was close enough to see his hair and realize that he hadn't dyed it very well lately. Some gray was showing through.

She felt a smidge of compassion for him.

Even more, she felt compassion for Ashley. No, she shouldn't have gotten involved with a married man, but she was paying for it, and would continue to do so. The old saying popped into Julie's head, almost making her smile: "The man who marries his mistress creates a job opening." But she truly didn't wish that on Ashley.

"Would you like to sit down?" she asked the younger woman. "There are comfortable chairs over by the fire circle. You can put your feet up. Make Melvin bring you a plate of food."

Ashley looked at her as if to figure out whether she was being mean or sarcastic, but she genuinely wasn't. She just knew that Melvin wasn't the most considerate husband. "You just have to tell them what to do," she said. "Melvin, get her a nice plate of food, and pile it up a little. She's eating for two."

He met her eyes and a tiny smile came to his face. Maybe he was remembering the same thing she was: how, when she was carrying Ria, she had made him go out to get her all manner of unhealthy foods in the middle of the night. Back then, it had bonded them together. Back then, he hadn't been so judgmental.

Maybe he could recall some of that and do better this time around. "Go on. Help her find a place to sit," she ordered.

"Okay," Melvin said, and took Ashley's arm to walk her toward the comfortable chairs.

"You're amazing," Earl said, and she turned back to him, surprised he was still there.

"I'm not," she protested.

"I don't think I could do what you just did." He had grabbed a handful of hush puppies and was eating them as he spoke. Then he studied her narrowly. "You wouldn't happen to be heaping burning coals on his head, would you?"

The Bible verse about being extra nice in order to shame your enemies made her laugh, loud and long. "Maybe a little of that," she said.

"My, my," he said, his eyes warm, "you are quite a woman, Julie. And Melvin's an idiot."

Hearing clear admiration in his voice, she looked thoughtfully at Earl. He wasn't a handsome man, but he was a good one. She could probably encourage him just a little and he would ask her out.

But life was good now. Did she want to add a man into the mix?

DON'T CRY.

The day after the motel picnic, Erica carried a bunch of empty boxes into the school, set them down in her classroom and looked around the place where so much love and learning had gone on in the past three months. It was still small, still dark, still smelling of sweaty teenagers. But to her, and to a lot of the kids, it had become a safe haven.

She'd started boxing up the classroom last week but hadn't been able to muster up much energy for the task, so she'd postponed it. Now, though, she didn't have a choice.

Just get to work. She tugged one of the empty boxes over to the bookshelf and began packing books. She was taking them with her, since they were all hers; the school hadn't provided any funding for a classroom library, so she'd scoured used bookstores online to find books she thought the kids would love.

The dog-eared copy of *The Outsiders* made her pause, and she turned it over in her hands. This was the book that had made Shane excited about reading for the first time.

Would that have happened in a different classroom? Would it happen for the next generation of kids who needed the extra help the support program could provide?

Heartbroken as she was about losing her class, she couldn't stop marveling at the kids and how great they'd been. Going to help out the elders had been exactly the kind of thing that she'd hoped for when she started the community service activities.

She had to recognize that if their altruistic behavior had caused the program to be canceled, then the program wasn't right for them. Or, at least, this wasn't the right home for it.

So she, Amber and Hannah would move on. She had talked to them about it, about how they would need to move somewhere else with a cheaper cost of living and more job opportunities for Erica. They were both sad. Hannah had started crying as soon as Erica had broached the subject, and Amber had come downstairs red-eyed the next day.

But they were both okay. They'd all talked and hugged and reassured each other that the most important thing was that they had each other. If they couldn't stay in this beautiful location, well, a lot of people didn't get everything they wanted.

Erica even had two job interviews lined up.

Having gotten the books into their boxes, she stood and looked around and realized she had to take everything off the walls. She reached for the framed photograph above the bookcase without really looking at it. But then she did look, and hot tears burned her eyes.

It was a photograph she'd snapped of Trey and the kids at the police station, kneeling around King. She remembered that day. Trey had been uncomfortable and ambivalent, but he'd stuck with it and the kids had had a good experience. That had been the first time she thought they might really bond together. And they had.

She studied Trey in the picture, a half smile creasing his beard-stubbled face, his hair curling a little longer than his collar. He was so handsome that her breath caught in her throat.

She could have had a chance with him.

If life had been different, if she hadn't had these wretched bad genes or if he had been more open to adoption or foster care, maybe they could have made it work. If he hadn't been so touchy. If they'd both been better communicators.

All that she had lost seemed to slam into her gut, and she wrapped her arms across it, trying to hold herself and hold in the pain.

"Hello?" A man's voice came from the door. "Is this the place?"

"The principal said she'd be in room sixteen," a woman said.

Erica brushed tears from beneath her eyes and turned to see a familiar local newscaster coming in the door, dressed in a colorful suit. Following her was a cameraman.

What in the world? Erica sucked in a breath and walked forward to greet them. "Hi. Can I help you?"

"Are you Erica Rowe?"

"Yes, I am." She belatedly reached out a hand to shake the woman's, then shook the cameraman's hand, as well. "What can I do for you?"

"We want to learn more about this fabulous program," the news anchor gushed. "At-risk kids working together with mainstream kids to help elderly people weather the storm, right here in our community? It's the best human interest story of the storm."

"It is?" Erica tilted her head to one side. "The behavior support program has a lot of great history, and the kids did do a nice job with storm assistance and cleanup. Is that what you want to talk about?"

"That, and your role, and we would like to get it all on camera if you don't mind." The woman set her bag down and rummaged through it. "Here's a release form for you to sign."

"But…" Erica hesitated. Did she want to announce that the program was ending? On TV? But then again, why not? Maybe it would find a new home somewhere.

"Hello, hello," came a fake-hearty voice from the door.

Oh, great. It was Principal O'Neil.

"I'm glad you're here to talk about this terrific program," he said to the TV people in a jovial voice.

Erica's eyebrows shot up almost into her hairline. Since when did he think the program was terrific?

"Oh, hello. You're the administrator in charge of this program?" The woman smiled at him. "We'd like to interview you, too."

"Why don't you interview him first while I get cleaned up a little," Erica said. It would be interesting to see what O'Neil had to say, considering that he had just shut them down.

Soon the camera was rolling and Principal O'Neil

was talking about how important the program was to the school and how wonderful Erica was.

Erica couldn't restrain a "Huh?"

"What?" The cameraman looked curious.

"Ask him how long the program is going to continue," she suggested, and he communicated the question to the reporter.

"We hope the program continues indefinitely," O'Neil said.

Happiness washed over Erica even as she rolled her eyes. Could it be true? Could she, Amber and Hannah stay at the beach where they were so happy?

But if O'Neil had said it on camera, he would have to stick with it. And indeed, he seemed to be doing so, obviously wanting to make a good impression.

"I've been very supportive of the program since it began," he said.

Erica blinked. The program had been ongoing for years. O'Neil couldn't have been more than a toddler when it had begun.

"It's excellent for the different kids to work together," he said. "We have the community connections and support. It's putting the school on the map."

Now the reporter turned to Erica and started quizzing her about the program and how the kids had helped during the storm. She talked a little about it, doing her best even though she felt self-conscious being on TV, especially in her clean-up-the-classroom clothes.

But if she was going to do it, she might as well do it big. "One thing we need is a new space for the kids," she said. "If you look around, you'll notice the facilities are limited here."

"Looks like you're packing up," the reporter said as the cameraman panned the dingy room. "Are you headed for a different classroom?"

"I certainly hope so," Erica said, looking over at O'Neil. He was rubbing the back of his neck with his hand and sweat was visible on his face.

She decided to take mercy on the man. "If people want to help," she said, "there's going to be a fund-raising campaign for a new wing for the academy. It's a very worthy cause and we hope people will be generous."

"I'm sure they will," the reporter said, and wrapped up.

As they were packing up, the sound of a throat clearing came from the doorway.

Trey.

What was he doing here?

CHAPTER TWENTY-ONE

EVEN DRESSED IN raggedy jeans and an old T-shirt, Erica looked gorgeous. And shocked.

And it wasn't totally obvious, but he suspected she'd been crying.

He walked into the classroom and stood quietly while the reporter and cameramen left, O'Neil at their heels. Then he turned to Erica. "Are you okay?"

"I...think so? But I'm not sure what just happened."

"Something good?" He was hoping against hope that it had turned out well, good for the program, good for Erica.

"I *think* we got our program back," she said, tilting her head to one side, a half smile crossing her face. "And I think we're starting a fund-raising campaign to build a new wing onto the school."

Relief washed over him. "That's great!"

He wondered if he should reveal his role in making that happen—the phone campaign, the strings he'd pulled to get the news team interested and out here to the school, the phone call he'd made to

O'Neil. He'd intended to break through her resistance with his admirable grand plan.

But now, suddenly, that didn't seem right. He needed to find out how she felt about him based on who he was, not on something he had done for her.

"Look, can we talk?"

She dipped her chin and looked up at him. "I thought there was no point," she said, throwing his own words back at him, which he definitely deserved.

"I'm sorry about saying that," he said. "And I'm sorry for putting the program in jeopardy in the first place. And for the attitude I've been carrying around. It was misplaced."

She was watching his face closely, and then she gave two quick nods. "Of course I forgive you." She paused, then added, "I heard you're going back to your old job."

"You did?" Funny, because that wasn't his intention at all.

She nodded. "Everyone hears everything here," she said. "Small-town life."

"Actually, I have another plan." He got out his phone and found the text exchange with Earl Greene. Wordlessly he showed it to her.

She read it. "He's offering you a part-time job on the force?"

He nodded. "And another part-time gig as a liaison to the support program at the school, if it actually survives. So it adds up to full-time, here in town."

"Is that what you want?"

"I think I do." He studied her face, the way her forehead was wrinkling. "What's wrong?"

"It'll be hard being together without, well, being together. To be honest." She hesitated, then added, "And maybe taking the job here sounded better to you before you knew that I was going to stay."

"Actually, I was hoping… Listen. I want to ask you something."

She looked totally confused. "What?"

His stomach kept knotting and his throat felt tight. He was such a wimp. He reached in his pocket and pulled out the little box. Took a deep breath. "Erica, I know it could take some time for you, but for me, I'm sure I love you. You're the woman I want to spend the rest of my life with." As soon as he said the words, his heart relaxed and warmed. At least he had told her. "I know you love kids, and whatever the reason you're set against having any of your own…together, I think we can work it out."

Her eyes glittered with tears. "Oh, Trey." She hesitated, then added, "Thank you."

"Thank you? Is that yes?"

"I still can't," she said.

Of course she couldn't, the old voice in his head harangued. No good woman would want him.

But there was a new voice there now, that came from the kids, from Earl, from his father, from the community. A voice that told him not to back away yet, to ask questions instead of giving up.

"*Why* can't you?" he asked.

She sucked in a breath and looked up at him, still with those glittering eyes. "When I told you I wasn't having children, I meant...I *can't* have children."

He reached for her hand, stunned by her revelation and by the sadness in her eyes. She loved kids so much, was so good with them. "I'm sorry," he said. "It's related to the cancer your mom and sister have?"

"Uh-huh. And I know how much you want kids."

He nodded slowly. "I do."

"So it won't work." She pointed at him, then herself. "We won't work."

Outside, a seagull cawed an opinion. Through the room's one small window, a boat was visible on the bay.

"I want you more than I want kids," he said, setting down the ring, reaching out to grip her other hand, as well. "I love you more."

She was still looking at him, and now tears overflowed from her eyes. "You love me," she said, swallowing hard. "Oh, Trey, you have no idea how beautiful those words sound to me."

He wiped the tears from her eyes with his thumbs, then took her hands again. "They're true words."

She shook her head. "That's wonderful, but... even love can't fix it if you don't have the life you want."

"The life I want is with you," he said, urgent to convince her. "If we can build a life together, we can find a way to help children. In the academy. Foster care or adoption."

"But you don't want to foster or adopt. You told me."

"That's in the past," he said. "I realize now I'm beyond my past." It was true, and he felt like a great weight had lifted off him. It had been lifting all along, as he'd lived and worked in Pleasant Shores. After his dad had visited, he'd realized it was gone for good. Why had he carried that so long? "And besides," he said, "you're worth making any sacrifice for. You're fierce and kind and generous, and I'm crazy about you. I can't imagine life without you, but…only if you feel the same about me." Because he wasn't going to go through this again, loving a woman who didn't truly love him. He was starting to realize he was worth more.

"I'm still taking all of this in." Erica blinked. "Is that…?" She nodded down at the little box on the desk beside them. "Is that an actual ring?"

"It is," he said, half laughing, but with wet eyes and a choked-up throat. He sucked in a breath and let it out slowly, trying to regain his equilibrium. "I know this isn't how proposals are supposed to go," he said, thinking of the social media extravaganzas he'd occasionally witnessed. "Just…just say you're willing to explore it. Even that would make me really, really happy. I can do a big fancy proposal later."

"I can't believe I could have all this," she said, looking around the classroom, then at the ring, then at him.

"What?"

"You. Maybe a family. Work I love—" she squeezed

his hand, swallowed hard and looked at him through eyes glittering with tears "—with the man I love."

He lost his breath then, stared at her, his heart warm in his chest. "You love me?"

"I love you. So, so much."

He swept her into his arms and spun her around. "That's enough for me to go on," he said, filled with relief.

"And I don't need a fancy proposal. I don't even like that kind of thing."

"Then…"

"I'll marry you."

His heart flip-flopped and joy rose in him. He pulled her close, studied her precious face, then lowered his lips to hers.

A long time later, there was a pounding on the classroom door. Trey and Erica just barely had time to step away from each other when the door burst open.

It was Venus and Shane. "We just saw a video the TV station posted," Venus said. "Is it true? We got the program back?"

"Because of what we did?" Shane added.

"Because of what *he* did, dummy," Venus said, pointing at Trey.

Erica looked at him. "What did you do?"

Then the kids fell all over themselves explaining how Trey had come to them, how they brainstormed ways to get the word out, how they'd gotten their social media friends to spread the word while he had gone to talk to Principal O'Neil.

"You did that?" She hugged him tight, then gave each of the kids a hug, then hugged him again. "You're all wonderful people," she said, then looked up at Trey with eyes full of love. "You, most of all."

EPILOGUE

Ten weeks later

THEIR WEDDING DAY dawned with a little rain shower, but soon, golden sun peeked through blue-gray clouds. Gulls cawed, their voices trailing off in the August heat. A breeze blew off the water, rustling leaves and cooling the picnic area between the church and the motel. So they wouldn't necessarily need the tent they'd put up to shelter their guests.

A perfect day, but Erica would have considered any day perfect when she was marrying the love of her life.

Amber and Hannah fussed with Erica's gauzy gown and her crown of flowers, while on the other side of the tent, Denny stood with Trey, talking quietly, laughing a little and getting Trey to laugh, too. They both wore light linen suits, and Trey had never looked so handsome. Denny's wife sat near them, hands folded over her very pregnant belly, smiling from Trey to Erica. In the months that Erica and Trey had been together, Denny and Laura had become their good friends.

Erica felt unbelievably blessed. Their fund-raising

was not only a success, it was going to be a roaring one; they'd just gotten word that they'd raised the money they needed to build a new wing on the school. It wouldn't be ready for this school year, so they'd have to make do with the small classroom for one more year, but that also meant they could get the kids involved in some of the planning. Erica was surprised and happy that she'd heard from most of the kids over the summer, claiming—in most cases believably—that they couldn't wait to come back for another year at the academy. Most of the local teens had been invited to the wedding.

Of course, the new school year would bring some new kids, each with their own issues, but Erica felt ready for that, invigorated, eager to take it on.

Even more important, Amber and Hannah could stay at the beach, fulfilling Amber's dream and allowing Hannah to stay in the school where she'd made so many friends. The two of them would live next door to Erica and Trey, who were moving into the cottage at the other side of their rental, allowing the Healing Heroes cottage to be open to another police officer in need once the high season was over.

A crab boat passed, loaded with traps, reminding Erica that not everyone was off work on a Saturday. The boat tooted and she squinted, saw old Henry Higbottom and his grandson headed out into the bay and waved.

Elegant Mary walked toward her, smiling, Baby-the-Maltipoo waddling on a leash beside her. "I'm glad you decided to make the wedding dog-friendly," she said, putting an arm around Erica to offer a brief hug.

"Of course we did!" Erica pointed toward the area where Ziggy and King were stationed with the teens who'd agreed to watch over them for the duration of the wedding. "Ziggy is getting better all the time, to the point where I may try him as a therapy dog. And King's doing great with his search-and-rescue training."

"Maybe he'll be able to loosen up and just be a dog for a while, after all that police work," Mary said, and then stepped back to study Erica from head to toe. "You look beautiful, dear."

"She does," Julie agreed as she came up from behind Mary and added her own hug to the mix. She'd become more and more of a mother to both Erica and Amber, and while she'd never take the place of the mother they'd lost, she'd added a new richness and security to their lives.

"You ladies had better look out." Amber approached, leaning a little on Hannah. She was still weak from a recent treatment, and Erica's heart lurched. Amber's future was far from certain. They'd figured out that her pain episode wasn't a recurrence, but she had a lot more tests and scans to do before they could begin to think she was healed.

"Why should we watch out…? Ooooh." Julie and Mary looked toward the entrance to the tent, where Kirk was approaching, resplendent in a summer suit and with a determined glint in his eye. "I think we'd better go check on the flowers," Julie said, and the two of them hurried away, arm in arm.

Erica, Amber and Hannah watched, giggling, as Kirk changed directions and sped up his pace.

"Old people aren't that much different from high school kids," Hannah said, shaking her head. "I thought Julie liked Officer Greene, but now it looks like Kirk is hitting on her, too. But I thought Kirk liked Mary."

"Drama is drama, no matter what your age." Amber turned to Erica. "Honey, I have something for you," she said, and pulled out a box containing a silver-and-sapphire heart locket.

"Mom's locket!" She met Amber's eyes, her own filling with tears.

Amber nodded. "She gave it to me and told me it was for my wedding. It's old and it's blue and now, for you, it's borrowed. From me."

Erica hugged Amber carefully, and then Hannah fastened the necklace around her neck. They all hugged, and both Erica and Amber shed a few tears.

"She's watching from heaven," Amber said, her voice husky.

"I know she is." And she did.

A man on a bicycle approached the church. He leaned it against a tree, straightened his ponytail and unhooked a gift-wrapped package from the back of the bike. He looked around the crowd.

Erica sucked in her breath and caught Trey's eye. She nodded sideways, pointing at the man.

Trey's eyes widened, and he said something to

Denny and then strode across the grass. He wrapped his father in a bear hug, then tugged him toward the seats and introduced him to a couple of guests.

"It's almost time," Hannah said, and fussed a little with both sisters' dresses.

Erica watched Trey as he walked back to the front of the gathering, greeting people and then going to stand by Denny, and her heart seemed to expand. Trey looked so, so handsome that she got a little lost.

She'd learned an incredible amount from opening herself to Trey, and this glorious love was the result. A family, too, because it turned out LJ would be living with them as a foster child when they returned from their honeymoon.

Trey caught her looking and smiled, wide and true. His dreams were fulfilled, too. He'd gotten serious about counseling, wanting to avoid the mistakes he'd made in his first marriage and be the best husband possible—and that had been his idea, not Erica's, since she already thought him pretty much perfect. Still, he'd shared with her some of his childhood wounds and she'd shared her fears about the future, and just the ability to talk about it made it better. Like Erica, he'd fully immersed himself in the life of Pleasant Shores.

The wedding was beautiful. The teenagers were quiet and respectful, but cheered and applauded at the right times. Amber gave Erica away, and Hannah served as her maid of honor, and Denny, of course, was best man. Julie and Mary sang a duet about love, their voices ringing rich and true.

Trey and Erica had just finished their vows when a sharp bark sounded. Suddenly, Ziggy broke away from Shane, who'd been charged with keeping him under control. The big goldendoodle took off after a seagull, and King took off after Ziggy.

"King!" Trey called.

"Ziggy!" Erica stood on tiptoe to see her dog over the crowd. "Stop! Sit!"

Ziggy stopped and looked from Erica to the seagull as if he were pondering his decision. King turned and trotted back to Trey, and Ziggy followed more slowly, looking back at the gull, who cawed laughter at him.

Rather than returning to the teens who'd been watching them, King came and sat at Trey's side, attentive, and Ziggy took up the same posture at Erica's.

"So adorable," one of the guests said, and almost everyone raised a camera.

"Looks like the dogs have stolen your thunder," the pastor said, a big smile on his face. "Trey, you'd better hurry up and kiss the bride."

Trey pulled her into his arms, and Erica felt all the excitement in his touch, the anticipation of their wedding night and honeymoon.

But first, they would spend the evening with their friends and family and lovable dogs in Pleasant Shores, this beautiful community that had become their home.

* * * * *

ACKNOWLEDGMENTS

MANY PEOPLE HAD a hand in getting The Off Season series off the ground. I'm very grateful to my agent, Karen Solem, font of sensible ideas; to my editor, Shana Asaro, who pushes me to make my stories the best they can be; and to HQN's editorial director, Susan Swinwood, who took the time to meet with me during the RWA conference in New York and got me thinking about shifting this book's setting from the Jersey Shore to the Chesapeake Bay. The art and marketing departments at HQN have been patient and dedicated, and I am grateful to them for their hard work.

My writer friends give me so much support, and I am blessed to have them. Kathy Ayres read a draft of the proposal and gave valuable feedback, and my Wednesday morning writers' group offered thoughtful critique of several sections. Sandra Belle Calhoune, Dana R. Lynn and Rachel Dylan are continual sources of writerly encouragement and sympathy. The amazing Susan Mallery has been extremely generous with her knowledge of the publishing world, and I am beyond grateful for her very kind endorsement of the series.

On the personal side, thanks are due to Bill, my companion of the heart, always willing to drop what he's doing and take a research trip that turns out to be the best fun ever. My beautiful and resilient daughter, Grace, puts up with subpar cooking and housekeeping, keeps me young and makes me laugh. The goofy young goldendoodle who frolics through *Cottage at the Beach* is modeled on my Nash, whose antics keep me on my toes.

Cottage at the Beach deals with the difficult topics of ovarian cancer, chemotherapy and genetic mutations that run in families, putting certain members at increased risk of developing the disease. My mother, Janet L. Tobin, survived melanoma and ovarian cancer before finally succumbing to pancreatic cancer. Much of my knowledge of the emotional impact this horrible disease can have on a family comes from Mom's difficult battle. Just within the past year, genetic testing let me know that I've inherited a mutation that increases the likelihood of breast and gynecologic cancers, and facing that challenge brought me into contact with many much younger women who face the same sort of heartbreaking risks, difficulties and decisions as Amber and Erica. Hence this book is dedicated to my mother and to the many young women who face their genetic predisposition to cancer with courage and grace.

Read on for a sneak peek at the next book in
The Off Season series,
Reunion at the Shore,
from Lee Tobin McClain!

CHAPTER ONE

RIA MARTIN SHOULD have enjoyed the chance to escape the month-end paperwork for the Chesapeake Motor Lodge, should have relished the soft fall breeze. But as she hurried toward her teenage daughter's school, her stomach churned.

Can you come pick up Kaitlyn, Mrs. Martin?

October, and it was the third such urgent text message since Kaitlyn had started eighth grade. Her heart ached for her sensitive younger daughter, and she wished she could just hug her and make everything right again. But hugs hadn't helped; Kaitlyn had skipped three classes in a row, again. Her grades were slipping and her reputation as a star student was morphing into that of a star troublemaker. What had happened to her sweet daughter?

She knew at least part of the answer: adolescence, an AWOL father and a too-busy, stressed-out mother. Guilt clawed at her. She needed to find a way to connect better with Kaitlyn, figure out what was wrong, make sure she knew she was loved. Needed to plain old spend more time with Kaitlyn, even though they seemed to grate on each other's nerves these days. Typical mother-daughter stuff, but Kaitlyn took everything deeply to heart. She always had.

Kaitlyn needed her father, now more than ever. She'd always been a daddy's girl. Anger at her ex made Ria's heart race and her steps quicken, and she deliberately slowed down and took a couple of deep breaths. It would do no good to take that anger out on Kaitlyn. She needed to put it where it belonged.

The private school's parking lot was small, the place surrounded by trees on two sides and backed by the Chesapeake Bay. She paused a moment, deliberately, made herself look at the natural beauty that usually calmed her. She'd been fortunate to get tuition assistance when they'd moved here last year, part of a displaced-homemaker scholarship program. Such a great opportunity for her girls. Or so she'd thought.

Obviously, a great school wasn't enough to help Kaitlyn, not now, anyway. She needed to get Drew reinvolved in his daughters' lives. She paused at the bench outside the school's front door, sat down and tapped Drew's number on her phone.

This time, it wasn't even him asking callers to leave a message. "The mailbox is full," recited a mechanical voice.

For just a second, worry overrode anger. Had something happened to him?

But no. If it had, she'd have heard. Yes, he was two hours away in Baltimore, but his department had her number and would let her know if, God forbid, he'd been killed in the line of duty.

No, this was just Drew being irresponsible, which was totally out of character, but then, men went nuts when they got divorced. It was the nature of the gender. She thrust the phone toward her purse, missed the pocket and grabbed for it as it fell to the ground.

"Ria! What are you doing?"

Her mother's voice startled her. When she looked up to see Mom's concerned face, she felt like bursting into tears. But she didn't, of course; she was a competent adult. "Being an idiot," she said as she snagged the phone and looked at the face of it. "I think I cracked it. What are you doing here?"

"I got a text about Kaitlyn."

Ria stood and frowned. "I did, too. Why would they text both of us?"

Mom shrugged. "Sometimes, when they can't reach you…" She trailed off.

Her perpetual mom-guilt ratcheted up a couple of notches. It was true; sometimes she couldn't be reached, caught up in the day-to-day management of a busy motel.

She'd never wanted to be *that* mom, focused on her career instead of her kids. But when she and Drew had split, working only part-time hadn't been an option anymore. Thank heavens they'd moved to Pleasant Shores and were close to Mom, who'd picked up a ton of slack for Ria over the past year and a half. Especially when the disaster had happened, the one Mom didn't even know about, because nobody knew. "I'll take it from here, Mom. You do too much for me already."

"Are you sure? I'm glad to help."

"No, it's fine. You go ahead back to work."

"I'm done for the day. I'll meet you at your place, if you'd like."

"That would be great. Thank you."

As Ria watched her mother walk away, she longed to call after her: "Please, stay. I don't know what to do."

KAITLYN SCRUNCHED DOWN in the chairs outside Pleasant Shores Academy's administrative offices and watched her mom talk to the school counselor. Despite the fact that she was sure to get yelled at, seeing Mom was a huge relief.

Both foreheads wrinkled, and both women kept glancing her way. Poor Mom, always so stressed, was just getting more so with this new problem. It was all Kaitlyn's fault. She wanted to throw herself into her mother's arms and cry like a six-year-old, but that wasn't an option. For one thing, her mother drove her crazy these days. For another, she'd be tempted to tell Mom what she'd done.

That could never happen. Thank heavens she hadn't told Mrs. Gray, the counselor, anything substantial.

Maybe the woman sensed it, because she and Mom both turned and beckoned to her. "There's only one period left, so why don't you go ahead and go home," Mrs. Gray said. "You and your mom have some talking to do."

She stared daggers at the woman, who patted her shoulder. "It's not always easy for mothers and daughters," she said, "but communication is so important."

Well, duh. Unfortunately, communication wasn't exactly her family's specialty.

They got halfway across the parking lot before Mom started in on her. "I know eighth grade isn't easy. But you're old enough to keep control of yourself and stay in class."

Kaitlyn pressed her lips together, because what did Mom know about eighth grade? What did she know about Kaitlyn's life? At a school where everyone else had been together since kindergarten, Kaitlyn was still considered a new girl and a summer person after a year and a half of living here full-time. It didn't help that she was the biggest and tallest girl in her class and had gone from an A-cup to a D-cup practically over the summer.

In the car, she breathed a sigh of relief. Getting away from school felt so, so good. She wished she could get away from Pleasant Shores entirely, just go back to Baltimore for a month like they'd been supposed to do over the summer with Dad.

Not that Pleasant Shores Academy was a horrible place, or at least it hadn't seemed to be when she'd started there last year. It was much smaller than the public school she and her sister had attended before their parents' divorce, and she'd liked that, thought it would be easier to make friends. It was definitely easier to stand out as a star student.

But when everything went south, a small, gossipy school wasn't what you wanted. She'd learned that the hard way.

"So what exactly happened?" Mom asked as she started the car.

"Don't yell at me!"

Mom opened her mouth, closed it, took a yoga breath. She had no idea how irritating that was obviously. "I asked a question," she said, speaking slowly and clearly now, as if Kaitlyn were a toddler, "in a normal tone of voice."

The fact that she was right didn't matter. "Just leave me alone," Kaitlyn said, and her voice started to shake.

"Oh, honey." Mom reached out and rubbed her arm as she had when Kaitlyn was little and scared. "Whatever it is, I'm sorry it hurts."

Tears welled up and she jerked away. "Don't!" If Mom kept on in this sympathetic voice, she would fall apart.

Mom's jaw clamped, and she didn't speak again until they walked in the door of their house, adjacent to the motel. Grandma was there—thankfully—and from the smell of things, she'd cooked a lasagna. Normally, Kaitlyn loved her grandmother's lasagna, and she hadn't eaten anything since the granola bar Mom had forced on her this morning.

But her stomach felt too upset to even think of eating.

She headed up to her room, ignoring Mom's protest, then stopped halfway up the stairs to listen to what Mom would say about the whole scene. She only had to wait a few seconds.

"Is she okay?" Grandma asked.

"I don't think so. I'm going to go up and see if she'll talk to me."

"Give her a little time," Grandma said. "Sometimes Mom is the last person an upset fourteen-year-old wants to talk to."

"But...well." Her mother's voice sounded sad, almost hopeless. "I guess you're right, but it's frustrating not being able to do anything to help."

"Have you talked to her dad? He always connected so well with Kaitlyn."

"No, because I haven't been able to reach him. His mailbox is full and he's not answering his phone."

Her grandmother tsked, and they talked a little bit about whether Kaitlyn's sister, Sophia, could help.

As if. Sophia was too caught up in her own excellent social life to give more than a pitying glance to Kaitlyn.

"You know what," her mother said to Grandma. "This isn't Sophia's responsibility, and like you said, I'm not connecting real well with Kait these days, no matter how hard I try. I'm going to go find Drew."

"Oh, honey," Grandma said in exactly the same way Mom spoke to Kaitlyn. "Is that a good idea? I'm glad to stay with the girls, of course, but..."

Kaitlyn closed her eyes. *Yes, yes, please yes.* Having her big, strong police-officer dad in the area might get Hunter Gibson and his crew off her case.

"It's the only idea I can think of. I know I can get information out of Michael or Barry." Those were the officers Dad was closest to on the force. They'd been coming to their house since Kaitlyn was small.

"But if he doesn't want you to know where he is…" Grandma trailed off.

"At this point," Mom said, "I don't really care what he wants."

"You don't want to catch him in an awkward position."

Kaitlyn almost gagged. She did *not* want to think of her father in an awkward position.

"Just because Dad ran around within seconds of leaving you, that doesn't mean Drew is doing the same thing."

"Of course it doesn't, honey, but you still might not want—"

"He hasn't seen the girls for three months. Totally outside our visitation agreement. The excuse he made for not taking them over the summer was ridiculous, especially since he texted it to me. Didn't even have the courtesy to call."

"Are the support checks coming?"

"Yes, he's great about that, but being a father isn't just about money. They need to see him. Kait especially."

They went on talking, but Kaitlyn didn't linger to hear any more. Her mom would go bring her dad home, and Dad would make everything better.

As RIA DROVE through their old Baltimore neighborhood, memories flooded her. She'd walked through these tree-lined streets, holding Sophia's hand and pushing Kaitlyn in a stroller. There was that little corner restaurant where she and Drew had gone on date nights. Their old church, where they'd attended in the early days, before Drew got too busy with extended shifts and Ria got too bitter.

She lowered the window, and the smell of autumn leaves brought back more memories. She tried to focus on the city noises: cars and horns and sirens from a busier street nearby. She didn't miss that. She loved the quiet of Pleasant Shores.

There was the park with walking paths beside the little lake they skated on in winter. She and Drew had taught both girls to ride their bikes on those paths.

She drew in a deep breath and let it out, blinking back tears. This was why she avoided coming back to Baltimore. *Thanks a lot, Drew, for making me fall apart again.*

But that was what Drew did. One look at him and she remembered all the good times. But if she spent an hour with him, she remembered exactly why they'd split.

She pulled into the same gas station where they'd always filled their tanks and ran inside to get something to drink.

"Ria! Is that you?"

Ria turned, and there was Sheila Ryan, one of those mom friends with whom she'd been thrown together for years. They didn't really like each other, but they pretended to because that was what you did for your kids.

"Hi, Sheila. How's it going?" Ria prayed that Sheila wouldn't ask her the same question.

Sheila went into a description of her thirteen-year-old daughter's ascent up the cheerleading squad ladder, her status on the honor roll and the volunteer work she was doing to help shelter animals.

"How are Sophia and Kaitlyn doing?" she asked.

"Oh, just great. We love living at the shore."

"I was sorry to hear about your divorce. That must be a big adjustment, for you and for the girls." Sheila's words were kind, but her eyes were just a little too avid and curious. Whatever Ria said would find its way around the gossip circuit.

She sucked in a deep breath, let it out and forced a smile. "Thanks. It's definitely an adjustment. But I'm running a little motel, and that's fun." *Except that it's always at risk of going under.* "And the girls love their new school." Well, Sophia did, so that was at least half-true.

She made an excuse and escaped, and only when she got to the car did she realize that she hadn't gotten the drink she'd gone in for. She'd never been good at the competitive mom games. They had always made her uncomfortable.

As she drove the rest of the way to the police station, she wondered whether it had been like that for the girls, too. Had they felt the competition of their upper-middle-class neighborhood, where she and Drew had stretched so hard to be able to afford their little brownstone?

At the police station, more memories assailed her. She'd come here so often over the years, to pick Drew up, to bring him something he'd forgotten, to just say hello, when the girls had been small and she was a stay-at-home mom.

Now she didn't fit anymore. The new receptionist didn't know her, couldn't tell her anything about Drew, citing confidentiality. Fortunately, she found his friend Michael and begged and pleaded her way into getting Drew's address.

"He shouldn't have fallen out of touch with you, Ria," Michael said. "But he's had a tough time. If you want, I can try to call him and let him know that you need to see him."

"Thanks, but I've come this far." Then what he'd said registered. "He's not working here anymore?"

"He didn't tell you?"

"Tell me what?"

Michael studied her, slowly shook his head. "He's on a leave," he said.

"Is he okay?" Her heart pounded wildly.

Michael opened his mouth to say something, then closed it again and nodded. "Pretty sure he is," he said. "Honestly, I haven't spoken to him for a few weeks." He looked like he wanted to say more, but someone called him from the back hallway, and he patted her shoulder and left.

Something was definitely going on. And she was going to find out what it was. It wasn't right that

Drew had left her out of his life this far. Not that she had to know everything—they were divorced, after all—but they had kids together, kids who needed him. That anger mixed with worry, because Drew was nothing if not responsible. Had he changed that much?

She drove toward the address Michael had given her. The neighborhood wasn't nearly as nice as where they used to live. Unwanted sympathy washed over her. Drew did provide enough child support to allow her to live in Pleasant Shores with the girls. He'd taken the hit to his own lifestyle, unlike a lot of divorced dads, and she appreciated that.

She turned onto his street and was looking for a parking place when she saw Drew across the street.

With a woman.

A stylish, laughing, tall, thin blonde. She seemed very animated as she talked with Drew, who was looking straight ahead. They were both tall enough that she could see them over the row of parked cars. She pulled crookedly into a parking place, nearly hitting the car parked in front of her.

He replaced her, he'd really replaced her.

She had never thought that would happen. Her chest contracted around a hole where her heart had been.

It was true, then. He didn't love Ria anymore. She'd gotten too stressed, too focused on mother-hood instead of marriage, too fat. But she'd thought in her heart of hearts that they'd get back together someday.

Drew stumbled a little, and the woman leaned closer, seeming to steady him. Drew never stumbled. Had he been drinking? During the day?

She got out of her car, closing the door quietly, and sneaked across the street to watch them. The woman glanced back once, and Ria waited for Drew to do the same, but he didn't. He was focused straight ahead. His walk was a little halting, not his usual confident stride. Had he been injured?

There was something about the way the woman was poised next to him, like she was ready to grab his arm, but not quite touching him. Ria walked closer and her heart nearly stopped when she saw the white cane Drew was holding. It had a little rolling ball at the end, and he was moving it back and forth to feel his way down the street, and the truth slammed into her like a gale-force wind.

Drew was blind.

CHAPTER TWO

DREW MARTIN USED his cane to find the curb and leaned forward a little, listening to the traffic sounds. "Is it…?" he started to ask Meghan, and then shook his head. "Wait. I can figure it out."

"Good." She waited with him, and he sucked in a deep breath and started across the busy street.

"Just a little to your left," she said quietly behind him, and he looked down. In his small remaining window of vision, he could see that he was veering off the crosswalk. He corrected, then finished his way across and navigated the steep curb easily.

"That was great," Meghan enthused as they continued on down the street, and Drew felt a small rush of pride.

Ridiculous, when all he'd done was to cross the street.

"Drew?"

Drew froze. He knew the sound of that voice better than he knew the sound of his own. He had heard it raised in anger, racked with childbirth pain, husky with passion. He had heard it say, "I do."

And he didn't want Ria to see him like this. He

turned away and started back in the opposite direction.

"Drew! Wait!"

Meghan gripped one of his arms and Ria—it must be Ria, it smelled like her and it felt like her—gripped the other.

"Hey, you were about to walk out into traffic," Meghan said. "You know better than that."

But he couldn't listen to her when his wife's soft voice drilled into his ears, his mind. "Drew. It's Ria."

"I know," he said. He wished desperately that he could see her face, see how she was reacting to the person he was now. On the other hand, he wasn't sure he wanted to know. "How did you find me?"

"Oh, you know each other!" Meghan sounded happy, and he knew why. She was worried about him, thought he was too isolated. Not that it was any of her business—she was just his orientation and mobility specialist—but she took an interest, as they said.

"This is perfect. Our session was just ending. I'm Meghan," she said, obviously to Ria.

"Ria." His ex-wife sounded a little dazed, and that was understandable. She had just learned that the father of her children was blind. But, warm like always, she reached across him to shake Meghan's hand.

"Do you want help going back to your apartment, Drew?" Meghan asked.

What was he supposed to say? He did need a little help still, but that was humiliating in front of Ria.

"I'll help him," Ria said, and that was worse.

"Great!" Meghan reminded him about their next appointment and left, and he was standing on the street with a rapid heartbeat, his face and neck and ears impossibly hot.

"Do you want to…take my arm or something?" Ria nudged him with it. "You're in the brick building, right? Apartment, what is it, 3B?"

"Uh-huh." He held her arm reluctantly and breathed in the smell of her, a smell as familiar as life to him. Their hips jostled as they went up the steps to his building, and he was so disconcerted that he stumbled a little going inside. Sweat dripped down his chest.

Between his explanations and her eyes, they got to his door and he pulled out his key. Of course, it took him four tries to unlock his apartment.

Navy gave a bark of greeting and pushed her nose into his hand, and his blood pressure went down a little just from the friendly feel of his former police dog, now pet.

"Navy!" Ria sounded happy—much happier than when she'd seen Drew—and he tipped his head back and could see her kneeling to pet the yellow Lab she'd loved.

"Come on in," he said. Then his face heated when he realized he didn't know whether the place was really neat and clean, or a mess. They hadn't done much with that after his initial orientation and mobility session, because his main concern had been to figure out how to navigate the world outside.

The two-month residential program where he'd gone as soon as he'd gotten out of the hospital encouraged setting priorities.

Unfortunately, they'd given him no guidance on what to do when his ex-wife paid a surprise visit.

"Have a seat," he said, gesturing toward his small living room. "Want something to drink?"

"Sure," she said. "Do you have a Coke?"

"Think so." He made his way into the kitchen and leaned way into his refrigerator, hoping to cool off. He studied cans, which was mostly what he had in there, as he wasn't much of a cook. He found one that he was pretty sure was Coke. Grabbed that and a beer from his beer shelf—he knew exactly where that was and he also knew he really needed one—and carried both to the front room. He felt his way to the couch and sat down and then realized he was way too close to her. He felt her scoot away at the same moment that he did.

"Your friend Michael told me where you were living. And don't be mad at him—I needed to know. Drew, what happened?" Her voice held curiosity and sympathy, but not pity. It was a fine line, but one he'd learned to recognize in the past three months.

"Head injury," he said. At his feet, Navy leaned into him.

"Is the vision loss permanent?"

"They don't know."

They sat in silence for a couple of minutes. He

wondered why she'd needed to find him. He kind of hoped it was because she missed him, but he doubted it. Anyway, now he was even less likely to be able to make a success of their marriage.

When they'd gotten married, it had been under duress. All his long hours in rehab had given him time to reflect, and he'd figured out that they'd never really recovered from their rough start.

"The girls need you," she said.

That was another personal failing: he wasn't living up to what a father should be. "I'll come and see them, make it up to them, after I figure this…" He waved a hand, vaguely. "Figure a few more things out," he finished. "How are they doing?" Truth was, he missed his daughters terribly.

"Sophia is fine, of course." She paused, then added, "She misses you a lot."

His firstborn daughter, beautiful and competent and smart. His throat tightened as he thought about not being able to see his children, not now, maybe not ever. "What about Kaitlyn?"

"She's not doing so well."

An icy hand gripped Drew's heart. He loved both girls equally, of course, but Kaitlyn was his special child. She needed him the most, and when Ria and Sophia had gone off doing the girlie things like shopping, Kaitlyn had usually chosen to stay home with him. When she was small, she'd sat and talked to him for hours while he puttered around the house, and he'd loved it. "What's wrong?" he asked.

"I just can't communicate with her."

Relief washed over him. Just mother-daughter stuff. "You push it too hard."

Ria sucked in a breath audibly. "I've had to go into school three times already this year. She's having some kind of trouble with the other kids."

"Bullying? Fighting?"

"She did get into a shoving match once, but mostly she just skips classes and hides in the bathroom."

"Why would she do that?"

"If I knew that I'd tell you!" She blew out a breath. "Like I said, I can't communicate with her. She won't talk to me about it."

"Maybe I'll come to Pleasant Shores." The moment he said it, all the problems inherent in such a visit flooded into his mind. He couldn't drive. He would have to learn to navigate a hotel room, new shops, new streets. He was somewhat familiar with the town from their visits to Ria's mother, but knowing a place when you could see it wasn't the same as knowing it blind.

"*Maybe* you'll come? When you feel like it?" Ria let out an exasperated snort. "Nice, Drew. Way to put your kids first."

His blood boiled. Could she ever, just once, look at things from his side?

But he knew the answer. They were from different worlds, and they'd never managed to quite cross the gap between them. And she was right: no matter his own issues, kids came first.

"Just don't even bother. I'll manage." He heard her stand up.

"Give me a minute to think!"

"Oh, take your time," she said sarcastically. "It's only your children, after all." He heard her steps click across the floor, heard the door slam shut.

Navy whined a little.

He let his head drop into his hands. Yes, he'd failed on so many levels, and, yes, he blamed himself. But Ria still had the power to totally piss him off.

THE NEXT FRIDAY, Ria walked down to the end suite at the Chesapeake Motor Lodge, wanting to check on the cleaning job done by a new worker. She unlocked the door, walked in…and froze.

What was her ex-husband doing here?

"Who's there?" Drew asked. He reached a hand toward Navy, the yellow Lab who was so often by his side. "Check them out," he said, and Navy trotted forward, tail wagging. She was a police dog and would stop any unknown intruder, but she'd been Ria's pet.

"It's me," Ria said as soon as she could find her voice. She knelt and rubbed on Navy, whom she'd always loved. "Sorry to walk in on you, but…what are you doing here?"

Behind her, there was a sharp knock and then her mother was calling through the door. "Oh, no," she said. "You beat me."

Ria shot a glare back at her mother. "We're both a little surprised," she said.

"I should've called you or something," Drew said. "It was just a lot to pull together, getting the transportation down here, canceling appointments. With this." He waved a hand at his eyes, now covered in dark glasses. "The only ride I could find got me here a little early, and they gave me the key at the desk."

Then there went any option Ria had for being angry at Drew, because how could you be angry at a person struggling with his disability? Instead, she focused her anger on her mother. "Can we talk a minute?"

"Sure, honey. Drew, we'll be right back to help you settle in." And her mother led her out to the old-fashioned metal chairs outside the door of the suite.

Ria was too agitated to sit down. Instead, she paced back and forth. "What did you do? How is he here?"

"He needed a place to stay. He needs to be close to his kids, reconnect with them."

"Granted, but he didn't seem at all interested in coming a few days ago. And now he's here, in my motel, without my knowledge?" Her voice rose to a squeak as she glared at her mother.

"He called me."

"He called you and not me?" Heat flashed through her body. "Why?"

"He's worried about Kaitlyn, honey. And I would never have gone over your head like this, but…I'm worried, too."

"So am I!" Her chest tightened, and she glanced toward the house, toward the window of Kaitlyn's bedroom. She'd pleaded cramps and stayed home from school today, and Ria honestly didn't know whether allowing that had been the right thing to do.

Maybe having Drew here would help—she prayed that it would—but why had he acted so unwilling the other day? "Did you know he was blind?"

Her mother nodded. "*Visually impaired* is a better term, I think. He told me he still has some sight. But he'll need some extra help getting around, and that's the only reason I suggested he stay here at the motel. I'm sorry, honey. I know it was interfering of me, but…" Her lips tightened and she, too, glanced toward Ria's house. "Kaitlyn talked to me about Drew possibly coming, and she brightened up. It's the only smile I've seen out of her in a long time."

Ria had opened her mouth to continue semi-yelling at her mother, but Mom's words snapped her mouth shut. She bit her lip. Mom was awesome at this motherhood thing, and had a good sense about what kids needed. Ria, on the other hand, had made so many mistakes, a terrible, secret one in particular. She needed to defer to those who were better at parenting, for Kaitlyn's sake.

"I'll help Drew as much as possible," Mom said. "I was planning to come in and do a quick clean of the place, because that new cleaning guy didn't get to it yet. He seems a little…eccentric." She gestured down the row of rooms to where a frizzy-haired man in a tie-dyed shirt was rocking out to music on his earbuds.

Ria puffed out a breath. One more thing to worry about, but it paled in comparison to worry about her daughter.

Her mother put an arm around her shoulders and squeezed gently. "I know it's got to be hard for you. I'll just run in and make up the bed, and then I have to scoot. Mary has an emergency and needs me to come in and cover for her at the bookstore."

"Go on. I'll help him settle in." Mom did so much for everyone, Ria and her kids most of all. But as she hugged her mom and thanked her, a knot of dread settled into her stomach.

Being around Drew while he visited Kaitlyn was going to be tough. She only hoped this week would go fast.

"Listen," Drew said as soon as she greeted him, "you don't have to clean. I can do that. I could just use a tour of the place so I can get my bearings."

Ria looked around. The place wasn't dirty, but— she checked the bedroom and bath—they needed to put out clean linens. "Why don't you unpack and I'll put sheets on the bed and towels out for you at least." Then she hesitated. "That's if...*can* you unpack for yourself?"

"I can unpack." The words were said through gritted teeth.

"Sorry! I just don't... You let me know if you need help, okay? Otherwise I'll assume you don't. During your whole visit." She headed into the bedroom as she spoke and pulled the spare set of linens out of the closet.

He came into the bedroom, and she watched him move around touching the furniture, getting his bearings. Strange to see this big, proud man who'd always stridden rather than walked now moving tentatively. "I've been doing orientation and mobility training pretty heavily," he said when he got to the side of the bed where she was. "And I have some limited vision. I do okay."

"What's going to happen with Navy?" She dreaded the answer, knowing how much Drew loved his dog.

"They're letting me keep her. Some grant for disabled officers." He winced and started taking clothes out of a duffel and putting them in drawers, all by touch. "Hate that term."

She finished making the bed, watching him furtively. He was still so handsome. And she was still so attracted. Ridiculous.

Of course, the attraction had never been the problem between them, even though she'd lost her confidence about actual intimacy. Even their last fight had been fiery, and when he'd grabbed her shoulders in frustration, she'd wanted to kiss him, and she'd seen in his eyes that he wanted to kiss her, too.

But the physical side of things wasn't enough. They'd never communicated all that well in actual words, and as the hurt had built up on both sides, their ability to understand each other had declined even further. When people—even good friends—

asked what had happened to their marriage, she'd never been able to say exactly. It wasn't cheating or drinking or abuse. But it had been conclusive, just the same.

"Tell me about Kait," he said as he moved to the doorway. "When can I see her?"

"Anytime. She's home from school today, in fact."

"You let her stay home?" Drew grabbed his cane and started moving around the room, restlessly exploring. "Why?"

Her chest tightened. "She said she has cramps."

"That's not an acceptable excuse. She can take medicine for that, right?"

"Right, but—"

"You argue with her and then give in to her. It's not the best strategy."

"I've been doing the best I can, alone!" She forked her fingers through her hair. "Believe me, I question myself every day, but I just have to make a decision and go on. She looked so miserable this morning that I let her stay home."

"She's not going to solve a problem by running away from it."

"Neither are you," she snapped. "Look, I get that you've had a major challenge with this…this blindness thing—"

He made some sort of noise in his throat.

She pushed on. "But that doesn't absolve you from responsibility, nor give you the right to question my decisions. She's more than I can handle alone, Drew, so I hope you can do some good, at least, with this visit."

She spun to leave, and froze. There in the doorway was Kaitlyn, looking from her to Drew, her face stricken.

Don't miss
Reunion at the Shore
by Lee Tobin McClain!

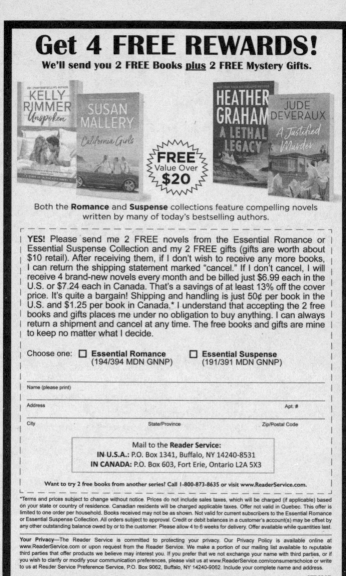